REVOLUTIONARY DEAD

KEVAN DALE

GET SORCERY OF THE STONY HEART
FOR FREE

To instantly receive the free novella *Sorcery of the Stony Heart* and the exclusive novelette *A Spark of Will* (unavailable anywhere else) sign up for Kevan's free Readers Club at kevandale.com

For Leah & Lila

1

A TERRIBLE THING

April 23, 1775
West Bradhill, Massachusetts

It was a terrible thing they were doing. Thomas Chase didn't understand why they'd brought him along, or what they planned on doing with his dead cousin, Nathan, out by the old lake—only that it was terrible. He supposed his uncle, Joseph, was mad with grief, but that didn't explain why Father didn't stop him. They left Thomas and his questions to watch the horses. He shivered, glad not to see the body any longer. A deep chill held the midnight woods. His breath hung in the air in rolling clouds, and steam rose off the horses' backs. He barely knew those woods, being so far out from the village, out in the lonely stretches that folks avoided. He didn't like them, either—too dark and still, with old trees close together.

A cold half hour passed before a hand fell on his shoulder. Thomas recoiled, but his father steadied him, the older man's face grim. He motioned and Thomas followed, pushing through branches and thickets until the trees opened on the lake.

Thomas looked around but didn't see the body.

At the lake's edge, moss-patched granite overhung the water. Moonlight shimmered on the water's surface a dozen feet below. His uncle grabbed his shoulder. Thomas flinched and looked up into his uncle's wide eyes and twitching mouth. Joseph shook him by the front of his cloak and pointed to the water. Thomas tried to pull away.

"Told you he wouldn't do it," Joseph said. His sour breath washed over Thomas.

"He'll understand," Samuel said. "He can't see your lips, that's all."

"This's why I didn't want him here in the first place, he's useless. Just have him do it," Joseph said. He shoved Thomas toward his father.

"You can't do this," Samuel said. "Leaving him out here won't make it go away—you of all people know that."

"Meaning what?"

When his father had nothing to say, his uncle leveled a pale finger at him.

"You don't stop now," he said.

Samuel stared at him for a long minute and stepped over and put a comforting hand on Thomas's face, turning his head toward the water again.

"Right there," he said.

His father pointed to a spot above the water. At first, it looked like another gray outcrop of rocks and moss. Then Thomas saw the body. Bent saplings and broken plants marked where it had slid down the face of the rocks toward the water. It hadn't made it all the way—a thick root held it in place.

His cousin Nathan.

Looking at the body made Thomas want to run back into the woods—he couldn't swim and didn't like heights, and the thought of having to touch Nathan twisted his stomach. Still, he hated everyone thinking of him as useless. He stepped forward and picked his way down. He slid in spots, feet shifting for traction, hands grabbing what they could to steady himself. Saplings and mossy fissures in the rock allowed him to work his way to the steep drop. His hands grabbed at the granite, his eyes drawn to the dark water below him. At one steep spot, he missed a foothold and nearly slid past the body and into the water. A few more steps and he stopped next to the body. Nathan's eyes stared at the moon, dry and empty. His head lay at a funny angle to his shoulders. A matted patch of hair and bone on the side of his head marked where he'd smashed against the edge of the wagon—Thomas didn't look at the wound.

He inched closer. A rock came loose and tumbled into the lake with a *ploonk*, rippling the surface. Steadying himself, he reached over and yanked on his cousin's jersey, hoping to free the arm over the root. The material ripped. Thomas grabbed the arm instead and shuddered at the feel of the flesh—like cold clay. Thomas pulled, scared and wanting to get the horrid task done with, wanting to get away from the dark lake.

The root let go from underneath the arm. The bag of stones tied to Nathan's ankles pulled his body to the water. Thomas lost his footing and slipped next to the corpse. Terrified of plunging into the black water with Nathan, he cried out. At the edge, his pants caught on a stone as his legs hung out over the water. He looked down just in time to glimpse his cousin slipping into the water. For a moment more, Thomas could see the hands, pale fish swimming into the depths. Once the trickle of dirt and stones ceased, the surface of the water smoothed and the moon shown on it. A few bubbles rose from below and soon ceased.

THE STARS to the east faded into a deep indigo sky as the two men and the boy came out of the woods and onto the road. Frost thatched the ground. Thomas rode the smallest horse, leading the riderless horse by the reins. His hands ached from the chill night. He wanted his own bed where he might forget the long night. Joseph turned around and spoke to them.

"I'll not lose him, I won't. This bloody curse won't take everything from us," his uncle said. "That's what this is. Do you understand?"

Thomas looked to his father, but Samuel kept his eyes forward.

Joseph turned to him. "And it's not anything like before. Not a single bit. This was an accident."

Thomas didn't know what he meant—only that he couldn't let go of the feeling of dread the lake had put into him.

"He's my boy," Joseph went on. "A good boy, not fit for leaving. Not yet."

The horses passed through a grove of birch. Dawn lightened the sky to the east.

"My good boy," Joseph said. He pleaded with them. Tears slid down his face. Thomas thought he should say something. Instead he looked away.

2

THE LAKE: PART ONE

A day came and went, and the sky drained of color, the final light of sunset painting the tips of the trees before fading to night. The dark woods stood silent. Stars poked out, their reflections riding still on the deep black water of the lake, smooth as marble. In the middle of the lake, a ripple broke and rode out in circles. Then another. It was nigh on midnight when something pale neared the surface.

3

———

THIS ISN'T RIGHT

Thomas sat on a fence rail, waiting. Lamps came on in the kitchen of the farmhouse behind him as the road faded to a silver river in the dusk. He'd been waiting two long days and was about to burst for wanting to see his brother, to have Jonathon explain to him why they'd done it. A wagon pulled by a single horse came riding toward the house, coming from the Boston Road. In the twilight, Thomas made out the driver.

"Jonathon! Hey, Jonathon!" He waved his arms, and the driver returned the gesture. Thomas sprinted toward him.

"Easy there, little man," Jonathon said. He held out his hand and lifted Thomas up onto the driver's bench.

"Cousin Nathan's dead," Thomas said.

Jonathon smiled and then looked confused. "Nathan's what?"

"Day before yesterday. He fell from the loft swing at the mill when we were moving the powder and guns because word came that the British are coming for them. He hit his head on the wagon below and broke his neck. And we buried him that same night out in the lake past the Stag Jump Brook."

His brother stared a moment longer and then looked up at the house where the lamps burned yellow against the darkness.

It fell on Thomas to take care of the horse and wagon, so by the time he got into the house, he didn't know what was going on. Jonathon and their father were next to the hearth in the kitchen, arguing. The embers of the fire were a muted orange. Jonathon swung his arms as he spoke, sometimes even getting up on tiptoe to make a big point. The lanterns fluttered with the breeze as Thomas slipped into the kitchen, to where he could see both their faces. He'd lost most of his hearing during the horrible winter when he'd been six, but he could read lips—and it was easiest with Jonathon and his father.

"—but now you need me," Jonathon said.

"That's right," his father said. "I need you. Here. It's your responsibility."

"How can you say that? Liberty is all of our responsibility—isn't that what the pamphlets say? What you've said."

"It's not that easy."

"But we need every man. Especially with Nathan not here."

"We put him in the lake," Thomas added.

His father looked at him with fury—he took two steps over and slapped Thomas hard across the cheek with the flat of his hand. "Enough! No more of that, young master. You will never speak of that again."

Thomas stepped backward, touching his hand to his stinging cheek, his eyes filling with tears of shock. His father had never struck him before, ever.

"Look," Jonathon said, ignoring Thomas. "They're calling up the militia, our militia, and we may have only one chance to bring the fight to the king's men. We can't fail. We can't—and that means we need to bring the fight. All of us."

"Absolutely not. You're to stay here and watch Thomas; watch the house and shop."

"I'm sixteen—" Jonathon cut in.

"And that means nothing."

Thomas shifted and said, "I'm old enough to watch myself."

"No, you're not," Jonathon said—Jonathon, of all people.

"I'll go, too," Thomas said. He reached into his pocket and pulled out the cracked fife he'd found a month back. "I can play with the fife and drummers. We can all go fight together."

"That's all we need," Jonathon said. "A deaf fifer. Why do you always carry that broken thing around?"

Thomas pointed the fife at him and raised his voice. "I can still help, and I can shoot. I'm not afraid to shoot a Brit. And I can shoot a better musket than you. Uncle Joseph said so just two weeks back."

"I let you win," Jonathon said.

"You didn't." He frowned and put the fife back in his pocket.

Their father took the musket that hung over the mantle and gathered his powder, cartridges, and other items. "We're mustering outside Brewster's at first light and we march from there. I have work to do."

"How long will you be gone?" Thomas said.

"Time will tell. In the meantime, you keep up with your chores and help your brother." He turned to Jonathon, who was downtrodden. "You need to finish the Currier job for me. I've laid half the type, you do the rest. And you keep an eye on the property. If you spot or hear anything strange, you find old Corey Lane, tell him about it."

"Nathan and I were supposed to go, too," Jonathon said. He turned and walked out of the kitchen. Thomas looked at their father. In the lamplight, he looked older. He motioned him over, and Thomas stood before him, nervous.

"Listen," Samuel Chase said. "I'm sorry for hitting you, but you're never to tell anyone else about what your uncle and I did with your cousin."

"But why did we—"

"No one, and I mean that. I know it doesn't seem right. Maybe it's not—but Nathan was all he had. He's family, my brother."

Thomas still didn't understand.

"And you forget anything else he said. That's all gone now and best left there. Do you understand?" his father said.

Thomas nodded his head, pretending he did.

In their bedroom, Jonathon rolled up a shirt and stuffed it in a haversack.

"What are you doing?" Thomas said.

Jonathon waved his hand, annoyed. "Close the door."

A lantern burned on the small writing table by the window. Thomas threw the cracked fife onto his bed and stood by Jonathon. "I'll tell." He kept his voice quiet.

Jonathon spun on him. "No, you won't."

"But father said—"

"He's just worried. These are important times, and if we don't show the British what we're made of, they'll hang the militias and occupy every town."

"Not West Bradhill."

"Yes—even here. We've got a good militia. Father and Uncle Joseph are patriots. Known far and wide."

Thomas could come up with no counter to that. He took another tack.

"He won't let you."

"He can't stop me."

"But what about me?"

Jonathon smiled. "You said you didn't need watching after, didn't you? You can't always wait around for me to help you."

"I do not."

"You do, all the time. Now it's time to watch out for yourself. Until I'm back from the war. Nathan and I trained for this, so I can't back down now. For him." He gathered his sack and put it over his shoulder and then swung open the window. The night air was rich with the scent of pines.

"Jonathon—" Thomas said.

His brother climbed out the window, out onto the starlit grass.

"Well, then...what about Carolyn?" Thomas asked. He kept his voice to a whisper.

Jonathon frowned. "You don't understand, do you? Of course not. Ask her father—or better yet, ask Nathan."

"What do you mean?"

"Whose fault is it that the Brits found out about our powder house? That's why we had to move it, isn't it? That's why Nathan was there. Treachery."

"But Carolyn—"

"Forget her and forget all the other traitors."

With that, he turned and ran off into the darkness. Thomas watched after him until he disappeared, and when he tired of fretting and pacing, he sat on the edge of his bed. He had to tell his father, otherwise Jonathon would be off in the morning to fight, leaving Thomas alone. He stood at the window and looked out at the starlit fields. Nothing moved. His father stayed up for an hour more, shaking the floorboards as he walked about the house. Then all was still. Torn, Thomas blew out the lantern and got into his small bed, and he fell into a worried sleep.

His eyes opened hours later. Moonlight shone through the window. It was late, past midnight. Thomas didn't move—he was terrified to move. His gaze snapped to the window. Cool air rolled in. His hand found the broken fife next to him. He set his jaw and slid from the blanket, afraid to make a sound. The night outside the window frowned, as though something had just passed through it, close by. Something horrible.

The urge to pull the blanket back over his head and hide took hold. Thomas did just that when he felt a floorboard groan. Father was up, too. Thomas dropped the blanket and crawled to the door, wanting to stay below the level of the window. The front room was all shadows, charcoal and pewter. One of the front windows was open, the faded curtain shifting in the breeze. A tall figure appeared from the darkness of the kitchen. Thomas pulled his head back into the bedroom, then inched his face forward again, peering around the door. Samuel Chase stood in his night clothes, his hair shooting out in several directions. He held his musket.

"Father?" Thomas whispered.

Samuel swung the musket around. He eased up when he recognized Thomas. Even in the dark, the fear on his face was clear. His father came closer. "A voice. Calling for us."

Something cold gripped Thomas's heart.

"Get Jonathon," his father said.

Thomas was furious at Jonathon—he had to tell now, and he would have to bear the brunt of father's wrath. "He's gone. He climbed out the window. Before I went to bed."

"He's calling for him, for your brother," his father said, as if not hearing him. "To play. Play in the fields."

He left the bedroom and crossed the front room. Thomas followed him, crouching. The kitchen was darker than the front room, being on the side of the house away from the moon. The windows showed clear the moonlit trees and fields that led to the woods. Someone stood in the field, a dozen paces from the kitchen, a silhouette against the lighter grass and trees beyond. Not moving. The fear he'd woken with swept over Thomas again.

"Is it Jonathon?"

"Don't you listen if you hear it. Lies, horrible lies. This isn't right."

"But who—"

A quick shake of his shoulders by his father. "No. You need to go and get your uncle, and you need to do it right now. Tell him it's come back on us. Get him here—and find Jonathon, too."

The thought of leaving the house was terrifying. "But Jonathon—"

Another shake from his father. "Listen. Once you've told Joseph, you ride to Corey Lane, and you tell him what's happened. Straight to him. Take Gunther and don't stop to saddle him or for anything else, just go right to the barn and out over the field. Cut through Wilkinson's place. Tell—"

His father stopped again, cocked his head. He and Thomas looked out the window. The figure was a few paces closer, a mish-mash of shadow and hints of pale features. There was something wrong about the way it held its head.

THOMAS HURRIED to get his uncle. He closed his eyes as the horse leaped over the brook at the edge of Israel Wilkinson's field. He barely held on. It had to be the British coming after the militia, the Chase brothers first. Both his father and his uncle had fought in the French and Indian War—his father had served under General Bradstreet at the capture of Fort Fron-tenac—and they led the village's minutemen. Thomas scanned the empty roads, looking for companies of lobsterbacks on the march, half-imagining the glint of muskets in every other shadow. If they blockaded the road, he'd still be fine—he knew the fields and woods as well as anyone, and no soldier of the king could keep up with him there. He wished he'd brought his fife, in case he should need it. By the time he crossed Boston Road near his uncle's mill, the moon was waning. No lamps burned in homes. He stopped in front of his uncle's home and slid off the horse.

The mineral scent of the river carried in the night air, a spray of water thrown up by the small waterfall next to the mill. The water drove the great grinding wheels inside—Thomas could still remember the sound of the wheels and the roar the water made from before he'd gone deaf. He ran to the house attached to the side of the mill and knocked on the door. When no answer came, he pushed, but it was latched from the inside.

"Uncle Joseph!" he called out.

Movement from the mill caught his eye. Something flashed in one of the top windows. He rushed to the wide doors and pulled, but they were also locked. The left door was loose on the bottom, so Thomas pushed against it, leaning in hard with his shoulder. The bottom of the door moved in a little, not much more than a foot, but it was enough. He wedged himself in, crouching and forcing his head and shoulders in, then pulled the rest of his body through. As he came out on the other side, the door swung back with a boom. The inside of the mill was dark, save for where moonlight came through the narrow windows. It was strange to see the mill so still—it was normally loud and busy, his uncle directing the activity of his cousin and the others like a general.

He looked up all the way to the high ceiling and the walkway that ran along two sides. The machinery and tools lined the walls, the tall grinding wheels were still. Below the walkway a swirl of dust spun silver in the air. Thomas noticed a motion in the shadows.

"Uncle Joseph?"

He moved toward the stairs that ran along the walls. As he put his hand onto the wooden railing, the hairs on the back of his neck stood. He turned to find his uncle barreling straight toward him, eyes wide and a pistol in each hand, shouting. Thomas fell back on the stairs, raising his arms. His uncle grabbed him and dragged him to the doorway that connected the mill to the house. Thomas barely got to his feet. Joseph stumbled in behind him and spun around to close and latch the door. He looked past Thomas and sprang forward to the dining room table. With a sweep of the pistols, he knocked the table clear—plates, knives, candlesticks, and a mug clattered to the floor. He put one pistol down and swung around again to face Thomas. He pointed at the table, then the door. Understanding, Thomas ran to the other side of the table and pushed while Joseph pulled. They wrestled it across the kitchen, flipping the table onto its side so that its top blocked the doorway.

Joseph handed a pistol to Thomas and motioned for him to follow. He turned and headed toward the back rooms. Thomas looked back at the barricaded doorway and then followed. They passed though the main room, passed the stairs leading to the bedrooms upstairs, and then came to Joseph's cluttered study. Joseph closed the door and hurried to his writing desk. With a few quick motions, he lit a lantern; the wick sputtered and spit. He knelt in front of Thomas. In the lantern light, his features were more pronounced—eyes deep-set, his mouth a shifting cavern. He put the pistol down and grasped Thomas by the shoulders and leaned in close.

"I thought it would work this time; work because he was so young, and it was an accident," Joseph said. His eyes widened, and he turned to the door—he'd heard something from the other side of the house. His gaze turned to the window and then back to Thomas. "I was wrong, wrong. Again."

The words came but nearly too fast for Thomas to decipher. His uncle stood and shoved Thomas toward the window. Standing in front of the small panes in the crosshatched framing, he grabbed Thomas's chin, made sure he could read his lips.

"And you tell your father I knew what he was doing, trying to do. And I did nothing when it would have mattered—and too much when it was too late. But he has to see it now, this is all part of it, their foul curse. Your father doesn't believe it, but that's because he doesn't want to admit that it's all around us, has been since back then. Taking everyone from us, pushing us to make it worse, as I did. Even took your hearing. Been a shroud on us since it started—it owns us. Now run to him."

Thomas shook his head. "I don't understand. Father needs you to come right away, there's someone—British, I think —and he—"

He fell to the floor in a shower of broken glass and splinters. He rolled and raised himself up on one arm. Joseph staggered back to the door. There was something on the floor between them, a large bundle of rags and pale stones. For a second, Thomas thought it was a scarecrow from the neighboring fields —but why would someone throw it through the window?

He looked more closely and realized that he was looking at a tattered cloak, and then his eyes found his cousin Nathan's face looking back up at him from a skewed angle. The flesh was gray and swollen, the eyes glinting a strange steely color. The lips hung open, and the mouth worked. With unnatural speed, Nathan rose and flattened himself against the wall, blending with the shadows in the corner. A burst of flame and a flash of yellow lit the room. Thomas felt the blast in his ears and stomach. Joseph stood near the door, a smoking pistol in his trembling hand, lantern on the floor. Tears streaked his face. The corner was empty. A dark form clung to the beams of the ceiling.

Thomas looked back to his uncle. The big man took two giant strides across the room and grabbed him by the collar and seat of his pants. He tossed him out of the window, knocking out the remaining bits of frame as he did so. Thomas hit the soft earth with a grunt, dirt in his mouth and nose. He looked back.

"Run!" his uncle shouted, leaning out of the window.

Before Thomas could do anything more, his uncle disappeared back into the darkness of the house, yanked back. Thomas crab walked backward, eyes huge. He scrambled to his feet. Behind him, the tall grass and trees that bordered the Shawsheen River shifted in the wind. Thomas ducked into them and sprinted as fast as his legs would move.

4

———

THEY DON'T STAND FOR IT

The common room of Brewster's Tavern in West Bradhill fell silent at the question. The aroma of ale and tea hung in the air. The men assembled watched and waited on Jude Brewster.

"Course not," Brewster said, "I'd never have done such a thing."

Beneath the low ceiling, two dozen of the village men gathered. News had ridden in the afternoon before that the Massachusetts Provincial Congress had ordered all local soldiers mobilized—the volunteers were to assemble and set out for Boston. Samuel Warren had sent the message around, and riders continued on in all directions, bringing the orders to the other towns and villages north of the city. Henry Salter, Lieutenant in the village militia, took a last swallow of cider and put down the mug.

"If that's the case, then why not join us, Brewster?"

"I've told you all before," Jude said. "My business is right here, and this is where I'll keep it. I don't have time for anything else."

"You had time for them British officers two weeks back," another militia member said. "Plenty of time. More'n enough to tell them where the powder was."

"They came for ale, nothing more. I didn't tell them a thing—and I'll thank you not to suggest I would, not here in my tavern," Jude said. "Especially after what happened to the Chase boy. We all know where those officers were before they stopped in here."

"That don't mean much," the same militia man said.

"Means plenty," Salter said. "We all know where Dr. Bucknell stands."

"I'd like to know where Samuel and Joseph are," someone said. "They ought to have been here an hour ago."

"I say we're better off without them," Eldridge Carrier added. "Too much of the grave about them as is. They'll only bring their ruin on the rest of us." He drained a mug of ale. Several of the men murmured in agreement. They'd heard the stories.

"Don't be a fool," Salter said. "The Chases do what's right by this village, always have. Neither one's a coward."

"Old Joseph ain't one to fear killing a man, I think we know that much," Carrier said. "Wouldn't you say, Brewster?"

"You'd best find him yourself, ask him directly," Jude said. The talk got under his skin.

"Right," Salter said. "Enough talking. We have our orders, and there's no reason not to get moving. Samuel and Joseph will catch up with us soon enough—they may already be on the road."

The gathered militia looked at him. Not every eye seemed glad at the prospect.

"Everyone outside and form up," he said, raising his voice.

The men emptied their glasses and hefted their muskets and packs. A few of them—Eldridge Carrier among them—gave Jude dark looks as they left. He heard one of them mutter "loyalist," but he let it go.

The sun shone on the chestnut trees across from the tavern. Most of the shops near the tavern were shuttered. Jude put away the plates and mugs from the militia. There was a knocking from the kitchen. He opened the door.

"I need to talk to you." Elizabeth slipped in past him, bringing with her a wave of spring air. She pushed the top of the cloak back from her head and turned to face him. "I'm sorry. I know I shouldn't be here."

Jude's heart sped up, being with her again. "They're gone."

"I half wondered if you'd be with them."

"And I half wondered if they'd drag me with them by my neck. Not more than a handful trust me."

Elizabeth stepped in close to him. A few moments passed before she spoke.

"I haven't been able to stop thinking about yesterday afternoon," she said. Her voice was quiet. She reached out a hand to his own—carefully, as if he might topple over. "I couldn't sleep. It was the first time I've felt anything in my heart—anything—for years. I didn't think it was possible again."

Jude glanced to the common room. "This isn't a good idea. It's broad daylight."

"He's off watching the men leave."

"Still."

It was hard keeping his thoughts straight, and even worse when she kissed him, as she had the day before—soft as a gentle rain. Her arms slipped around his back, and she pressed against him. Jude forced himself to pull back.

"We can't," he said. It was hard to find his voice. "It's not that I don't want to—"

She leaned in and kissed him again. He couldn't not kiss her back. After a few seconds, he pulled back again.

"No. Yesterday was a mistake. We can't. We're asking for trouble," he said.

"I don't care."

"But people. The village. They don't stand for it."

She took his hand and slid it into the top of her dress, between her breasts. She turned just so, and her breast filled his hand. All the words he'd had ready for her fell apart in his head.

"You're a wonderful man with a kind heart, and I don't care about any other thing," she said.

She kissed him again, and her nipple rose under his touch. Every muscle in his body hummed. They moved into the morning shadows, pressing up against the table. The trees out back sighed with the wind and broke up the sunlight. Her hands fumbled with his breeches, and he lifted her dress.

5
_____

A DARK RUST

The afternoon shadows lengthened as a rider on horseback emerged from the woods behind the Chase farm. Major William Pomeroy sat back in his saddle.

"Now, come along, dearies," he called over his shoulder. "You'll be happy to learn that this tiresome forest isn't quite as endless as that dreary marsh was."

He flicked a sprig of pine needles from his shoulder and prodded his horse out onto the edge of a field. Behind him, two soldiers came out from the trees, leading their horses and one other. A third soldier hunched over on the last horse, eyes squeezed shut.

"Where are we, Major, sir?"

"Look, Hutchison," Pomeroy said, "I'm starting to rather worry about your constant 'where are we now, where are we now?' Strikes me a tad unhealthy. It's perfectly clear we're"—he swept his arm forward—"in back of this lovely farm."

The two soldiers leading the horses exchanged a look, no longer even careful not to let him catch it. Pomeroy ignored them and headed straight across the field. His men could damned well think what they want—he was past caring.

"Let's see if our hardworking folk of the land would be inclined to assist a few of their good king's loyal troops," he said. "Maybe we'll get lucky, and they'll have one of their ingenious home-remedies-got-from-the-natives that can help Hawkes with whatever it is he's come down with."

"His leg's broke, sir," Private Hutchison said.

"Ah, yes," Pomeroy said, setting his hat at a practiced angle. "That was quite a spectacular fall, now that I think about it."

They crossed the field and approached the farmhouse. The smell of smoke coming from a hearth carried on the breeze as the shadows deepened in the surrounding woods.

"We may even glean information about the location of the cannons and powder we're after," he added.

"You're sure this is West Bradhill, sir?" Hutchison said.

"As sure as the days spent listening to your constant questions are long, Hutchison."

They came around the corner of the house.

"A well," Hutchison said, heading straight for it.

Pomeroy didn't stop him. Their own water had run out earlier, and they'd found nothing but rank marsh water, black with muck and skimmed over with algae.

Pomeroy stayed on horseback. "Get Hawkes some first," he said, tossing Hutchison his own canteen. Pomeroy rode to a corner of the farmhouse. Over a few gentle rises, he spotted distant chimney smoke and the tip of a steeple, painted deep orange with the lowering sun.

"Hutchison!" he called back.

The private came walking up, wiping water from his chin. "Sir?"

"Where is everyone?" Pomeroy said.

Hutchison looked around, scratching the beard on his pale face.

"Don't know, sir," he said. "Maybe inside?"

The horse stamped. Pomeroy looked down at the private after a few moments. "And the reason you're still standing here?"

"Yes, sir," Hutchison said. He hurried over to the door of the farmhouse.

He knocked three times.

"'Allo," he called. "Open up."

Pomeroy dismounted, throwing the reins around the hitch set before the porch. Hutchison pushed open the door.

"Not locked, sir," he said.

Pomeroy walked past him and stepped into the house. The front room was long and narrow, the hearth cold. He bent and picked up a piece of metal.

"Curious," he said, looking at it. He tossed it to Hutchison.

"Bit of the latch, sir?" Hutchison said. He turned to look at the doorframe. Splinters angled out from a spot over the handle.

"It would appear to be," Pomeroy said. He sniffed the air and caught a lingering hint of powder. "Bayonet forward, check the other room."

Hutchison brought his weapon around and held it in front of him. He stepped through a narrow doorway next to the fireplace.

"Bloody hell! Sir..."

What struck Pomeroy first was the blood crusted on the beams of the ceiling—little bits had collected and dripped, forming small stalactites. Blood and bits of flesh smeared the floor. The streaks of blood on the opposite wall were a dark rust in the muted sunlight.

"Christ on the cross," Pomeroy said.

Hutchison turned and stepped to the doorway, seeking air that wasn't heavy with the coppery tang of blood.

"I believe supper is usually slaughtered outside somewhere, don't you, Hutchison?" Pomeroy said. He wrinkled his nose. The private pointed near the large fireplace.

"Ah. Handy," Pomeroy said. He stepped over and nudged the severed hand with the toe of his boot. Behind him, Hutchison lost his stomach. All the water he'd guzzled splattered on the wooden floor, along with the last of the biscuit he'd eaten earlier.

"Just a little joke, Private," Pomeroy said. Kneeling, he inspected the hand. The edges of the skin were torn, the bones pulled clean from the end of the arm it was once part of. It was cold to his touch. He stood up and walked across the kitchen. Blood trailed into the hallway. "Go get Cooper and have Hawkes keep watch as best he can."

As Hutchison hurried back outside, Pomeroy walked down the hallway, listening. A staircase climbed to the second floor. The trail on the floor stretched to a small door set in beneath the stairs. The cellar, likely. Hutchison and Cooper came through the kitchen. Cooper's eyes widened, following the trail of blood on the floor.

"I'm rather curious now," Pomeroy said. He nodded to the door beneath the stairs. "Privates first."

"Sir," Hutchison said, after a moment. "It goes right through that door and all—but we're after cannon and powder stashes. Not this."

Pomeroy looked at him. "I see."

A few moments passed in silence. Both privates kept their eyes straight ahead.

"And you, Private Cooper?" Pomeroy said.

Cooper cleared his throat. "I agree with Willie, sir. I think we should get Hawkes fixed up and rejoin the regiment. We ain't found nothing but bugs and marsh and woods, and I don't see as how getting involved in something like this is, er—for us. Sir."

"Admirable candor, gentlemen. I wouldn't want soldiers under my direct command to feel as though they were doing something that wasn't for them. I know—let's all just sit down and think this through." He lifted the pistol he carried and waved it toward them. "On second thought, you'll do as commanded by your officer—unless you'd prefer six months in the stocks and an ongoing relationship with the lash for insubordination."

He stepped over to the door and turned the knob, keeping his eyes on the other two. "Now, I'm ordering you to go down there. Let's see if we can find out what happened here."

The soldiers exchanged a glance but went through the door, ducking their heads.

"Dark as anything, sir," Hutchison said. "Can't see me own hands."

Pomeroy stepped into the room at the end of the hall and found a lantern. He lit it and handed it forward to Hutchison. As they went down, their shadows flickered on the stone walls, the shadow of the railing to their left spilling out across the floor. The air was musty, and Pomeroy felt the crusted blood beneath his boots. They paused at the bottom.

"Where does it go?" Pomeroy said.

Hutchison held the lantern low to the floor. The blood smeared across the floor, away from the bottom of the stairs.

"What was that?" Cooper said.

"What?" Hutchison said.

Pomeroy had heard nothing—the time he'd spent commanding artillery in the Scottish Highlands two years earlier hadn't left his hearing the better for it.

"A groan," Cooper said.

Hutchison held the lantern out, driving back the shadows to the corners. Narrow shelves lined with bottles and preserves became visible on the wall to their left. The base of the chimney cast a dark shadow behind it.

"Something's not right," Hutchison said.

"Just see where it goes," Pomeroy said.

They didn't move, listening to and watching the other side of the basement.

"And then we can go," Pomeroy added. Hutchison went first, Cooper a pace behind him with his musket lowered. Pomeroy watched as the deep shadow behind the chimney base shifted to the right as they got closer to it. Just as Hutchison came up even with it, a dead body appeared. Hutchison gave a sharp inhale.

"Mary help us," Cooper muttered.

The trail of blood ended in a wide pool. A body hung upside down over it, the ankles tied together. The rope was looped over the end of one crossbeam of the ceiling. Both arms hung free— and the left arm was missing a hand. The man's face was swollen and discolored, splotched with blue and black, the mouth open wide from the pull of gravity on the rest of the head. Hutchison lowered the lantern. The eyes watched them. From the darkness of the distorted face, the gaze follow the three of them. Hutchison stepped back, and the eyes followed the lantern. To the horror of the three men, the man's mouth moved, darkened lips curling. But no sound came out.

"My God, sir." Hutchison gagged and took a step back, leaving a bloody footprint.

During his stint in the artillery, Pomeroy had once seen a soldier get his arm blown off by a misfired shot. The blood loss had been massive, and the fellow hadn't lasted the hour. Looking at the pints of blood on the floor—not to mention what had covered the kitchen and trailed down the stairs—he could find no good way to explain why those eyes and mouth should move at all.

"Perhaps you soldiers were right," he said, standing up straight. "This isn't our business. No one loses that much blood and lives. Not that I've ever seen."

"But—" Hutchison said.

"Let's go, privates," Pomeroy said over him. As he reached the bottom of the stairs, there was a sound from the darkness.

"Something moved," Cooper said.

"I see you. We both see you," someone said from the darkness.

The three of them froze. A cold voice, from the shadows beyond the root cellar door. Pomeroy put a hand on the rough railing and started up. Hutchison followed. The shadows moved with the lantern.

"It's over there," Cooper said, still not moving from the chimney base.

"Come hold me," the voice said.

A figure crossed the low ceiling and landed in front of Cooper. It appeared to be a young man. Pomeroy made out a tattered cloak with boots below the hem.

"Sir, the eyes—" was all Cooper got out before the figure leaped at him. The sound of snapping vertebrae filled the cellar. As Cooper dropped to the floor with a moan, the figure spun on Hutchison. For a second, Pomeroy saw a pale face underneath muddy hair. The eyes caught the flames of the lantern. Hutchison yelled, hurling the lantern at the figure. The glass shattered, spilling oil and flame down the front of the figure. Pomeroy turned and bolted up the stairs. He put his shoulder to the door at full speed. His left foot caught on the top step, and he spilled out into the dark hallway, sliding on the floorboards and the trail of dried blood.

A scream tore from the cellar.

Pomeroy pushed himself up and looked back to the dark stairwell. In the light of the flames, Hutchison stood at the bottom of the stairs, looking up.

"Sir!" Hutchison called. "Help!"

Pomeroy pulled back the hammer on his pistol when a sudden movement to his right caught his attention. A boy stood off to the side, looking at him as though he were just a tad less terrifying than the horrors in the cellar. The boy looked at him and slammed the door closed.

"Open that up!" Pomeroy commanded, waving his pistol.

"Guns won't work," the boy said. His voice was muted as if his hearing was very poor or gone. Pomeroy pointed the gun at the door.

"They're gone," the boy said.

"Out!" Pomeroy ordered. He motioned with his gun for the boy to come out. From behind the door to the cellar, another scream. The boy didn't move so Pomeroy shoved him forward in the house and then stumbled after the child, down the hall, and out the door.

"Sir?" Private Hawkes called out, astride his horse. Through his pain, he'd still kept watch. "What was that?"

Pomeroy grabbed the boy and lifted him up onto Cooper's horse, thrusting the reins into his hands.

"No questions, Hawkes." Pomeroy mounted his own horse. "We're leaving."

"But—"

"No!" Pomeroy shouted. He looked at the farmhouse for a moment and then toward the road. "Bloody hell. This way."

He spurred his horse toward the fields, now growing dark with the setting sun. The others followed. In the twilight behind them, the flames in the cellar of the Chase farmhouse spread.

6

———

THESE DARK WOODS

The waters of the lake were black, reflecting stars that, summer or winter, never did quite match the night sky elsewhere. Ripples touched the rocks along the shore where Corey Lane stood looking out from the trees. Little wind broke the still air, and no frogs or crickets sang. His bones ached, and this place weighed on him worse than ever.

Something had disturbed it. The worry crept up on him when he'd awoken two days earlier, and it had only grown since. He'd tried to write it off as an old man's imagination, but standing here, he couldn't ignore it. He made his way around the shore, looking for signs on the ground, in the grass and reeds: he found hoofprints fifty yards from the lake. Looking closer, he spotted bootprints with them, ones that went to the rocky southern end of the lake. Three, maybe four days old. He stared at them a long while.

Chase wouldn't have done it again. Not after the last time.

Word had reached him about the young Chase who'd broken his neck; the news had stayed long in his head through the days and nights since. Joseph hadn't come to him, and Corey left him to his grief, knowing he'd let him know if he needed help with the boys. Over the years they'd come to an understanding, and now he felt for the man whose family had had its own share of tragedy. Corey looked out across the still water where the moon rose through the tree line. He wasn't going anywhere. Alma would complain—especially after all her haranguing him about leaving.

The lake needed watching: so simple to him, so difficult for his daughters to understand.

Corey did it because of a friendship long-gone. Because of vows made in youth, and a promise made at the side of a deathbed. And because he was the only one left who could.

He reminded himself of all of it as he watched the water from the eaves of the dark woods. A dread came over him, made worse by the sight of the black surface. It was too dark to search the rest of the shore for signs. There was one thing he could do, though— a way to tell. Corey took pained steps to the water. At the edge, he kicked off his light shoes. The mud was cool under his feet. He stepped into the water. His feet sunk into muck and the icy water grabbed his bare ankles.

At first, he heard nothing more than the lap of the water on the shore and the wind rustling the reeds. For a minute, relief grew as he realized that he'd been wrong. As he turned to go, he froze.

The voices filled the air. Voices of the damned.

To the eye, the lake was still, but whispers surrounded him. Here and there, fragments of speech——some in English, most in tongues he didn't understand. Voices moved past him. Cries and screams, mutters and laughter. Women and children pleading in agony. He grimaced and shifted in the mud. The voices grew in number. He struggled to hear anything else.

With a yell, Corey pulled himself from the water, stepping back up onto the grass. All around grew quiet again, nothing but the gentle creaking of the birch and pine trees. The lake stretched before him, scraps of mist clinging to the surface. With a falling in his gut, he turned from the lake. As he took the path that would bring him to his cabin, he cursed old age, cursed the passage of time, cursed the weight of memory and oaths. Mostly, he cursed the lake. He spat on the path. He hated this place, these dark woods where the dead talked.

7

AS GOOD A PLACE AS ANY

The boy led them along a narrow lane beside a brook. Hawkes slumped over his horse's neck. Pomeroy spotted a light up to the left. A cabin nestled at the edge of a clearing, moonlight sketching in the tall grass around it.

"Wait," he said.

Thomas kept riding. With a frown, Pomeroy spurred his horse and came up beside him. He reached across and slapped his shoulder. Thomas startled, staring at him with big eyes.

"Wait," Pomeroy said again, raising his voice.

"It's farther on," Thomas said. "I know a place. Corey Lane will know what to—"

Pomeroy held his hand up and shook his head. "I don't think so—and whoever you're going on about will have to wait. Hawkes can't go any further, and this cabin will do just fine. Housing the king's troops is an honor."

He was exhausted. It had been thirty hours since he'd slept, and he couldn't stop hearing Hutchison's screams in his head. He turned his horse to the cabin and reached long to grab the reins from Hawkes, leading his horse along, too. Looking back, the boy didn't follow.

"Well?" Pomeroy said. "I can't lift Hawkes in there myself."

"We're not far enough. Another few miles and—"

"I'm in no mood to tramp along any further without rest. Now, come along—that's an order."

Thomas looked up the path, then back in the direction they'd come. After a moment, he followed, his face pinched up in worry. There was dim light shining through the lone window on their side. Pomeroy dismounted, every muscle in his legs and back stiff, then limped to the door of the cabin and knocked.

"Open up," he called.

Silence. He stepped to the window. It was a single room and empty by the looks of it. A fire in the hearth was down to red embers. The latch was free, and the door opened. There were leather-working tools in one corner, a cot in another, a hide rug on the floor. A shelf with tin cups, knives, a bag of powder, apples. Faded clothing—but no occupant. Pomeroy turned and approached Hawkes.

"Come," he said, "let's get you down."

The soldier's eyes were still closed, his face a mask of pain.

"Hawkes," he said louder. He reached up. The private trembled. Pomeroy looked over at the boy.

"Help me with him," he said.

A breeze gusted, knocking the door of the cabin against the frame. Together, they wrestled Hawkes down and got him through the doorway. By then, Pomeroy's arms were on the verge of giving out. He blew a rivulet of sweat from his lip. They got Hawkes onto the musty smelling bed. Thomas stared at the injured private's leg. All that jostling hadn't even brought a word from him.

"Tuck him in," Pomeroy said. Thomas nodded and tried to get the blanket on top of Hawkes. Pomeroy straightened up and tended to the dying fire. He put more wood in the center of the embers, blowing on them until sparks rose and the flames caught. There were two squat tallow candles nearby—he lit these off of the flames and put them on the table. A pewter plate and cup were on it, fish and greens still on the plate. A wooden fork was on the floor. He lifted the cup and sniffed. Mead. Looking around, he spotted two small casks on a low bench by the door. He hefted one, then the other. The first was empty, the second untapped.

"First good turn of luck in four days," he said. He carried the full cask to the table.

Thomas stared at him. Pomeroy drained the cup—strong—and poured another, knocking it back in four swallows. The warmth slid down his tongue and throat and blossomed into his chest. That was more like it.

"Your name?" Pomeroy said. The mead was flushing his cheeks.

"Thomas. Thomas Chase."

"And why do you talk that way, Thomas Chase?"

Thomas looked at the floor and turned red. Looked up again.

"I lost my hearing to a fever when a pox came through," he said. "I was six. My mother died of it. My aunt, too. Mister Lane saved me."

Pomeroy poured more mead. "Just not your hearing. Not much of a physician."

The boy frowned. "He'll know what to do—he always knows what to do, and my father told me to go find him. Before what happened at the house."

"Dreadful luck. And yet you can read my lips?" Pomeroy said.

"Unless you mumble, or you're turned where I can't see you well."

"Well, then I shan't mumble. And the rest of your family?"

No answer.

"That was your house?" Pomeroy said. He got a slight nod for an answer. "I see. And what happened? What was in the cellar?"

Again, Thomas said nothing. Just thinking of all the blood in the kitchen—let alone the horror of the cellar—Pomeroy couldn't blame the child for not wanting to repeat or relive it.

"Fine," he said, standing up and draining the cup for the third time. "I suppose it hardly matters at this point. Fetch the horses."

Thomas glanced at the door, then back at him. "I shouldn't be helping you."

"More gratitude would be more like it—unless you've already forgotten who rescued you."

"My family wouldn't want me to."

"The family in your cellar, do you mean?"

The boy looked positively torn, and Pomeroy understood. "Don't tell me you come from a family of uppity malcontents? Colony is rather bristling with them, isn't it? Well, don't believe everything you hear, boy—or, in your case, read on others' lips. Now to the horses."

"They're patriots, known far and wide," Thomas said.

"Well, three cheers for them," Pomeroy said, raising the cup and then taking another long swallow of mead. He pointed to the door.

"But it's dark," the boy said.

"It's night, now snap to it. They'll wander off otherwise."

Thomas hesitated still.

"Have no fear," Pomeroy said. "I'll be in the doorway, both pistols. We're miles from your house." He pulled the pistols from his belt. "And bring Hawkes's musket when you come back in."

Still the boy hesitated, eyeing the night beyond the doorway.

"To the horses, lad," he said.

"I was supposed to get my uncle, and I was supposed to get Jonathon, but I couldn't get either," Thomas said.

"Is that all that's bothering you? Don't let a trifle like letting people down bother you, boy," Pomeroy said. "I've made a veritable career of it—yet look at me now. An esteemed officer. Now, the horses."

Thomas stepped outside and Pomeroy leaned in the doorway, pistols hanging. The night around the cabin was alive with wind and crickets. Pomeroy watched as the boy rounded up the three horses and brought them to a small trough by the side of the cabin, then tied them to a pair of posts. The lad was frightened—and he'd also likely stand on his head if Pomeroy ordered him to.

"Have no fear, young Tommy," he called out to him. "You're under the watchful eye of one of the finest officers of the King's Own Regiment, a strapping young major who's risen through the ranks nearly as fast as his dear father could purchase his commissions."

Thomas struggled to reach Hawkes's musket. Pomeroy raised the pistols, admiring the shadow he cast in front of him.

"Beloved by his men, trusted and respected by his superiors, he represented the cream of British might. Why, even his own family eventually noticed that he'd been shipped off for his gallant postings—oh, how the tears must have flowed," Pomeroy said.

The boy came back to the door, and Pomeroy stepped aside with a flourish. Thomas carried the musket, careful not to let it smack the door.

"Ah, you seem a natural with that musket, young master Chase," Pomeroy said. The boy wasn't looking at him, but that didn't stop him. "A right grenadier-to-be, and with my officiary brilliance to model, you'll go far. Just ask Hawkes. Or Cooper and good Hutchison."

Thomas put the musket against the table and searched the cabin for more food, coming across potatoes and half a loaf of bread.

Pomeroy put his pistols on the table, locked the cabin door, and poured another cup of mead. "It might have gone much worse without my leadership. And that, young Tommy, is precisely why I'm the officer to lead a secretive and dangerous powder-hunt, to catch the local militias unawares. So secret—

now listen up, young master—so secret that not even his commanders knew about it."

Pomeroy winked at the boy and drained his cup yet again. The boy looked confused. Pomeroy shook the second cask—it was still two-thirds full.

Yes, this was more like it.

WHEN HE OPENED his eyes the next morning, Pomeroy winced. It was cruelly bright. His back and neck were stiff from sleeping on the floor. He lifted his head and worked his mouth, his tongue as dry as velvet. The boy sat before the fireplace—and he held one of Pomeroy's pistols, pointing it right at him.

"Put that down and tell me you haven't fed that fire all night," Pomeroy said.

"You're an officer. I'm taking you prisoner," Thomas said. "And we'll get Corey Lane."

Pomeroy sat up with a groan. He reached over and took the pistol, grabbing it by the barrel and pulling it out of the boy's hand with little resistance.

"Hardly," he said. He looked at the pistol—it hadn't even been properly cocked.

"I could have shot you in your sleep."

"And I'd probably have felt better," Pomeroy said, setting the pistol to rights. "This is dangerous and you're too young to go fooling with it, boy."

"I can shoot better than my brother."

"Well, so can I," Pomeroy said. "And yet I'm here in these miserable Colonies while he enjoys the wine and women of Hampshire. Not to mention Father's wealth and hearth."

He cleared his throat and looked around the room. His head pounded. What a bloody mess. He got to his feet with care and went to the window. Midmorning sunlight dappled the trees and meadow near the cabin. Pomeroy grabbed the water-skins from the table and walked over to the boy. "Have you heard of a tavern by the name of Brewster's?"

"It's in the village, next to my father's printing shop."

At least that was something. Pomeroy held out the water-skins.

"Well, then, Thomas, go fill these in the stream," he said. "We have things to do."

Thomas stared at the skins without moving. Pomeroy tossed them, and Thomas caught them.

"Look, if this is about me being an officer and you being from a family of rabble-rousers, then don't get too knickered up about it," Pomeroy said. "You'll show me the way to town, show me the way to the local physician, and then the tavern—and that's it. I'm hardly about to drag you around by way of an example of the king's might."

The boy still didn't appear convinced.

"I can hang a sign around your neck reading 'Not Colluding' if you'll just get the water."

With a frown of resignation, the boy left. Perhaps he'd run off now—though the fact he hadn't during the night when he could have danced a jig an inch from Pomeroy's mead-filled head and not woken him made him suspect that the boy was either very frightened or very confused. Pomeroy assumed he could find the way to the heart of the village without too much trouble on his own, if need be. He turned and walked over to the bed.

"And what about you, Hawkes?" he said. He tapped the leg of the bed. Hawkes didn't stir. Pomeroy gave his shoulder a nudge, but he still didn't wake. He held his hand under the private's nose, checking for breath. The man's forehead was hot, and the blankets soaked through with sweat.

"The unstoppable Royal Grenadier," he said.

He'd have to deal with this. Too much mead, too little

thought. Not much had gone right on this powder hunt. He frowned, thinking about the farmhouse. Cooper and Hutchison. The boy came running in, pulling him from his ruminations.

"Where are the water-skins?" Pomeroy said. The boy's hands were empty.

"Come look," Thomas said. He spun around and ran back outside.

Pomeroy looked at the open door for a moment and then followed him, not bothering to put his boots on. As he jogged after the boy, he grunted—it felt as if the inside of his head was full of broken crockery. And if the sunlight coming in through the window had been bad, being outdoors in the morning was brutal. Thomas led him over to where the brook cut across a strip of cleared land. The water ran fast over the stones, a foot deep in places and two strides wide. Stepping into the water, Thomas waded upstream, to a point where the brook widened into a slower moving pool, where the water filtered the sunlight into waving bands of gold on the bottom. Maple trees hung over the left side, while a large elm marked the start of a clump of woods on the right. Thomas stepped along the large rocks at the edge and pointed to the bank. Pomeroy followed, his feet slipping into the icy water.

"Now I'm awake," he said.

He saw nothing at first. The bank was thick with roots from the elm and mossy stones. He looked more carefully. White sleeve and the brown of homespun breeches nestled underneath the earth and twisted roots. With a splash, he stepped deeper into the water, his feet sliding on the smooth rocks on the bottom. It was a man, arms folded across the chest and the legs crossed—as if he'd taken a leisurely nap among the roots by the brook side. Blood caked the back of his head. The body was wedged in good, and quite dead—the skin was a drained white gray, cold to the touch. Pomeroy turned to the boy.

"Do you know who he is?" he said.

Thomas watched his mouth and then shook his head. Pomeroy turned back and grabbed the man's shirt near the shoulder and gave it a careful pull. The arm was stiff. With a grimace, Pomeroy pulled harder, until the body slid free. The head hung back, matted hair pointing out in several directions. Thomas splashed in closer behind him. The man had been in his thirties and thin. Several of his teeth were missing. Around his nose and mouth was a black substance. Pomeroy reached up and grabbed a twig from the bank and then scraped some of the black matter from the face. He brought it to his nose and sniffed. It smelled of rot and clay and made the back of his neck tighten. He tossed the twig into the water. Lifting the shoulder, he bent and looked underneath. Absolutely lovely. The back of the man's head was shattered, a mess of skin, bone, hair, and dry blood. He lowered the body and pushed it back in until it was where it had been when the boy had found it. He stood up.

"As good a place as any," he said, wiping his hands on his breeches. "I have no inclination to wrestle him out and lug him around until we find a better place. Being in the roots and stones is the least of that fellow's problems."

Leaning over, he splashed his hands in the water, forcing himself to splash his face. He climbed back to the grass. Thomas stared at the body for a moment longer, then turned and followed. He was tripping over Pomeroy's heels to stay nearby. Pomeroy felt queasy and weak but tried not to show it. Back at the cabin, he gathered his boots and dressed. Thomas stood looking at Private Hawkes.

"Is he all right?" Thomas said. He turned to look at Pomeroy.

"No, he's not all right," Pomeroy said, pulling on a boot. "In fact, I think he's closer to our friend out by the stream there than he is to us. Private Hawkes fell from a tree he'd climbed to take a peek around."

Thomas lifted the damp sheet, and his jaw fell. The soldier's right leg was swollen and discolored, the toes black.

"What are you going to do?" Thomas said.

Pomeroy got his other boot on and stood up. "I will wait right here while you fetch those water-skins. Then, we're off to fetch this lovely rural hamlet's physician. I will then press him into service of the king's army, so he can take care of Hawkes here. You will show me the way." He looked at Thomas. "Now hurry. Private Hawkes is waiting for us."

Thomas looked from the private to him to the fireplace, which was down to shifting embers again. He nodded his head and ran outside.

They made their way across meadows until reaching a road that led west, crossing stone walls and low fences in the warming April sunlight. The roads were empty and often in shadow from the overhanging trees. The boy turned in the saddle to see Pomeroy's face.

"There's someone who can help," he said.

"Hawkes?" Pomeroy said.

"No. Us. Corey Lane, and he knows my father and watches over my brother and me, and he lives north of the—"

"Is he a doctor?"

"No, but he'll know about what's happening."

"As will our good doctor, lad."

"It's the other way."

"The doctor and then the tavern," Pomeroy said. "Everything else will wait."

And not be my problem, he added to himself. They crossed a wooden bridge over a stream. A white steeple came into view along with a handful of buildings. The center of the village lay to the left, but the boy pointed to the right, where a rutted lane wound through tall trees. A white house came into view, dark green shutters open on the many windows.

"This is the one?" Pomeroy said.

The boy nodded. The house was enormous and well-kept. They rode up to the front. A carriage stood off to the side, next to a low carriage house. Pomeroy dismounted and tossed the reins to the boy.

"Hold," he said. He walked to the front door and swung the brass knocker twice, two quick taps. He straightened his hat. The door opened, and a young woman looked out. She wore a dress of quality cotton, trimmed with deep blue. Her eyes were the gray of a London sky.

"Dr. Bucknell, if you would," Pomeroy said.

"And you are?"

"Major Pomeroy, Fifth Regiment of Foote. The King's Own is in need of the good doctor's services."

She looked at him, up and down.

"And did the King's Own just crawl through a swamp?" she said.

Pomeroy knew that his uniform had developed an aroma that was noteworthy. Like all soldiers in the king's service, he had to keep several sets of breeches and shirts and to keep them fresh. He'd left them back at the regiment on the night he'd taken the men and headed north—the haze of rum having obscured such details.

"Well, if spotless, silken finery is more to your tastes," he said, "we regrettably weren't able to bring along the regimental tailor."

She looked past his shoulder.

"Thomas Chase?" she said. It was an accusation. She pushed out the door and past Pomeroy, to the gravel path where the horses were. She stopped in front of the boy. "What are you doing here? Have they forced you to do this—and where are Jonathon and your father?"

Thomas frowned. "He told me what your father did."

"What my father did?"

"Told the British of the powder store, and Nathan died because—"

Pomeroy followed after her, irritated. "This is all quite interesting, but I'm here for your father—not for you to tongue-lash my young companion."

"His family is no friend of the king's army, sir," she said, "and he will not take kindly to his being pressed into your service."

Pomeroy raised his voice. His headache had returned. "The king's army will press into service whosoever it sees fit, Madam. And at this moment, Dr. Bucknell is required. As for any other details of our operations, I should thank you to restrain yourself."

She ignored him and turned back to the boy. "Have they hurt you? Get down from there. You can stay with us until Jonathon and your father are back."

The boy set his jaw and shook his head. His look was daggers, clear enough for Pomeroy to wonder what had gone on between them—for something had.

"We have business to attend to, I'm afraid," Pomeroy said, "and young master Thomas has important tasks ahead of him. Is Dr. Bucknell here?"

His tone insisted on no more distractions. She turned to him and stepped in, pointing a finger at him.

"Let me tell you something, Major," she said. "If even the slightest bit of harm comes to him when he is in your company, you'll not only have to answer to the Chase men but to me as well. Perhaps your filthy uniform and horses have impressed a child, but few around here care to see a Chase boy in the company of English soldiers."

Pomeroy thought of a crow, the way she pecked at him with her finger and squawked at him. He was all too familiar with such young women, growing up a Pomeroy in Hampstead. Well-to-do by virtue of their family, convinced of their own rightness, driven to tell everyone else how they ought to behave in every situation.

As she spoke, he noticed that the gray in her eyes was flecked with green.

"The locals may think what they wish," he said, "but the boy is perfectly safe and providing a necessary service to my company. Now, your father—where is he? I really must insist."

She stepped back and folded her arms across her chest. "Not here. Rode into town an hour ago."

"To where?"

"Brewster's Tavern," she said.

Pomeroy smiled. He took a step back, swept his hat off in an elaborate bow, then turned to go.

"I thank you indeed, Miss Bucknell," he said. He stepped to his horse, and the boy tossed him the reins. Pomeroy lifted himself onto the saddle. "Come, young master Chase. Our mission takes us to the tavern—lead the way, if you would."

THE CENTER of West Bradhill was an arrangement of small businesses and houses in the shape of an L on the northeast corner of a green. A church stood on the far side. Next to it, an old man wearing all black—the town reverend, Pomeroy assumed—was gesturing to a man on a wagon.

"You know her," Pomeroy said to the boy.

"Carolyn? She's in love with Jonathon."

"Jonathon?"

"My brother."

"The one whom you shoot better than?"

The boy nodded. "She's more in love with him than she'll admit—that's what Jonathon says."

"Well, he would, wouldn't he? They are betrothed?"

The boy looked at him, shook his head. "Her family are loyalists."

"Your tone tells me you don't think much of loyalists, boy."

"I told you, Jonathon and my father and uncle are patriots."

"Oh, are they?" Pomeroy wasn't sure the boy's father was much of anything anymore, judging by what he saw in the cellar of their house.

"Jonathon chides her that her father will only be happy to see her married to an officer. A British officer."

"A sound theory," Pomeroy said. "All things considered." She had seemed rather taken with him when she first saw him at the door.

He brushed dried dirt off of his uniform as they rode past a cooper and a blacksmith and came to a stop in front of the tavern. The largest of the businesses in the village, the tavern was two stories tall and painted green. The shutters were black next to windows of six-over-six lead panes. A painted sign—decorated with a frothy mug—read: Brewster's Tavern & Victuals, Jude Brewster, propr. Twin lanterns bracketed the doorway. Pomeroy got down from his horse and then helped Thomas from his.

"Stay with the horses," he said. He motioned to a water trough off to the side where an old nag stood. Pomeroy pushed open the tavern door, a rich red that shone in the sunlight. He stepped into a common room. It took a moment for his eyes to adjust to the darkness inside. Long tables and benches stood before a wide hearth. Lanterns hung from the low ceiling beams. The air held the pleasant smell of fresh ale; Pomeroy inhaled deeply. Two men stood near the hearth. They stopped talking and stared at him.

"Gentlemen," he said, walking in, "your king requires the service of Dr. Bucknell."

Neither man moved.

"And you are?" the older man said. The other man appeared to be his servant.

"Major William Pomeroy, Fifth Regiment of Foote. Of the Pomeroys of Hampshire, sir."

The older man's eyebrows rose, and he tilted his head in approval. He looked at the other man. "As I said," he said, as though concluding a debate. He stepped forward and bowed. "I could hardly have asked for better news, Major. Rest assured that not all the countryside shares the madness of rebellion. Israel Bucknell, physician, at your service."

Rebellion? Pomeroy smiled at the doctor. What on earth was he getting at?

"Tell me, Major," Dr. Bucknell said, "are the other communities pacified? And the troops surrounding Boston—have they been dispersed?" He approached Pomeroy and lowered his voice, putting a hand on his shoulder. "All along I trusted the king's men would not tolerate such aggression—and though much of our village and the nearby towns have mustered their weaponry —I should be glad to see your men garrisoned here," he said. "Anything is preferable to the entire colony crawling with armed militia and more coming in every day."

Pomeroy had a bad feeling. "Quite," he said. "And about your services, Doctor. One of my men has been injured—an accident with a tree and his leg. And the ground, I suppose."

That was it. Get the doctor to Hawkes. Hawkes will have to take care of himself after that. This talk of militia and troops wasn't making his head ache any less. A drink was what he needed—now that he was, finally and after all, at the legendary Brewster's Tavern. Pomeroy caught the attention of the doctor's servant.

"Run and fetch the tavern keep, would you?" he said.

The servant gave him a strange look. "Well, Major Pomeroy of the King's Regiment, I am the tavern keep."

He was a Negro—in the northern colonies, one could never be certain who was a free man and who wasn't. Pomeroy swept off his hat and bowed.

"A thousand pardons, sir," he said. He put the hat back on. "I am a fool—please forgive me. If it brings consolation, I can tell you that word of your brewing prowess has spread far and wide, and I'm most eager to find myself on the outside of one of your legendary ales. I've not had a drop in days."

The tavern keep looked at him. "Be glad to, in one moment."

With that, he disappeared into the kitchen, toward the back of the tavern. Dr. Bucknell tapped the floorboards with his cane. "And how has the fighting been?"

Pomeroy ran a hand across the stubble on his chin. "I've lost some men," he said.

"Pity."

"Indeed."

"And how many troops do you command, Major?"

"My company is small—but tenacious," he said.

The tavern keep returned, a tall pewter mug in his hand. A head of froth jiggled across the top. Pomeroy's mouth watered. The aroma of hops, spice and fruit, and finally yeast touched his nose. The door to the tavern opened and the boy stuck his head in. He looked at Pomeroy, who shook his head and made sure the boy could read his lips.

"Not now, boy," he said.

"But—" Thomas said.

The door opened wider and two tall men walked in. Behind them, a large troop of men stood in the road before the tavern, muskets shouldered, a small forest of them. The two men paused for a moment—eyes adjusting from the sunlight—and looked at Pomeroy. He paused with the mug two inches from his lips.

"Redcoat!" the first man yelled, raising the bayonet end of his musket. Before Pomeroy could do anything, more militia barreled in through the doorway.

"Oh, bloody hell." With a heavy heart, Pomeroy threw the mug into the face of the leading militia man, foaming ale splashing everywhere. He turned and blew past the tavern keep, knocking a few chairs over as he passed them, and ran into the kitchen. With a spin, he threw over the heavy table in the center. He ran to the back door and opened it. He hurried by a stable, toward a copse of trees. Men spilled out the back door of the tavern. A shot went off and some leaves above his head fluttered down as the ball sang through them. He sped into the thicker evergreens beyond, gasping for breath.

"Good Christ!" he yelled as he ran.

8

WORDS TO REMEMBER

Darkness fell across the land, bringing cool night with it. A pair of crows argued in the trees by his cabin. When the stars appeared, Corey entered the hut behind his cabin, lantern in hand. Along one wall hung some of the things the villagers had given him: brooms, hand tools, ceramic jars from the preserves they often gave him in exchange for his remedies or finding a spot for a well or lending a hand with whatever needed fixing. Over the years, he'd used it to store firewood in the winter and dry his rye and barley in the warm months, a testament to creeping practicality. He stood for several minutes, looking around the hut he'd built, remembering the week they'd built it. Young men, then—he twenty, twenty-one, and Pannalancet a year and a half older. The hut was for ceremonies; now the tiny room smelled of must and mouse droppings.

Corey pulled out the wooden box he kept deep in the storage trunk. He put the box on the floor and propped the lantern next to it before kneeling with a grunt. With a puff, he blew the dust off the box and opened it. Folded up sheets of paper. Feathers. Bones. Rocks. Tins of powder. Pouches of herbs. He wondered if maybe he'd be better off stuffing the box back into the trunk and uncorking the last jug of whiskey instead.

It reminded him of Pannalancet. Not the rail-thin specter he'd become before consumption had taken him shy of his thirty-third year, hollow-eyed and gaunt. No, the instructions and ingredients were from the young man, hale, hearty, and brimming with spirit, years before that.

Don't forget what you promised. I may have been dying, but I was more serious than I'd ever been.

Corey shook his head. "I know. Don't nag me."

Unfolding the brittle paper, he squinted at the faded ink. The lantern shifted in front of him, orange hearts and yellow tendrils dancing. He brought the page close to his face, and he read.

The lantern burned low by the time Corey returned to the present. His hips ached as though packed with red coals. For several minutes, he stared into the lantern. He got to his feet, unsteady at first. He put everything back into the box and tucked it under his arm, then shuffled to the door with the lantern. The air outside was cold. He tried to forget about what now roamed the night near West Bradhill. Once inside his cabin, he drank water and wrapped himself in blankets, getting in bed. His eyes focused past the ceiling above him. He understood what he needed to do and which words to remember.

I have to do this, he thought, over and over.

Words.

The dawn woke him, tired as he was. With hardly a pause, he climbed from his bed and got ready to ride into the village. Once dressed, he put on his hat and used the tree stump to get up onto his horse. It took more than one try.

"Don't give me that look," he said to the horse.

As he rode, he saw the lake through the trees. He recalled what he'd read, the notes from Pannalancet: the ceremony of skulls and clay to shut the gate, the ceremony of bloodfire to seal it.

That was what he had to remember. He grimaced as he watched the glints of morning sunlight on the surface of the cursed water. The lake had been disturbed, used yet again in the pursuit of the impossible. And the embers he'd thought had long ago grown cold and gray hadn't. This time, the curse could spread, flaming to life, consuming everything nearby—and he was on his own in stopping it. Much as he tried to convince himself that it was early enough to seal everything up before the veil between this world and the others opened any further, a voice in his head reminded him that Pannalancet had been alive the last time. That now he was alone. Now he was old.

The whiskey sounded better.

The ride to town was long, and with each step his worries grew. When he at last came to the tavern in the center of the village, he was sweating in the April sunshine. He dismounted with a groan and hitched the horse out front. Before going inside, he looked around the village. The streets were empty. No clanging or smoke came from the blacksmith or the cooper. A few women talked near the front of the church. The reverend emerged from the shadowed doorway and looked about.

It had been better before that one came, Corey thought. Back then, a morning like this would have seen handfuls of Pennacook people alongside the English, living well. Enough that the lake gave no trouble to anyone. It wasn't just time that did its worst—it was people, too.

He spit into the dirt before pushing the tavern door open. Jude Brewster was at the big hearth, pouring sliced vegetables into a giant simmering pot. There was no one else there.

"You missed your chance to join the fight," Brewster said, nodding toward the road outside.

"I'm an old man. What's your excuse?"

"I'm old in spirit."

Corey waved his hand in dismissal. "Where've they all gone?"

Brewster put down the cutting board after flicking off the last of the potatoes and went over to one of his casks. He told Corey about the militia and the other troops, the officer from earlier in the morning. He filled a mug with a dark ale, brought it over to Corey, who took it with a nod of thanks.

"Samuel with them?" he said. He took a sip of the malty brew. "I need to talk with him."

Brewster shook his head, told him what he'd seen, what he'd heard.

"Burned?" Corey said.

"The troops mentioned seeing their house burning from the road. Young Thomas was here, looking for help."

"Here?"

"Wouldn't stay—I tried to get him to, but he wasn't making much sense, trying to get through to the troops, going on about his house, his father. In all the commotion, he ran off."

The ale suddenly didn't taste of anything in his mouth. They stood out front a short time later. Across the green, the reverend spotted them, pointed, and said something to the women out in front.

"He's a sour one," Brewster said.

"Worse than sour. He's dangerous."

A pair of riders came down the way, each with a musket on his back. They tilted their hats and kept on riding.

"Been no friend to the village, though many think he's the best we've got," Corey said.

"I wouldn't say many. You know better than most. Yet you've never raised a hand against him."

"I've got more important worries."

"You stuck it out here through some hard years. No one would have blamed you if you'd have moved on."

"You sound like my daughters."

"Even after everything that happened."

"Because of everything that happened." He beat the dust from his hat and put it back on his head. "Thanks for the drink. I need to find the Chases. They're in trouble."

"English soldiers around, they likely are."

"More than that. You see them, send them out."

He untied his horse. Brewster came forward, gave him a hand up onto the saddle.

"Old in spirit's one thing," Corey said. "Old in body's for the birds."

"I'll keep my eyes open for Joseph."

Corey pulled the horse around. "For anything else, too."

"Anything else?"

"Anyone mentions seeing anything odd. You see anything strange, trust your instinct. Especially at night."

9

A BRUISE IN THE DARKNESS

They hadn't been with the militia.

Jonathon kept worrying that thought—worrying it sharp—as he made his way back to West Bradhill. The day faded into cool evening and then darkness as he reached the apple orchards at the edge of the village. None of this was working out. He'd gotten as far as Andover before stopping to rest. To his chagrin, he'd slept most of the afternoon, waking to the noise of the West Bradhill militia itself marching along the road he was next to. He decided he'd follow them, then step out when they reached Boston—his father couldn't well send him back at that point.

But they hadn't been there. Not his father, not his uncle. It looked as though old Henry Salter had been leading the men. The thought stung him that his father and uncle were still in West Bradhill, looking for him. With that, he'd turned back.

He came out of the woods near his house and stopped. The acrid scent of smoke was strong—he'd noticed it off and on for a mile or more, but he had thought little of it. His breath caught. The farmhouse smoldered. Red glows brightened and dimmed with the wind around the ashen timbers. Jonathon put his hands to the sides of his head and let out a tortured cry.

He ran up the hill. As he got closer, he slowed. The house had burned to black beams; the roof fallen in, collapsed into charcoal. Carolyn's words from a week earlier echoed in his mind: "Father says he expects the garrison at Boston and the garrisons of Quebec to put down the whole countryside, one town at a time. Even West Bradhill will be under their eyes. And they'll be going after the leaders first."

Jonathon shook his head, breathing hard.

<u>Thomas.</u>

His exhaustion vanished, replaced with fear and anger. He took off in a sprint to the road and didn't slow until he reached the old fallen cabin that he and Thomas had often played in. He hoped that his younger brother might have escaped to it—but it was empty. He left his pack there—the straps had dug deep into his shoulders—and hurried to the river, following it south to his uncle's mill. The river splashing behind the building was loud in the darkness. The water wheel didn't turn, the lock before it closed, forcing the water to spill through an opening on the other side. Jonathon stood as still as the giant wheel, peering around the corner. He ducked back behind the building and followed the wall until he found the door and pushed, slipping inside. He found a lantern and lit it, taking it through the passage to the house. Once inside, Jonathon walked from room to room. It didn't look as if anyone had been there for days.

He stopped outside his uncle's study. In the room, shattered glass glinted, strewn across the floor. He crossed to where the window had been. He knelt. A few scratches marred the boards, but he found no blood nor signs of what might have happened to his uncle. He went to the stairs. A clump of soil decorated the second step. It was dry, with a tuft of grass still on one side. He started up and found more bits of earth. The narrow stairway took a ninety-degree turn to the right. Coming up to the second story, Jonathon stopped. The hallway led straight back and rooms lined the hallway. A foul odor hung in the hallway. The doors to the rooms were closed save for the last one on the right.

"Uncle Joseph?" he called.

Silence. A breeze stirred against Jonathon's face. There was a window at the end of the hallway. Open. The lantern didn't cut the darkness that far. Another three steps, and he stood at the top. He wrinkled his nose. The odor was strong—rotting flesh. Muddy tracks crossed the floor. He took a few steps, the lantern out in front of him.

Something slid behind one of the closed doors.

Jonathon jerked the lantern. The sound had come from a room on the left: Nathan's. Looking inside, he found the room disheveled, blankets thrown across the floor, and the bed flipped on its side, the window open. Dried dirt smudged the sill. The lantern flickered in the wind. He turned and looked over the room. Other than the disturbed blankets and bed, it was empty. Back at the door, he stopped, listening. A rustle of cloth came from the hallway. Jonathon poked his head out, but didn't see anything. He crossed the hall to the door opposite, then bowed his head and listened. After a moment, he opened the door. Folded cloth lined a shelf. Beneath, boots and candles filled the floor.

A thud came from behind him. The muscles in his neck tightened. He wanted to get out of the house, to run. Like a swift change in air pressure before a fast summer storm, the atmosphere in the house shifted. He looked toward the stairs. The chest on the landing was open, its lid leaning back against the railing behind it.

It had been closed when he'd come up the stairs.

Then he saw a figure with his back to the rail, shoulders hunched, the face a pale dough above dirty clothes. The figure raised its head, and Jonathon staggered back. His uncle stared at him, dark circles around his eyes and mouth, his skin drained white. His eyes shone in the light of the lantern.

"I had naught to lose," Joseph said, his voice choked, "because we already lost everything at the burning, when it settled on us. On me, on you."

"Uncle Joseph?" Jonathon asked.

The figure leaned forward to get to his feet, moving as though it were drunk. The stench of an animal carcass hit Jonathon.

"And it was true, that I was a cuckold, and I knew where it come from. I heard."

Joseph got to his feet and moved toward Jonathon.

"What's happened?" Jonathon asked.

"And he begged and wept and swore it weren't him but that didn't stop me. And I killed him, choked him until he turned black, black as the curse that stole our lives." He blocked the way to the stairs. His uncle's voice sounded as though he was speaking through a throat full of rocks. "Buried him out in the woods, just as I buried any hope I'd still had. They were both sick then, dying. But your mother came to me, boy—came to me and treated me right, treated me right half a dozen times, right in the mill, even with her sores weeping, and her fever burning her up inside and out, burning her between her legs."

Joseph staggered, hitting the wall as if he were blind. A terrible rush of wind rose from the first floor. Jonathon stepped back, sliding along the wall, and dropped the lantern. Something moved on the stairs. A figure in shadow behind his uncle. Whatever courage Jonathon felt earlier disappeared in a wash of terror. He backed off and turned into the open door on the right, sliding to a stop. The air was frigid and reeked of foul earth.

Half a dozen pairs of silver eyes broke the shadows. They fell on Jonathon. Hands grabbed him, strong, pulling him to the filthy floor. He couldn't pull himself free. One of them smashed his head hard against the floorboards and flipped him over onto his back. Glimmering eyes moved in and cold flesh pressed against his own, on his hands, on his neck. The figures turned from him. His uncle stood in the doorway, eyes burning like distant stars. Jonathon thrashed his arms and legs to break free. His uncle moved closer. The temperature plummeted and the other dead moved away from the door. His uncle staggered until he stood over Jonathon. Rough hands wrenched Jonathon's head upward, toward the lowering eyes of his uncle. The odor was putrid, overpowering, but the more Jonathon struggled, the harder the hands gripped him. Panic took him, and he screamed.

After a second, Jonathon's scream was cut short. His uncle was on top of him, icy lips clamping over his own. The touch was repulsive beyond measure. Jonathon couldn't turn away. His last breath was of the coldest air he'd ever felt. There was a gagging noise and then a thick liquid filled his mouth. As it worked its way inside of him, Jonathon could only stare into his uncle's silver eyes—and drown.

10

AND A BLOODY PLAN

Pomeroy stood on the bank of the brook looking up at the cabin. No horses, the cabin dark. After running and hiding for most of the afternoon, after stumbling through the darkened woods into the evening in a ridiculous search for the cabin and his horse, he was in no mood for this. He should have tied up the boy or locked him inside the cabin. First the child had neglected to mention that armed rebellion had erupted, then he'd set the militia on him—and now this.

He kicked the ground in anger and swore.

The door to the cabin was open. He stepped up onto the porch and paused. In the fireplace inside, the last hints of a fire glowed among ash. He put a hand against the door frame and looked around the inside. Hawkes sat up on the cot against the far wall.

"Hawkes?" Pomeroy said.

The man didn't move. His head hung, both arms stretched out resting on the knees. A sharp knock came from against the outside wall. Pomeroy leaned back and looked but saw nothing. The wind must have rattled the trees. He walked inside.

"Well, I see you're awake," he said. "Come on, grab your things and help me get mine. We're leaving."

Hawkes lifted his head and looked terrible. His eyes were black, his skin pale. A wet, rattling cough shook him, and a jet of black liquid spilled from his mouth to the floor.

Pomeroy stopped, staring.

Hawkes shook his head and spoke in a thin voice: "No good, Major. He come for me, and knows all of what I did. Every bit. The prison, he knew what I did—how'd he know about that? Now it's all inside me. Climbing up behind me eyes."

Pomeroy didn't move, didn't want to get any closer to the private. Something festered in this village, and it was spreading. All he wanted was his satchel and a weapon and to leave. "Where's your musket, Hawkes?"

The private groaned and lay on his side. He struggled for a breath and blew out another stream of fluid. It dripped from his mouth and chin, spilling off the side of the wooden cot. There was a sound from the roof, near the back, a sharp tap on the small single-paned window at the front. Pomeroy spun. There was a lightning-bolt-shaped crack in the glass. As he looked, there was another light tap, and a small rock bounced off the open door and landed on the floorboards. He looked back at Hawkes, faint in the darkness, then stepped to the door and looked out across the meadow in front of the cabin.

Someone waved at him from beyond the maple trees, not quite in the meadow. The moon slipped from behind the clouds, and Pomeroy recognized the boy, Thomas. He waved his arms with urgency, motioning him to come. Again, there was a noise from the roof, a quick series of muted thuds.

"His skin was white. And cold," Hawkes said. He retched again. Another thud on the roof

Pomeroy looked up. He leaped from the door and off the creaking porch. He sprang forward but something caught his cloak. The movement put him off balance, and he fell headlong to the ground. He rolled onto his back. A shadow draped the ground before him. The figure rose, the shape of a person—almost. The angles were wrong. Neck too long, arms differing lengths, thin and twisted. The face stretched and white, and the eyes a cold, rippling silver. The red of the British uniform shown maroon in the night.

"Cooper?" Pomeroy said.

It was Cooper but not at all the way he'd seen him last.

"Good God, what's happened to you?" Pomeroy said. He pushed himself backward.

The private cocked his head to the side and regarded him with those eyes. His head leaned forward, chin pointing at him. With an uneven long stride, he closed the distance to Pomeroy and leaned down, his back arching, his eyes fixed on Pomeroy's own.

"You left us, coward," the thing that was Cooper said. "Left us to our feast."

His voice was a harsh whisper. Fetid breath washed over Pomeroy.

"I didn't—"

"But now you'll taste what you missed and dream forever of her."

"Her?"

Cooper grabbed him by the collar and lifted him until he was an inch from that horrible face, gagging on the putrid smell.

"Young Darcy," Cooper whispered, "dancing in the night. Oh, you'll dream of her and dream of the times you touched yourself. Had her touch you, tricked her, used her. Dream as you crawl forever."

Pomeroy struggled to pull free. How could Cooper know about Darcy? His stepsister had been all of fourteen when they'd spent a summer hiding their twisted games from the entire family. It had ended with him being shipped off to the military by

Lord Pomeroy. She'd never answered a single one of his letters after that.

Cooper leaned close, and a dribble of black liquid slid from his mouth. Pomeroy pushed, but Cooper's hands and arms and chest were taught, unyielding as oak. An explosion belched from behind, and a flash lit the figure. Cooper flew backward, his head driven back. Still, he stayed upright. His right eye was extinguished, and his hand ran back and forth across his face like a crab, feeling around where the shot had gone in the socket. Pomeroy turned around and got to his feet. Cooper hunched over, his arms out in front of him, bent at the elbows. A second explosion went off, and the private's head snapped sideways, half of it a rain of bone and bloody fanning out over the grass.

"Run! Now!" Thomas shouted.

Pomeroy didn't need to hear it twice. He leaped from where Cooper staggered and sped toward the trees. Just in front of them, the boy stood, the musket still up to his shoulder. On the ground next to him was a second musket.

"Told you I could shoot," the boy said.

"What are you doing here?" Pomeroy said.

"Knew you'd be back. I waited," the boy said.

Cooper lurched across the rolls of the meadow, hands in front of him. The back of his skull hung loose and his one remaining eye glimmered. Thomas picked up the first musket and handed it to Pomeroy, then ran across the path and into the forest. Tracing the boy's path, he crashed through the slender branches that marked the start of the woods. Two horses were tied to low branches. Pomeroy knelt in front of the boy and took a handful of Thomas's shirt.

"What about Hawkes?" he said.

Thomas shook his head, his face unreadable in the darkness. "It's too late. He already got him."

Pomeroy let the boy go, staring back through the woods. "Piss on it all," he muttered.

Thomas turned and untied the nearest of the horses. He used a stone to step up, getting himself high enough to reach the stirrup. He swung up onto the horse and looked at Pomeroy.

"We have to go," Thomas said. "Now."

Pomeroy couldn't hold back the laughter. Just minutes ago, he'd feared for his life, appalled at what had happened to Cooper and Hawkes. Now he was taking orders from a child—a colonial child at that, too short to get onto a horse without aid. Pomeroy hurried to the other horse. At least someone had guts—and a bloody plan.

11

LONG ENOUGH FOR THE ROPE

Something woke her. Carolyn Bucknell sat up in her bed and listened, irritated. It had taken hours to fall asleep—the events of the day kept running through her mind, especially the thought of Jonathon running around somewhere, hunting or being hunted by British troops. The ticking of the grandfather clock in the hallway was loud. She got out of bed and wrapped a robe about herself, glancing out the window. The yard was darkness.

Off in the center of town, candles shone in the windows of the tavern and at Reverend Watts's home. This talk of invasion and rebellion was evidently keeping others awake. She crossed the room and out into the hall. Light came from the stairway. The tall clock chimed a quiet ring—it was three a.m. A lantern burned in her father's study. Carolyn went down the stairs in her bare feet and stopped outside his door. He was at his desk with a quill in hand, staring hard at the page. After a moment, he dipped the quill and continued writing.

"Father?" she said.

He startled and turned to her. His writing lenses were low on his nose. "You surprised me, child."

"I'm sorry."

"Why aren't you sleeping?"

"I was," she said. "Why aren't you?"

He sat back in his chair and took off his glasses, put the quill into the ink well. "These times are worrisome and won't go the way of those that don't rise to them. I'm sending out correspondence I pray will bolster our cause."

"Jonathon says liberty is their cause."

Doctor Bucknell lowered his chin and gave her a weary look. "Cheap talk, nothing more. Laid out by those who intend to steal away that which they already possess in abundance. These are coarse men, darling. Small of mind and brutish in nature. Likely you are unaware, but the Chase men themselves have quite a reputation in the village—a reputation you wouldn't want to have haunting you. They and all the others like them will, I'm afraid, pay a steep price for their talk. Talk is no substitute for character."

"Character," she said.

"Carolyn, I understand that the Chase boy seems like a fiery idealist to you—not much different from his father, truthfully— but idealism isn't character, no matter how hard he may wish it to be. What we have and what the king has given us are unbreakable. We're meant to have these ties—they can't be lost or stolen or broken. He has nothing to offer you—and the sooner you realize that, the happier you'll both be."

"At least he cares about something other than himself," she said. This wasn't the first time they'd had this discussion.

"A young man wears passionate beliefs as a Parisian wears fashion—always changing, and it is always about himself."

"You told them of the powder store," she said.

He put his glasses back on his nose and regarded her over them. "Who said that?"

"Did you?"

"Hardly. They never invited me to one of their parade exercises, nor did they volunteer the location."

"But the officers who were here—"

"I studied medicine with the Lieutenant Colonel's father, as I told you at the time. It was a social call—and, if you must know, an opportunity to introduce you to some worthy young suitors. Now if you're asking me if I would have told them of a weapons cache, had I known—well, then we might have that conversation."

"And the one who died because of it, Nathan Chase?"

"Darling, there will be many who die because of this. Some rightly, but most not. The price will be grievously high for those who seek glory in rebellion. They may in the beginning think they can control the course of events through the force of their intentions—but the end is hidden and fraught with peril."

The clock ticked in the hallway. She asked him the question that wouldn't let her sleep. "They wouldn't hang him, would they?"

"Sedition and treason are serious offenses. They well might hang all of them—if they even spare them long enough for the rope. They might bring them justice on the battlefield."

"But not Jonathon," Carolyn said, refusing to believe her father's words.

Dr. Bucknell sighed and turned back to his letters. Carolyn stepped to the window. She stole a glance at her father, then turned back to the glass panes. Outside, the stars were bright. The town was still.

12

A CURSED LOT

Elizabeth looked out the window and across the dark town commons. The tavern lanterns shone. She let the curtain fall and turned to the door of her room, listening. The pounding from the study had stopped. The reverend Adonijah had been having one of his spells—and was now likely sprawled on the floorboards, asleep. His spells had mystified her when she'd first arrived from London. Locked away in his study, he would mumble, sometimes rant, knocking on the floorboards. Peering through the keyhole, she could watch as he stood in the corner of the room, rocking back and forth, tugging at his own hair. He often knocked his forehead against the wall. On other occasions, he crawled around the edges of the room, speaking to the walls, cursing the demons that dwelt in the slats. During the rest of his hours, he was often no less strange. He complained that mice inserted their droppings into his Bible and accused Elizabeth of baking lye into their bread. He obsessed over an Indian whom he claimed lived below the stairs leading to the second floor. When he was in the throes of a spell, he forgot her entirely. A misplaced item here, a carefully planted mouse dropping there, a set of muddy prints made with his own boots in the night. Over time, Elizabeth learned the value of feeding these obsessions: a measure of peace.

This evening, it had taken no effort on her part to divert the reverend's attention. As the light had fallen, he'd made his way around the house, tapping on the walls with his walking stick, his face scrunched up in irritation. When she'd asked him if he wanted supper, he'd looked at her as though a statue had spoken and then continued his tapping, not saying a word.

Elizabeth hurried down the path that led back through the orchard against Boston Road. The trees were blossoming early this year, and the air was fragrant. In another minute, she came to the tavern. A pair of candles burned in the kitchen. She glimpsed Jude passing by the window. She bit the inside of her cheek, then stepped to the door and gave three quick knocks. Jude opened the door. The tavern's kitchen was warm. Fresh loaves of bread sat cooling on the table.

"Elizabeth," he said, "I didn't know what—he hit you?"

All day, she'd worried about what he would do when he saw. Her composure cracked. "It's nothing," she said. As though she had no choice, her hand grazed the swollen bruise around her eye.

"He found out," Jude said.

Elizabeth reached over and grabbed his hand, large between her own. "He doesn't know. He didn't even know I'd left and didn't hear me come back. I brought him a plate, and he started in on his nonsense about putting lye in his meals. Knocked the plate from my hands and struck me. Yelling at me for bringing the Devil into his home—"

"If he talks—accusing me—" Jude said.

"Adonijah accuses most of the community of being adulterers," she said.

"That doesn't mean that folks won't believe it, especially here. I'm the tavern keep, remember?" he said. "This village hasn't been kind to tavern keeps, not when they're accused of adultery—and no one knows that better than I do."

"People trust you."

"Don't be so sure. Most folks here already think I'm craven for not going off to Boston. And besides—we're not innocent of it, are we?"

"Adonijah is a hard man, with a bitter, cold heart. Some will listen because they want the world to be like that. Forget what they think," Elizabeth said.

"Didn't help Daniel Turner, forgetting what they thought."

"Then we'll leave. Start somewhere else."

Her words hung there for a moment. Jude shook his head. "I can't walk away from this."

"But you could sell it, buy another."

"Not so simple. Most towns, I couldn't afford a place like this. Salem, Andover, Ipswich—those places are different. Not a lot of folks find themselves out here, not on purpose, anyway. But I scratch by here. And it's mine."

Elizabeth walked around the kitchen, looking at the crockery, iron pots and pans, rows of tallow candles.

"Then what about us?" she asked.

"I don't know."

That hurt more than Adonijah's fist.

Jude cringed. "I—this is so fast."

"It's been there for a long time," she said, "at least for me."

"I never expected—"

"But we did. We are." She moved closer to him.

"Did you know?" he said.

"I wasn't thinking when I first got sent to Adonijah. My heart didn't work—I felt nothing." She stepped up to him and put a hand on his shoulder, high up and strong. "But I felt it when we first spoke. There was something that awoke in me again—like there was sunlight in a room long boarded up."

She kissed him. "I want to be with you, Jude Brewster."

Their tongues danced and their bodies pulled close, melting. He glanced at the door. She pulled him down to the floorboards.

LATER, she closed the latch with a soft <u>click</u>, flushed and satisfied. Dawn was an hour off, and she was exhausted. She still thought her idea of moving somewhere else was right; she had no ties here, and the shackles of matrimony to Adonijah meant no more to her than if she'd been told her husband was a cow or a tree. They could leave and start a new life—she only needed to convince Jude. She hung her cloak up on the peg in the kitchen and kicked off her shoes. Quietly, she walked to the hallway. The house was silent. Often, after one of Adonijah's spells, she'd find him on his study floor, breathing loudly through his mouth. He'd once curled up in the closet in the hallway. Stepping around the noisy floorboards, she headed to the stairs.

"No point sneaking, woman. The hour of deceit is long past."

Elizabeth froze. The door to his study was open, the room within black.

"I've heard you, I've seen you, I've sensed your sins," Adonijah said, his voice floating out of the darkness. "The corruption is all around us now, and you bring it back with you in your heart. Between your legs. Perhaps you carry sin now in your womb, a half-breed child."

He spat the last word out, convinced as always that not just ale and cider, but the Devil's will itself flowed from taverns.

"Adonijah, you've no idea what—"

"Stop, speak no further."

She went to the doorway. In the shadows, he sat in front of the window, slouched in his straight-backed chair. His gaze looked beyond the panes.

"We have drawn a cursed lot," he said, "and the ruin as written is to be ours. Ours. Your vile deeds are but a drop in the ocean that rises around us, to wash the earth clean as the sinners drown and choke on blackness."

He turned to her. "And even my wife betrays me, betrays heaven, bringing the Devil into my house. As for him, well—he'll go like the other. I saw to that. The same fate no doubt awaits him."

Elizabeth frowned. "Whatever devils are in this home have nothing to do with me," she said.

"Before the Lord you are my wife," he said, his voice soft.

"In name only."

"Before the Lord you spoke the vows of sacred marriage—"

"And I was out of my mind with grief," she said, raising her voice. "I despise you. Your mind is wrong, and your heart is dead."

Adonijah stared at her a moment, then turned back to the window with a snort. "The costs of our sin have come due. What we've planted in the fabric of this fallen world—the sins of our neighbors, by the sins of the godless, the sins we carry in our weak and dull hearts. The sins of rebellion, stored away in cellars and mill houses, weapons to blaze a path down into the fires. Oh, they scurry when they think they might be discovered."

He gave a dry sound that might have been a laugh. "Our seeds of sin. We've planted them and tended them and nourished them, watching as others weed out the scriptures, the God-fearing, the words of salvation, the signposts to a pious life. Members of our own community turning to an Irish whiskey-maker for advice, turning right into the Devil's arms, turning away from the path. The soil for this garden is rich."

Slowly, he got to his feet.

"You've joined them now," he said. "Joined the doomed, the blind. How many times have I worked to protect our flock from an evil that most scoff at? When the savages attacked us, who was it that organized for them to be removed? I protected us—for I've seen evil, seen it directly. Heard it calling out to travelers in the deep woods. Seen the Devil move the dead as though they were puppets."

He looked to the window again.

"And now the dead rise, climbing from the grave. As written, as written. They walk among us, they tread the earth."

He turned to look at her again, his eyes obsidian points. He fingered the white scar that ran along the top third of his forehead. "I have seen them, faithless wife. I have seen the dead prowling the night. One came to this very window, a crack in his head. From the Chase mill, risen from the grave, driven by the end of this shameful world. He told me things, told me what's coming. Told me what's been happening. Told me of your fornications—sang me a lullaby of them. Grave-talk whispers of your perversions."

"What are you talking about?" Elizabeth said.

He walked toward her. She stepped back to the hallway, and he brushed past her, his shoulders bent and his walk slow. He waved a hand in dismissal. "The end has come, and the faithless like you shall find no haven. Feast on the harvest of your sin. Those left with faith I shall gather as we wait for the golden rays to loft us to heaven. I must prepare my final sermons, the words to guide us on the last journey. I have no time to waste, not for you."

Turning his back, he climbed the stairs.

"You are lost."

13

THE VILLAGE

To the west, the sky held the last bit of night, the stars fading as the dawn approached. West Bradhill—nestled in the thick forests of the Merrimack River valley—had changed.

The night had been long, and the living dwindled.

OLD GOODWIFE BARKER—WHO had secretly stopped praying twelve years earlier when her husband drowned—prayed after seeing shadows cutting through her yard during the night, dragging things behind them. It felt worse than the night a dozen years back when she thought she'd seen Constance Chase walk past her windows three weeks after she'd died. This time, she heard voices—not just the screams and yells long rumored in the deep woods by the lake, but voices that made a promise to her, a promise to return and give her what she missed. As the sun came up, she muttered and worried and continued her guilty prayers.

Up Boston Road, Deliverance Draper and her daughter lay beneath their chicken coop. Noises in the walls and on the roof had stirred them from sleeping. The daughter had screamed

Deliverance awake when a face on the ceiling had spoken to her, a face of moonlight and shadow. Deliverance—as her husband had taught her—had fired off a shot from their musket, aimed at the strange figure in the kitchen doorway. The shot had connected, but the figure had climbed back to its feet, muttering a string of cruel promises. By the time she had almost finished reloading, another figure had crept into the kitchen, moving along the ceiling. They'd backed the mother and daughter into the kitchen corner and told them blasphemy after blasphemy. Now she and her daughter nestled in the cool earth with black smudges around their mouths and noses.

Henrik Graham curled up in his outhouse, shifting and moaning now and then. He'd not joined the militia—he'd no interest in the conflict, no sympathy for either side. Since leaving Prussia for the Colonies ten years earlier, all he wanted was to work his own farm and find a good wife. Some had told him that West Bradhill was a queer place, but the land was cheap. When he'd seen the figures slinking around his property as dusk fell the evening before, he'd assumed them militia or patriot sympathizers, come to enforce the message that one was with them or against them. He'd cursed them and fired a few warning shots with his guns, and they'd disappeared. Keeping watch into the night, his vigilance had been unexpectedly rewarded as the clock neared midnight: he'd gone to the outhouse, driven there again by the flux that had weakened him for half a month. As he'd done his watery business, he'd heard the sudden whispers—coming from beneath him. Before he could puzzle out what was happening, cold hands grabbed him where he'd never been touched. Another pair of hands slammed the door open as Henrik yelled, trying to free himself from the hands that attempted to pull him down through the hole. As Henrik had struggled, they'd whispered to him—described what he'd done as a soldier in the old country, things he'd tried for years to forget. As his insides were pulled down and out, it became clear to him they were neither patriots nor loyalists.

IN A DOZEN outlying houses and farms around West Bradhill, a silence held. The plows were still, the cows not let out to pasture. Chimneys cool. The mist in the fields was undisturbed, waiting for the morning sun to climb high enough to burn it off. In closets and cellars, beneath beds, in outhouses, in the dark of barn lofts, something was happening.

The night had been long.

14

A BIT OF BACKBONE

There was a clearing in the trees leading to the lake. Thomas searched the ground, at times crawling on hands and knees—here footprints, there an overturned rock. He followed the signs to the water's edge. The footprints continued in the mud, under the water. The rock outcropping he'd been at with his father and uncle rose twenty-five yards to his right—he could just make out the spot where his cousin Nathan had been stuck. Could it all have started right there?

Ripples on the water's surface moved out in rings from a spot behind him. He turned. The major stood at the water, squinting in the sunshine and pissing into the lake. He turned to Thomas. "And you didn't think to mention that bloody revolution had broken out? Those farmers with guns looked at me like I was a fox and the hunt was on."

The old, fallen cabin stood a quarter mile back in the trees. They'd reached it in the chill hour before dawn, the major stumbling exhausted into the corner, grabbing the one blanket that Thomas had thought to bring with them. Thomas hadn't been able to sleep, eyeing the dark forest until morning.

"See those footprints?" Thomas said. He pointed at the spot to the left of Pomeroy.

The major leaned forward and pulled up his breeches. "Someone went for a swim," he said, turning so that Thomas could read his lips.

"The prints come out of the water. From the lake," Thomas said.

The major stared at Thomas for a moment with one eyebrow raised. He took a step back and looked at the nearby ground.

"So they dove in over there"—he pointed past the rock outcropping—"and came out here. What on earth has that got to do with anything?"

"The bodies. This is where they came from."

The major gave the lake another look, scanning the black surface.

"Perfect place for a piss, then," he said, and headed back through the hemlock and old pine that bordered the shore. The air was cool where the sunlight didn't penetrate. They cut back to the tumble of rocks that marked the husk of the old cabin. The two muskets and the major's pistols leaned against a stone in the middle.

"I'm a man of very stupid ideas," the major said, collecting his gear, "and now look at me. This worthless little hamlet. I took four days to find it, two days to lose all my men in it, and a little more than that to end up next to a lake that makes walking—or I should say jumping—corpses. Bugger it all."

Thomas looked around the old cabin, seeing it in the light of day. He'd once mentioned it to his father, who had scolded his brother and him—Jonathon getting the brunt of it—and forbidden them from ever going near the spot; even when pressed, he'd never given the boys a reason. Thomas leaned over a wall and paused, noticing a leather pack. He searched it. A few wrinkled pamphlets, two dried apples, a scarf, quills, and a short knife: Jonathon's pack.

Thomas turned back and looked over the cabin again, excited. "This is my brother's."

"Lucky you. My brothers never gave me anything other than the odd beating," the major said.

"No. He was here. He left it here."

The major looked around the cabin and back up at Thomas.

"It means he's back," said Thomas. "He'll know what to do."

"That will make one of us," the major said.

Thomas paced back and forth. Jonathon would have gone to their house and found it burned. Had he gone to Uncle Joseph's, or had he come here first to work out a plan? He looked out at the trees toward the village. Maybe he would come back, since he'd left his pack here—he could help Thomas find Corey Lane, tell him what had happened.

The major looked around the woods and stepped over the rocks and went to the gurgling stream. It ran fast over dark rocks. Squatting at the bank, he lifted handfuls of icy water to his mouth and splashed his face. He lifted his head, water dripping from his nose, and straightened. He tucked his pistols into his belt and hefted his saddlebag, turning to face the boy.

"Best of luck, young master," he said. "I'm leaving before dark so I can—"

"You can't leave!" Thomas said.

The major put on his hat. "On the contrary, I most certainly can. Look, boy—you've seen what's going on here. You really want to face those things again?"

"Jonathon's out there, and he's my brother. It's my home."

"I'd find a new one," the major said. He turned to his horse. Thomas hopped over the stones and ran over to him. He grabbed at his jacket as Pomeroy stepped to his horse. The major tried to swat him away, but Thomas held him.

"I saved you!" Thomas said. "If it wasn't for me, they would have got you."

The major faced him. "And you have my hearty thanks—but no one asked you to."

"Carolyn did," Thomas said.

"Miss Bucknell?"

"She made me promise to find you, to help you."

"What are you talking about, boy?"

"The militia men wouldn't believe me, so I went to her. She kept asking me questions about you."

"Questions? What sorts of questions?"

"Stupid questions," Thomas said, "but she said—"

"What were the questions?"

Thomas shook his head in frustration. "Where you were from. Were you betrothed, had you asked about her—"

"She asked if I was betrothed?"

"—and I told her I knew you'd come back to get your horse, and she made me promise to watch for you."

"I don't understand—watch for me why?"

"She said you'd be the one to know what do to, that you were daring and noble. That you'd be the one to help me find Jonathon."

"What on earth would make her think that?" the major said.

"I told her what you did."

"What I did?"

"When you rescued me. And caring for Hawkes."

"I suppose I saved you," he said, "and made an effort by Hawkes."

"You almost saved him, too."

"And she knows what's happening?"

"It's why she thinks you can help."

The major looked at the woods, then back at him. "Perhaps we should discuss this with her, before the day gets on."

· · ·

THE SKY DARKENED, and the air smelled of rain as they left the forest. The road was empty. No drivers or drays making their way to the village, no herds of geese or pigs being led, no dispatch riders bringing messages from the city. Pomeroy noticed the boy wasn't looking at him, a trick he'd used to great effect when he didn't want to do or hear something. Since he never seemed to miss anything in his favor, Pomeroy suspected that the boy knew exactly what he was doing. The boy pointed to a field on their left. A body was visible on the ground among the red and yellow wildflowers and Queen Anne's lace. The corner of a dress and two feet, one of which was missing a shoe. It was the third body they'd seen since leaving the woods. After a short while, the boy pointed up ahead to a house.

"That's it!" he said.

"Miss Bucknell is here? She's meeting us?"

"No—it's my uncle's. It's on the way. Jonathon might be here."

"Look, boy—I'm willing to spare time to discuss the situation with Miss Bucknell, but I'm not at all willing to traipse around your village hither and thither, all day long. By evenfall I will be miles and miles from here."

"We still have time," Thomas said, but the boy turned and made sure not to hear Pomeroy's further commentary.

The mill was empty. Tools littered the floor, but there was no sign of the boy's brother. Broken glass glinted beneath the windows, and the door leading out back to the river was open. Pomeroy stepped out back. The water wheel stood still. He wondered how long it had been since the wheel had turned. Days, perhaps a week?

The boy tugged his sleeve and pointed. Pomeroy turned and saw dead animals by the river—a beaver, half a dozen ducks, a goat. The more he looked, the more he saw: jays and chickadees, crow, even fish floating belly up before the falls.

"If there were a painted sign that read 'Go Away, Now,' it couldn't be more clear, boy," he said.

"We should check the house," Thomas said.

"Do we want to leave Miss Bucknell waiting?"

"If we find Jonathon, she'll never forget it."

"He's one of her suitors?"

Thomas led Pomeroy inside his uncle's house. Mud and dirt decorated the floors, continuing down the hallway. As they passed the stairs, Pomeroy shivered. A draft of cold air flowed over the stairwell. He felt it as he stared up into the darkness of the second floor.

The boy's eyes were large as he surveyed the house. Pomeroy supposed that it was one thing to see a body lurching across a field—but seeing a place at the center of your normal world a short time ago turned into this, that was something different, larger and much more terrifying. And if the boy's brother was here, then Pomeroy was sure they wouldn't want to find him. He reached out and put a hand on the boy's shoulder. "Let's go."

Thomas looked around. His mouth was drawn and his jaw tight. He shook his head. "We need to search upstairs."

Pomeroy stared at him, and the boy stared back. "Look around. Do you think we'll find him?"

"He might be here."

"Doing what? Having tea? Taking a nap?"

The boy fixed him with that stare. Seconds passed, and the boy didn't look away.

"Fine," Pomeroy said. He'd give the boy one further moment of daring if it would lead him to Miss Bucknell. He turned and headed back to the stairs. As he drew closer, Pomeroy saw that the muddy tracks headed upstairs. Holding his pistol, he turned to Thomas.

"Stand watch here," he said, "and shoot anything that moves that isn't me."

He didn't want the boy to see whatever was on the second floor. With a dreadful resignation, he headed upstairs. At the top of the stairs there was a landing with a large chest. A fold of cloth hung out from underneath the lid. The hallway extended straight to the end of the house. A bureau blocked the window at the end of the hallway. A sickening odor filled the air.

Pomeroy wanted to run—as surely as though he'd heard a bugle blast. Still, the boy wouldn't be satisfied until he'd at least taken a look. And he was, or had been at any rate, a British officer. He stepped forward, pushing on in spite of the voice telling him to run the other way. Doors opened off the hallway, two on each side. He came up to the first one on the left and gave it a light push.

Christ on the bloody cross.

He noticed the feet first. Filthy feet, some with shoes, some bare. Bodies piled like rolls of cornstalks. The stench pushed him back, the putrid reek of decay. Of corpses. Worse still, they were squirming, moving dully like a newborn litter of rats. He stepped back into the hallway. Knowing what he would find, he crossed the hall to the opposite door and kicked it open with his foot. More bodies.

Pomeroy stepped back from the door and backed off. From the room on the left, he heard more movement as a figure crawled out of the shadowed doorway. Pomeroy turned and ran down the stairs.

"Out!" he ordered. "Now!"

He hit the bottom of the stairs and grabbed the boy by the shoulder. Pulling him with him, he dashed through the front room and kitchen. They flew out the front door into the rain. Outside, Pomeroy slowed and let go of Thomas.

"Jesus!" he said, breathing hard, shaking his head as if he could force the images out of his mind. "You don't want to go up there!"

He wanted the boy to understand. Kneeling in front of him, he spoke as clearly as he could. "The upstairs is full of them. Piled high. I don't think they're so dangerous now, during the day. They move, but slowly. I think there's a way we can take care of this problem. Right now."

The boy looked as though he understood where he was going with this.

"Jonathon?" Thomas said without hope.

Pomeroy wanted to be straight with him. "If he's there, he's one of them. If he's not, then you needn't worry about it."

Thomas looked over at the house. His eyes traveled over the front of it, as if looking for another way to see the situation. Finally, he turned back to Pomeroy.

"There's lamp oil in the mill," he said, "I saw it."

The frightened child of a few nights before was gone: the boy had grown a bit of backbone.

A MINUTE LATER, they each had two bottles of whale oil and doused the steps and slats of the house. Once they'd gotten all the way around the building, Pomeroy ran back to the mill and pulled out a few more bottles. He returned to the house with these and kicked open the front door. The kitchen and main room beyond it were still. He opened the first bottle and poured it out over the floor.

"Oh, hell," he said. He smashed the bottles on the floor. They broke with a shatter and splashed the oil all about. He turned and stepped out. Thomas handed him a flint box.

"Right. Nothing a little fire couldn't take care of," Pomeroy said.

It took a few tries but when it caught, a blue flame raced across the floor with a soft fluttering noise. Pomeroy turned and did the same to the edge of the house. It took longer to catch there but by the time it did, orange flames snapped.

They retreated to the horses. A column of thick, black smoke rose into the sky. The rain wasn't enough to stop the fire.

Soon, Thomas looked over his shoulder at the smoke rising

into the bruised rain clouds, as though it was the source of the world's darkness. The whole village had turned to ghosts—Thomas's life with it.

Pomeroy peered into the heavy rain and motioned to his left. "Isn't the center of town back that way?"

"She's meeting us at Corey Lane's. It's this way," Thomas said, pointing to his right.

"Why is she meeting us there—at whatever-you-said's?"

Thomas pretended not to understand and kept the horse moving. From the road to the heart of the village, a covered post chaise pulled by a single horse came around the corner, splashing through the puddles. After a moment, Thomas recognized Carolyn Bucknell. The major pulled his horse to the side of the road as the carriage approached. He tipped his hat as the rain danced in the puddles.

"Miss Bucknell," he said, "we were on our way to our rendezvous."

She pulled her carriage to a stop.

"I've been searching for you," she said. She spotted the smoke rising behind them. Her eyes widened, and she turned to Thomas. "Is that your uncle's mill?"

"We're searching the village for Jonathon—or anyone else of the boy's family," Pomeroy said.

"I have to tell you, Major," she said, "I fear I may have misspoken yesterday. Jonathon and the others have had little part in any of the troubles you and your troops are attempting to quell —it's the others of the town that drive the rebellion and the militias—"

"That's a lie," Thomas said. "They lead the militia, bigger patriots than anyone else in the village."

"And if I were you, Major," she continued, ignoring Thomas, "I would head back to safer grounds. The roads are, by all accounts, thick with armed militia. Dangerous."

"Miss Bucknell, the militia is the least of my worries. I can assure you that I'm determined to find Jonathon. While daylight lasts. As young Thomas here told you, faced with grave danger—and the black plague that has settled on this village—I've been determined to do the noble thing, as you so astutely surmised. Time and again, I've already done so."

He pointed to the rising column of smoke.

"My handiwork right there," he said. "I hope you'll recognize it as a small token of appreciation for your words of yesterday. And you have my word I won't stop until I find the elusive Jonathon."

She stared at him as though he'd told her he'd murdered her family. A shout carried on the damp air, and they looked behind themselves. A pair of rain-drenched soldiers came around the turn in the road to the north, heads and hats bowed to the weather, muskets on their shoulders. Four, half-a-dozen more, another dozen marched through the mud. The one who'd shouted pointed toward the house on fire. Carolyn put a hand to her mouth. Before she could say another word, Pomeroy was off his horse and across the road, leaping the stone wall. He dove to the other side and lifted his head high enough to see them.

"You're brother and sister, come to fetch the extra horse," he called. He ducked down again behind the wall.

Carolyn turned to Thomas. "This is your chance—run!"

"What did he say?" Thomas said.

"Never mind what he said. Let's go."

"He's helping me."

"Helping you?"

"Helping me. What did he say?"

The soldiers had spotted them. A few broke off from the rest and approached.

"How on earth is he helping you?" she said.

"He's helping me to find Jonathon."

"Thomas, he's tricking you—he wants you to lead him to him so he can hang him for sedition. Or shoot him."

"No he's—"

"Yes, he is! His men burned your uncle's mill. Don't you see what they're doing?"

"This is your fault," he said.

THE WORDS STRUCK CAROLYN, unexpected, leaving her stunned.

"My fault?"

"You told, you and your father told. About the powder store, and that's why we moved it, and why Nathan slipped, and why everything started, everything terrible."

"That's not true! Father told me himself that—"

"It is true—Jonathon said so! He hated you for it. He told me to forget you because of it—I don't even want you here. I hate you!"

Carolyn recoiled, but before she could even get another word out, the militia men approached. The soldiers didn't spare them more than a glance.

"What town's this?" one of them said.

"West Bradhill," she said.

"What happened back there?" he said. "The smoke."

"There are British troops around," Carolyn said.

"This far north?" he said.

"Right there." Carolyn pointed toward the stone wall. The major wasn't visible, only the empty field.

"They're headed to the green," Thomas said, yanking the reins of the horse and pointed them down the road. "Down this way, and they said they would burn the church and the tavern."

"No," Carolyn said, "there's one right there, right behind that stone wall. A major, the leader of their forces. This is his horse, right here."

The men turned in that direction. Thomas shook his head. "It's our father's horse. She's hysterical. They burned our house last night, and she keeps seeing them. Everywhere."

Carolyn leaned forward in the post chaise. "That's not true, and you know it. Just look on the other side of that wall. He's lying down, hiding."

"Our father was taken prisoner," Thomas said. "They said they'd hang him. She's been like this ever since."

"Why are you saying that?" Carolyn said. "He's right there."

She climbed down and stepped into the mud. Thomas caught the eyes of the nearby men and shook his head. Carolyn stomped through the mud and over to the stone wall.

"Listen to me," she said.

Mostly the men ignored her. A few spared her uncomfortable glances. The lines of men moved off toward the town.

"Wait!" she shouted. "He's right here."

She leaned over the stone wall, pointing. She leaned farther over, turning her head left and then right. "He was just here."

One soldier passing by Thomas reached up and patted him on the shoulder. "We'll give them back for what they done to your family, son. That and more."

Carolyn looked in both directions at the far side of the stone wall. The soldiers marched past the horses and carriage, off toward the center of the village. Soon, they were gone, lost in the rain and the trees that lined the curving road. Thomas turned. Carolyn strode through the muddy field along the wall.

Thomas wiped the rain from his forehead and looked north, and spurred the horse forward, giving it his heels until it splashed through the puddles into a gallop. He didn't glance back.

He'd find Corey Lane himself.

15

BLOODY, BLOODY HELL

When Pomeroy stood, mud slid down his front like thick gravy. He was twenty paces—hard earned in a frantic crawl—from where he'd first jumped the wall. His clothing was soaked, and he tasted wet earth. Behind him, Carolyn stood, drenched—minus the mud.

"What on earth was that about?" he shouted. "You nearly led them right to me."

"Of course I did—and they're not so far off that I can't catch them and send them after you."

He wiped mud off his uniform jacket and walked toward her. "How exactly is that going to help me find Jonathon? And where's the boy?"

"Safe from you and your men, Major. Now, I'd suggest that you return to them and move on. There's no one left in West Bradhill for you to be concerned with."

She turned and stepped over the stone wall.

"Good Lord, you make it sound as though I were the problem," he said, following her. "Have you lost your senses?"

"My senses?" she said. "You raided their house with your company and burned it, then took Jonathon's father. Your troops burned his uncle's. You just admitted as much—and quite smugly, I might add."

He turned to her, exasperated. He took off his hat and pointed it around at the empty fields and road. "Look around, Miss Bucknell. There is no company. No troops. No raiding parties."

"But Jonathon—" she said.

"Jonathon, Jonathon, Jonathon," he said, raising his voice. "My God, you all act as though he can walk on bloody water!"

"I suppose the Chase houses burned of their own accord?"

"It was me and my men, all three of whom are dead—or worse—by now. Do you even realize what was in that house? I'd suggest you see for yourself, but let me save you the trouble. Here is what you'd find: an empty farmhouse with dried blood all over the kitchen and a body hanging upside down in the cellar. And two more bodies. As for the mill, it isn't grain that's going up in smoke. It's bodies, Miss Bucknell. Not colonials, not my soldiers, not rebels. Worse than the lot of them. Dead, and yet not quite. Trust me, a spat over cannons and powder and tea and taxes is nothing compared to the horror of your little village." He stepped over the wall and went to his horse. "And if you must know, I didn't even know a bloody rebellion had broken out in the first place until my deaf assistant thought to mention it, though I probably should have guessed when I kept seeing long columns of troops filling the quaint roadways of West Bradhill. Christ, this whole thing has been nothing but one giant cock-up from the start!"

Carolyn climbed into the post chaise and wiped the wet hair from her face, picking up the reins. "I might suggest staying off of the main roads, Major."

"All that talk was nonsense?" he said.

"Talk?"

"About me knowing what to do about the situation, about me finding Jonathon?"

"I have no idea what you're talking about," she said, flicking the reins.

"Your questions about me. Being noble. Daring."

She frowned at him.

"Making the boy promise to find me."

"Thomas?"

"That little wretch," he said. He straightened his hat and lifted himself into his saddle. "Too clever by half, that one is. It's a pity he probably won't survive the night now."

The carriage horse was struggling to free the wheels that had sunk into the thick mud. The carriage rocked back and forth. Carolyn called to the horse, but the rocking only drove the wheels deeper in.

"He'll find his family, and he'll be fine," she said.

"He'll be lucky if they don't find him, given what I've seen. You're only making it worse," he said, pointing to the wheels. The rain had lightened, but the road was still thick.

"You could help," she said.

"Convenient now I'm not a prisoner of those farmer soldiers, no thanks to you."

She flipped the reins harder. "I thought it would be too much to expect from someone like you."

"Like me?"

"Yes, Major. I have more than a passing familiarity with the king's officers, thanks to my father's efforts to see me marry well. Haughty and arrogant to the man—and yet just below the surface, I always spot a petulant child."

Pomeroy swung down from his horse and approached the other animal.

"Then I'll happily leave the problems of your village to you and my betters," he said. He slapped the horse hard on the flank with the flat of his hand. The animal strained forward. While it did, Pomeroy grabbed the struts of the wheel and threw his weight into it. The carriage lurched forward and was free.

"Best of luck, Miss Bucknell," he called after her, "and here's to hoping that the magnificent Jonathon will be enough to rid your home of the darkness that's fallen on it, though I rather suspect you'll soon wish you had the stout resolve of one of the king's officers—despite what you think of us."

He watched as the carriage drove off through the puddles, the rain thrumming on its back. She didn't wave or offer so much as a simple thank you.

As the gray afternoon faded into twilight, Pomeroy tried to decide which way was west. The lane was muddy puddles, and the trees dripped every time the wind gusted. He'd ride until midnight, at least—maybe even straight on through until the dawn.

"Petulant child," he muttered. "As if. She should try a mirror."

He replayed their parting in his head, each time looking for an even more cutting rejoinder. She wouldn't have been so pleased with herself had he not been distracted by the close call with the soldiers—his wit could be quite keen, otherwise. He came to a fork in the road.

Which way?

He considered—for a moment—heading back to Boston, back to the regiment. He could spin enough of a yarn to make it workable and without consequence. If the outbreak of rebellion was good for nothing else, it would easily explain the loss of his men. And he was, after all, the son of Lord Pomeroy.

Then again—to hell with it. Why not be done? Done with the king and his bloody army. Done with gloomy England. Done with his whole wretched family and every demand they've ever made on him.

Sod them.

He yanked the horse toward the road leading west and started forward. All around, the dark trees that loomed over the lane gusted, shaking free cascades of raindrops from their leaves. In patches in the sky, the stars appeared. His horse took a strange step and balked, twisting the major's neck. Pomeroy pulled hard on the reins. The horse stutter-stepped.

"Easy," he said. The horse's nostrils puffed—he didn't want to go forward. Pomeroy peered into the dark lane ahead. Rain-sodden branches drooped. The horse snorted again and took a quartet of steps sideways, knocking Pomeroy into a branch stout enough to scratch his face before it snapped.

"Hold bloody still!" he said. He looked forward while he pulled a pistol out and pulled back the hammer, holding the reins in one hand. He strained to see. Blackened figures moved with the shifting of the trees. A clean shot to the head would take one down, he hoped. He pointed the gun toward the darkness ahead, in the direction at which the beast had balked. The horse threw back its head and snorted, nearly bucking Pomeroy off. It wouldn't stand still. Pomeroy looked down.

Silver eyes shone up at him from in front of the stirrup. A hand reached up and grabbed his leg. The body was on the underside of the horse, clinging, scrambling for a hold on Pomeroy. The major clenched his jaw and tried to steady the horse by pulling the reins as hard as he could. He lowered the pistol and aimed it straight at the quicksilver eyes. The horse pushed him once again into tree branches, and he had to lean far forward to stay in the saddle.

"Try this!" Pomeroy said. The muzzle of the pistol was half a foot from the eyes of the figure. He pulled the trigger, and the hammer fell with a dull click—the powder didn't fire.

Bloody hell.

He dropped the pistol to the muddy road and pulled his foot from the stirrup, kicking at the eyes while hanging on to the saddle. His boot cracked on the creature's skull. The horse neighed and staggered.

"Off, off, off, off!" Pomeroy yelled as he pounded the face with his boot. He pushed himself up in the other stirrup and jacked all his weight downward on the figure's neck, yelling as he did so. The horse bolted forward in a wild gallop up the road. Pomeroy saw the figure dropping. He pushed as much of his weight down as he could while still hanging on. By a stroke of luck, the horse veered to the side of the lane and a boulder caught the figure on the head, breaking its skull and snapping its neck. The body crumpled beneath the speeding horse, trampled by the animal's back legs. The horse stumbled and righted itself, not slowing. With the mud and rocks, Pomeroy worried the terrified beast would break a leg. He yelled and dragged back the reins, but the animal didn't slow. Pomeroy held on, risking a glance back. The figure looked like a bundle of sodden clothes.

He turned back around. The horse's ribs blew in and out like the fastest bellows at the hottest forge. It twisted its head to the left.

Its eyes shone silver.

Blood glistened on the horse's muscled neck. The horse galloped full speed toward the trees. Branches the thickness of his own leg were coming straight for him. Pomeroy leaned low and swung his left leg from the stirrup, then slid down the right side. With a combination prayer and curse that didn't even have time to pass his lips, he let go of the saddle and hit the muddy road. He landed on his side and slid forward, rolling and tumbling until the air was driven from his lungs and all sense of up or down gone from his mind. The thudding of the hoofbeats moved off in the distance.

He sat up, covered with mud. His shoulder gave him grief, and he felt as though, well, as though he'd leaped from a speeding horse. He got to his feet, checking to see if anything was broken, torn, or shattered.

"I never should have left the bloody regiment," he said, spitting out mud laced with the tang of blood from his split lip.

"Hold it right there, friend," said a voice.

Pomeroy jerked back. He turned and found himself staring at

the business end of a musket, not ten inches from his face. Holding it was a heavy man with a dirty face, a three-cornered hat pushed back on his forehead.

"Well, look here, boys," the man called back over his shoulder. Half a dozen figures ran down the road, all with muskets. The guns trained on Pomeroy, the hammers drawn back.

"Who is it, Zeke?" someone asked.

"I'll be damned if we didn't catch ourselves a redcoat. Officer, too," the heavy man said.

Pomeroy cursed. One of his pistols was back in the mud, the other was still in his saddlebag.

"Get those hands up!"

"You're making a mistake," Pomeroy said. He didn't move.

"Sounds like it's you might be making the mistake. I said get them up."

Pomeroy had no choice—after diving from the horse, the last thing he needed was to get shot. He lifted his hands.

"On your head. Slow."

He put his hands to his head. The men kept their muskets pointed at him.

"Andrew and Ben," the first one said, "you'd better see if there's any more of 'em. Where they's officers, they's likely regulars."

"But what do I do if—" the youngest of them said.

"Just do like I say and be quiet about it. We'll be right here."

"All right, Zeke," the boy said.

Pomeroy turned his head and looked at the man nearest him holding a gun. "You wouldn't happen to have any rum, would you?"

Zeke stepped up and eased him back with the tip of his musket. "Now, that's enough of that. Best if you keep it shut for now."

Pomeroy sighed. Bloody hell.

"Nothing up here, Zeke," the older of the two boys said. "Road's empty. That horse is long gone, too."

Zeke stepped up in front of Pomeroy.

"Now, ain't this strange," he said, looking him up and down.

"More than you'd ever guess," Pomeroy said. All around them, the dark trees and fields were silent. Bloody, bloody hell.

16

THEY WANT TO COME INSIDE

Elizabeth paused. Firelight shone from the inside of the tavern and the pair of lanterns that hung on either side of the door. Behind her, the church shone from within, the faint sound of Adonijah's voice carrying out the windows. Another step and there would be no turning back. Frowning, she crossed the road. The sound of a rider came from the darkness to the north. A horse bolted out of the black—riderless. The reins dangled across its back, and its eyes shone white and frightened as it galloped past her, disappearing into the night.

She hesitated, spooked by the lone horse, but steeled her will again and hurried to the tavern door. The common room was lit by four lanterns and an armful of tallow candles. A blaze filled the hearth, roasting a pair of chickens, their skin crackling. A barley soup simmered and filled the room with the rich scents of carrots, onions, and broth.

"Elizabeth," Jude said. He sat at a bench, supper plates in front of him.

"I've left him," she said.

Jude stood. Relief lightened her shoulders the moment she shut the door. He looked at her, searching for a bruise.

"No, it's not that—it's everything else," she said. "I can't—won't,stay with him anymore. I won't."

"But where are you going to go?"

"Here with you. What do you mean?"

"But what—is that a good idea?"

"Jude," she said. She put down the sack containing the few possessions she'd carried with her and stood in front of him, hands on her hips. "You don't feel the same way?"

"It's not that. I do."

"Then what is it? Three days ago we made love in the kitchen and yesterday right in this very room. I haven't felt that alive—that close to someone—since well before I crossed the Atlantic. I want to be together."

"But you're married—"

"I was married when we made love," she interrupted.

"But it's one thing to have that between us, and another to put it out in front of everyone."

"So it's fine—as long as it's a secret? As long as we pretend it's not happening?"

"That's not the problem," he said. "It's people, people in the village."

"People who might come to your tavern?" she said.

Jude turned away from her, looking at the fire. She could tell his hands wanted to fuss with something—a lantern, a mug, anything to occupy himself.

"It's about your business," she said.

"No, not the business—though it's been hard enough for some around here to live with a Negro owning a tavern." He turned to her, anguish on his face. "West Bradhill isn't kind to adulterers. You know that."

The fire snapped with grease from the chickens. He used a wooden-handled instrument to take the spit down, then carried it into the kitchen. She followed him.

"I lost everything I had, Jude. Back in London. I had a lovely husband. I had a child, an angel named Joshua. Lost them both in the same week from the fever that spread through the city, my little one first. And my spirit died."

He stopped. "You never told me," he said.

"Because it still tears at my soul. Those days were so terrible that I didn't care what happened, where I ended up. And I ended up here, payment for a debt. But everything's different now. We can do this, we can make a life together. A family."

She reached out to touch him, but he pulled away. That simple recoil was a splash of cold water on her face. The realization hit her that she had nothing but what was in her sack— nowhere to go. Again. It was all gone.

"Don't," she said, quietly.

"You make it sound so simple. But it's not—not for me. Not here. It can all go away so quickly."

He placed the spit with chickens on the large table and worked the birds free of the sizzling metal. She looked past his shoulder and saw a pale face outside the window. She gasped and Jude followed her gaze to the window.

"There's someone there." He put the utensils down. The face had pulled back into the darkness beyond the candlelight. "Did anyone see you come here? Did your husband?"

"He's at the church—giving a sermon. On the end times."

"You're sure? You weren't followed?"

"Jude, no. It wasn't him."

The fear was plain in his eyes. He pulled open the door, looking into the darkness behind the tavern.

"Could he have had someone watching you? Someone who would—" He stopped. "I think there's someone out there."

"He hardly knows I'm still here," she said, "and all he talks of now are his spells, the dead rising, the end coming."

"Dr. Bucknell talked about the British," he said. "Coming to sack the village, put down the militia. Corey Lane said to keep an eye out for anything strange."

"But you're not in the militia."

"I let them meet here. That would be enough."

"You've done nothing wrong."

"Doesn't matter. I need my musket."

"That's crazy—let them alone. They'll go away."

He went past her and took his weapon from the wall, checked that it was loaded.

"What are you doing with that?"

"Whoever it is, they went to the stable. I won't just sit and wait for it."

"For what?"

"For any of it—the British, your husband. Whoever."

"You're not making any sense."

"I will not do this again. I won't. Latch the door after me."

Outside, the night was cold, the moon rising over the stable. There was a soft click behind him as Elizabeth latched the kitchen door. She was at the window a moment later. He lifted the flickering lantern and headed for the stable. A soft banging sound came from it. Although he was sure he'd shut the stable door earlier, it was wide open, the wind knocking it against the wall of the stable. Against the moonlit yard, the doorway was black. All was still save the shifting branches of the trees and the banging of the door.

Stepping up to the doorway, he lifted the lantern and paused. The flame jumped and lit up the first few yards. He looked around. The moonlight threw a slice of light to the earthen floor by the wall. The farthest corners of the stable were untouched by the shifting light of the lantern. Seeing no movement within the deep shadows, Jude made his way to the horse stalls.

Shifting sounds came from the other side of the stall doors. He hung the lantern on an iron hook set in the support beam. Readying his musket, fingers tensed, he reached for the wooden crossbar. The door opened and the lantern's light filled the stalls. One horse stood facing him, the other horse facing away. Jude looked over the stall—it was just as he'd left it. Patting the horse on the nose, he stepped out and once more closed the door. He reached up and took the lantern. The stable door slammed shut. Startled, Jude dropped the lantern to the hard dirt floor, extinguishing the flame and sending the stable into darkness. He wasn't alone. Behind him, a horse snorted. A sickening smell reached him. The horses didn't like it and stamped in their stalls. By the door, there was a deeper shadow.

Jude lifted the musket to his shoulder. "Get out, whoever you are, or so help me I'll put some lead in you!" he said.

The shadowy figure moved several feet toward him. Jude clenched his jaw and pulled the trigger. The explosion was huge. The flash from the end of the barrel lit up the scene for a split-second. A pale figure stepped backward, to the left as a fist-sized hole appeared in the wall where the shot had gone. Low whispering filled the stable. Jude stood frozen.

"I'm nothing but a worm in the emptiness. I can see the fires and the lights, and I can see you, can see you, can see you. Come here, come here. Come, come. Are you cold?"

"Jude?"

It was Elizabeth, calling from outside.

"Go back inside!" Jude shouted.

The stable door swung open, and the figure leaped out into the yard. Jude ran out after it. Stepping into the wind, he found no sign of the intruder in any direction. Elizabeth stood in the kitchen doorway.

"Close the door, lock it!"

The dark figure stood at the corner of the tavern, pale face and hands. The eyes gleamed silver, shimmering. Jude caught the stink of the grave.

"I'll have you, you and yours, and share the cold and take the warmth."

Behind him, the horses snorted and screamed, kicking the walls. Jude spun around as a hand grabbed his cloak. The figure was on the low roof of the stable, leaning down with a filthy hand. The eyes shone out of a mottled face, dotted with mold.

"We'll play with you," the figure said, breathing out the air of a charnel house. Jude recognized him as one of the dairy farmers from the edge of the village, Benjamin Frye. Jude threw his weight backward. The fabric of his cloak tore, and the figure lost whatever balance it'd had and came tumbling forward, clammy skin brushing against Jude's face as he did. He hit the ground with a thud and tried to grab Jude's legs. Jude swung the rifle around and clipped it under the man's jaw, snapping its head back.

"We'll play inside, yes. Our games can last all night," the voice behind him said.

Jude kicked at the one in front of him, hearing the crunch of snapping teeth as his boot slammed into its mouth. Freed from its grip, he turned, swinging the rifle in a fierce arc. The figure leaned back, missing catching the rifle butt in the face.

"Come with us and feel the darkness," it hissed. Jude swung his musket. It clacked the figure on the side of the head before spinning off into the shadows. Jude bolted for the kitchen door. A shadow raced up the wall. For a moment Jude saw something near the roof, then all was still again. The figure who'd been on the stable was gone—footsteps crunched on the ground outside. Jude stared at the shadows, taking deep breaths. Dragging his gaze away, he ran to the kitchen, jamming the lock closed behind him.

He fetched his other musket and reloaded it while he told Elizabeth what he'd seen. The front door tugged and shook. Jude lifted the musket. Three knocks rang out, quick raps on the door.

"Jude Brewster?" came a voice. "Are you in there?"

Jude lowered the weapon and went to the window near the door. In the light from the lanterns outside, he could make out two horses on the road—one with rider—and a figure standing by the door. He stepped over to the door.

"Who's that?" he called out.

"Benjamin Maguire. Why you closed up?"

Maguire was one of the town militia who'd ridden off to Boston. Jude turned and motioned for Elizabeth to go to the kitchen. She shook her head.

"You can't be seen here," he said.

"I will not hide."

Another round of knocks on the door. Jude shook his head and slid back the locks on the door.

"Hell, Brewster," Maguire said, stepping in, "not even Reading or the Heights are rolled up as tight as West Bradhill. Lights off all over the place, tavern locked. The British are in the city, and that's where they're staying for now, so I wouldn't—"

He stopped when he saw the empty common room and Elizabeth.

"Mrs. Watts," he said, tipping the corner of his three-point hat. He couldn't keep the curiosity from his face. Maguire turned to Jude and spoke with voice lowered. "Now, it's none of my business, what's going on here—"

Jude felt his face flush though the darkened room hid it. Maguire took off his hat and knocked it against his leg, a spray of rainwater coming off of it.

"Thought you were in Boston," Jude said.

"We were, all right, and you should have seen it, Brewster. Men from all over the colony come down, ready for a fight."

He ran a hand through his greasy hair and scratched the side of his unshaven face.

"A cup of beer would go down right easy, if you've any," he said.

Jude nodded, stepped to the serving wall, and drew a mug full of ale. He handed it to Maguire, who nodded his thanks and took a long sip. A line of foam clung to his lip when he pulled it away, and he used the back of his sleeve to wipe it.

"I missed that," Maguire said. "No one can touch your ale, Brewster. No one."

"So what happened?" Jude said.

"Nothing. That's the problem. It was turning into a lot of standing around and sleeping on the ground. The Brits are holed up tight. Word is that they've got a fleet racing to the harbor even now. Now, the captains and other militia officers were busy. Busy talking. Working things out, I suppose. But truth is, it doesn't seem like nothing is going to be happening for a while. No storming the city, no driving them back across the water. Not yet, anyway. So a bunch of us figured that we'd come back. Our fields and businesses won't take care of themselves, now will they?"

"And Henry didn't mind?" Jude said. He was growing uneasy with the night outside the door, only half paying attention to Maguire's story.

"I wouldn't go that far," Maguire said. "He and Eldridge Carrier had words, no doubt about that. Henry wasn't happy, but Henry don't have a farm to look after."

"How many of you came back?" Jude asked.

"Ten. Eldridge and Zeke, my boys. Some others." His eyes strayed over to Elizabeth again, and he stepped in close to Jude and lowered his voice further. "Your business is surely your own, Brewster, but I can't imagine the reverend doing anything less than shooting up into the sky to pull down the wrath of Jesus Hisself if he knew his wife was sitting in your tavern."

Jude couldn't think of what to say. The British officer earlier, everything with Elizabeth, what he'd seen in the stable out back and the yard: none of it seemed able to pass his lips as Maguire stared at him. The sound of horses and a wagon outside gave him a reprieve. There were a few shouts back and forth and footsteps outside the door. Zeke Morrill stepped in, his eyes lit up. With his mouth hanging open, he looked around the room, clearly expecting to see a full common room, with light and voices and townsfolk. Confusion passed over his face as he took in the very different scene.

"We got one of 'em," Morrill said, looking at Elizabeth. "British officer. He was on the road leading out of the village. Didn't see no one else, but everything is still out there, and there's smoke on the wind. Let's figure out what to do with him."

Both Morrill and Maguire stepped out to the wagon. Jude followed. In front of him, half a dozen men and boys from the town's militia stood around a wagon, pointing their muskets. In the back was a British officer, the one that had come into the tavern and fled from the militia. His arms were bound.

"Wait'll Henry hears about this," Maguire said. "Instead of coming down hard on us, he's gonna shake each and every one of our hands. Don't think any other militia found themselves no officer."

The other men nodded their heads.

The major turned and looked at them from the back of the wagon. "Yes, and what masterful tactics and precision you displayed. Why, it was as effortless as if you had simply stumbled across me when I wasn't looking."

"I don't think I asked you to—" Maguire began.

"Well, I don't wait to be asked, and certainly not by some unwashed hayseed who was apparently high-tailing it as fast as he could away from where the fight is."

"Well," Maguire began, "you're not in any kind of position to tell me—"

Major Pomeroy cut right in over him again, the disdain plain on his face in the flickering light of the lanterns. His words were fast, with a hard edge to them. "Trust me, you're the one not in any kind of position to start crowing about catching a prisoner by accident. You've no idea the mess you've walked into. What's your name?"

Maguire's mouth hung open, his eyebrows raised. He looked at the other men and back at the major. "I'm not—"

"Your name," the major said, raising his voice.

"Ben Maguire."

"Well, Ben Maguire, perhaps you'd care to take a close look at your little village. I'll wager you're in for a surprise."

"What kind of—"

"Uph, uph," Pomeroy tutted over him, "you'll let me finish. The darkness is crawling with problems, Ben Maguire—and British troops aren't one of them, I assure you. No matter what the situation might be down in Boston, you'll soon wish you'd stayed there."

He shifted, eyes taking in the scene.

"Now," he said, "untie me. I'll be heading straight away from here."

"What in the hell are you talking about, mister?" Maguire said.

"Major."

"Fine. Major."

"Look, Ben Maguire—don't take my word for it. Ask a few questions of the local citizenry, if you can find them. Or perhaps you hadn't noticed the empty, quiet, and dark quality that's fallen over the village. Perhaps you should ask our old friend the tavern keep."

The men turned to Jude.

"What's he going on about, Jude? Is there more troops here, or is he trying to vex us?" Maguire said.

"Yes, do tell, Brewster," the major said. "Am I trying to vex them?"

Everyone stared at Jude. Maguire and his boys, Morrill, Daniel Gerry from out by Miller's Hollow, the Cooper brothers.

"I can't say as he is," Jude said.

He looked over across at the town green.

Elizabeth came over and stood in the doorway behind him. "You should tell them," she said, softly.

"Benjamin, Morrill. You and the boys better come on inside.

Not too safe out here. Bring him in, too," Jude said, pointing at the officer. "As long as he's tied up, he won't do no mischief."

A few minutes later, the common room of the tavern looked nearly back to normal. Men sat around the handful of tables, candles and lanterns were lit, and the fire in the hearth warmed the room. Jude brought out bread for them and poured ale. The officer was still bound, but Jude felt it only right to loosen one arm and feed him, too.

"Good Lord," the major said, taking a gratifying sip of fresh ale. "It's nearly worth it."

He raised his mug in a silent toast. Jude nodded his thanks.

"Jude," Maguire started, "some of the boys been wondering if maybe you don't have more to tell us than you've let on." Maguire's boys passed a glance between them.

"Like maybe how you didn't look too surprised when we showed up with that officer," Maguire said, motioning over to the other table. Some of the others were nodding their heads.

"You might want to—" Jude began. Maguire held up his hands.

"Now, Jude," he said, "you know I've always respected you and wouldn't be saying this if it didn't look to be so curious. But you were plain about not coming to fight with us, and now we find the village empty with a British officer about—and they usually don't travel all on their own. You'll have to allow as to how a man might start thinking—"

"Thinking what?" Jude said.

"Thinking that maybe you have something to do with this," one of the Cooper boys cut in.

"You're heading down the wrong road, boys," Jude said.

Joshua Cooper nodded his head, his lips folding away into a tight line. "Of course he's gonna say that. But just look over there. He could've just as easily kept that one tied up, but here he is, providing him food and drink. He didn't even put a hand to his head and say 'Lord, a British officer!' when we showed up. Hell, he didn't even raise an eyebrow."

Jude looked at him. "It's because I've seen him before. Passed right through here the other morning." With that, he told them what had happened. As he told the story, the men shot astonished glances over at the officer, who watched them, not speaking.

"And what about the rest of their troops?" Morrill said. "You seen any of them?"

"Yeah," one of the boys said. "They been rounding up folks? Looking for us militia?"

Jude shook his head. "I don't think it's been like that."

"Well, where is everyone?" Maguire said.

Jude looked into the fire for a moment, then told them what he'd seen out in the stable.

17

SING-SONG

The village was dark. Carolyn rode up the lane that led to her house, bouncing in the driver's seat of the carriage. The wind blew from the west, sweet with rain and pine. Her house loomed up against the night sky and the backdrop of moving clouds. Lanterns burned on the first floor. She would tell her father everything—surely getting admonished in the process for traveling alone, for taking the carriage—but he would calm her worries. The nonsense Major Pomeroy had gone on about would crumble before her father's logic.

She slowed the horse and guided him into the carriage house. The animal's steps and the creak of the wheels were loud in the enclosed space. She pulled him to a stop. Water dripped from the carriage as she stepped down and felt about for the lantern and tinderbox. The horse snorted and pulled the carriage forward an arm's length.

"Easy, hold on," Carolyn said.

"Carolyn."

She froze. A voice, thin and sharp, came from just outside the big door. Her heartbeat jumped. She looked around, then turned to the doorway.

"Yes?" she said.

The wind outside sighed through the big chestnuts in front of the house.

"Father?" she called out. The little light coming in from the house was clear, and she noticed a shadow stretching into the open door across the ground.

"Carolyn, I see you."

It was a voice, and not her father's. An unexpected tide of fear swept in, threatening to bear her away. The major's words came back to her.

It's bodies, Miss Bucknell. Dead, and yet not quite.

She backed away from the doorway, leaving the tinderbox on the chest. Panic bloomed in her chest. The voice. She took a few steps farther back into the darkness, trying to be as silent as a draft. She stared at the shadow on the ground. It took a step forward. She held her breath, afraid to make the slightest sound. A partial profile appeared at the door, the warm light from the house behind it leaving the face in darkness. Carolyn froze.

"My love," someone whispered just outside the door.

Jonathon?

She tried to stop that thought from rising to the surface, but there it was. It was his voice—but that didn't explain the waves of fear and cold darkness. She'd imagined a dozen different ways she might greet Jonathon when she found him: she'd let him know she'd been the one to throw the soldiers off his trail; how furious the search for him had been; teasing him that the major in charge had clearly been smitten with her. But she didn't want to see him now because something was wrong with him. That voice. Boots stepped into the carriage house.

"Please—help me put my mind back. Please."

His voice was so dry. Carolyn held on to the side of the carriage as though she might otherwise fly away. With those few rasping words, so much disappeared. Then a thought came to her. It was a simple thought: take ten steps, stand in the doorway, and be with him. She bit her lip.

"Hold me, I'm scared. Let me kiss your white throat."

The silhouette stepped inside. In one horrid moment, all the romance, all the arguments, all the promise of bright days crumbled. That voice dashed all such hopes. Nothing would be fine again. She turned and bolted to the other side of the carriage house, to the wide doors. In the blackness, she fumbled with the sliding iron latches.

"The cold deep inside me is more real than springtime, you'll see. I'll give it to you. My uncle showed me how."

Footsteps shuffled closer. Carolyn didn't turn around, she worked furiously at the door. With a yell of frustration, she slid the bottom latch free and shoved the door open with her shoulder. She stumbled out into the night air. The horse bolted out behind her, catching the side of the carriage on the door and struggling, the carriage slamming against the wood, but not giving. The animal kicked and cried out, cracking the wood, blocking the doorway.

Carolyn ran around the corner. Father owned a gun—he'd know what to do. She cut across the driveway between the house and the carriage house. Just as she was about to leap to the front porch, she stopped. A thin figure stood before the door.

"Please, Carolyn. I need to touch you."

She screamed and tried to go around him. He blocked her path, pale skin and glimmering eyes—not the Jonathon she remembered. A foul smell wafted from him. Black liquid quivered from his mouth and down his chin. His hands flew up to her face, and the mere brush of his fingers was ghastly, the touch of a dying snake, dull and thrashing.

"You'll taste my lips . . ." he said.

Behind him, the front door of her house opened, and her mother lurched out, awkward. Her eyes were closed, her face slack. A limp arm raised.

"Mother!" Carolyn said.

"Come inside," a voice said, coming from behind her mother. Her mother's arm motioned inward. That's when Carolyn noticed a pale hand wrapped around her mother's arm, another around her waist, holding her up, forcing her into that gruesome pantomime.

"We'll have such fun," the voice said. A hand rose and ripped off the front of her mother's dress, exposing her bare bosom. Her mother's head rolled forward, her hair spilling across her face. Carolyn screamed and fell backward. She landed on the dirt. With a twist, she was up and running off, away from the house, away from the terrible sight of her mother, away from Jonathon.

Away.

She hardly knew of where she ran to—it was all the blues and blacks of night, trees and dark houses, lanes and greens. Eventually, she dared to look behind her. The lights of her house were just visible, up the hill from town. A stitch in her side slowed her. Her shoes and the hem of her dress dripped mud. She needed help, someone to escort her past the horror of her yard, into her house, to her father. As she considered what to do, she noticed someone come up the road in her direction, coming from Boston Road. It was a thin man, staggering. He wasn't wearing a shirt, just a pair of loose breeches.

"Hello?" Carolyn called out.

The figure stopped and looked in her direction. The eyes were dark hollows. "I'm lost, you're lost, I'm lost, you're lost. Come, come here."

Carolyn stepped back.

"If there's no sun, we can hold each other," the figure said in a harsh whisper.

Carolyn yelled and ran off the road, following the edge of a meadow until it ended where the road turned and crossed River Road. A pair of figures—faces pale ovals—moved toward her. The road wasn't a safe place to be. She crawled back to the corner of the meadow and ducked beneath low branches, turning south, toward the center of town. The woods were black, heavy with the smells of earth and fallen leaves. The footing was difficult among the roots, branches, and wet leaves that covered the wood's floor. Thick bushes and deadfalls drove her deeper into the woods. She tried to keep the road in sight as much as she could through the trees, but it became difficult the farther she went. Noises were all around: the creak and groan of high branches shifting on the gusting wind, the constant drip of rainwater. Every splash of moonlight was Jonathon's face, every glint of rainwater the shimmer of his eyes, every shadow his long arms. Panic drove her, and tears blurred her vision. She pushed through wet hemlock branches, finding the going easier once she entered a grove of the tall, long-branched trees. The ground wasn't as wet and her steps were quieter. The trunks of the trees rose around her, the branches forming a roof overhead. Small twigs snapped underneath her feet as she hurried.

"We can play house-time, Mummy. And I'll nuzzle your neck."

Carolyn froze. The whisper floated in the darkness. Drops of rainwater hit her face, landed around her. She looked up. Silvery eyes gleamed from a pale face in the trees.

"My bones are cold. You'll see, Mummy."

The eyes dropped toward her. Carolyn screamed and stepped aside just as the figure crashed through the branches and hit the ground where she'd been. Turning, she bolted between the trunks. A high giggle erupted in the blackness behind her. She crashed through the low branches and came out past the thick hemlocks. There was movement just in front of the black of the hemlock. A pale face, low to the ground. The eyes shone a silver that danced. The face came closer.

"He wanted you, he wanted you—but I got you. I get to climb on you, you, you."

The child's voice was a terrible sing-song. Carolyn took a pair of steps backward, tearing her gaze away from that pale face with the cruel eyes. She turned and barreled in the opposite direction, heedless of the branches and roots and briars that grabbed at her dress and scratched at her skin. She crashed through twisting pricker bushes and burst out onto the road. Winded, she looked back. The branches behind her jostled. A small figure came out onto the road, pale in the moonlight: a toddler, stumbling through the brush. Wispy hair and tattered clothes, with a rotted leaf clinging to her face. Her skin was as white as the bark of the birch trees. The silver-eyed creature found her.

"Don't run, don't leave me, don't run, come hold me. I'll wrap your head, your head."

Sing-song. Carolyn ran, staying to the edges of the road, where the mud wasn't as treacherous. Ahead, she saw the center of West Bradhill. The stars shone and the moon—a slender presence—climbed above the horizon.

18

____

THE FIRELIGHT WAS PAIN

The firelight was pain and the darkness a welcome shawl. Even the candlelight hurt, in sparks and bursts that traveled through his swollen eyes, deep into his head. Something bad had happened, and he'd only wanted to go home, wanted to be with his mother, with Thomas, to be with his blankets. To be safe. But it was emptiness, cold and hard and agonizing—they weren't in the burned timbers of his house. And in that silence, he'd changed further, down in his bones, down in the back of his skull, down where the sound of churning wasps filled his own head. It had driven him out into the fading day, on to where his smashed memories hung in shards, broken and destroyed.

And then she'd arrived, clear to him as a last glimmer of sunlight to a man sinking into watery depths. He wanted her, wanted to tell her things. Wanted to give his new mind to her. Walking was difficult, even though the new strength was growing, hour by hour. His legs and arms felt like branches sewn to a sack, loose and no longer connected right, not letting him chase her as she dwindled. He couldn't swallow or make a sound. So room to room he went, the scent of the living overpowering and inarguable. He knew what to do, the corruption in his lungs snaking out. After, he crawled down the stairs, pushing out the door. The light of the stars was almost too much, the openness. He groaned.

Carolyn.

Outside, he no longer understood the road or the fields. What was inside him drew him forward to the darkness—he looked for the glint of her radiance. When the wind came, it was like a beating, but he kept going.

Carolyn.

19

THE STRANGEST FEELING OF ALL

orey sat by the fire at the edge of the lake, getting himself ready. Beside him sat a pile of the plants he'd gathered, those that Pannalancet had shown him so long ago and written out carefully in his instructions. In the proper order, he tossed them onto the flames, where they burned and gave off a fragrant smoke. The night sky cleared, revealing the stars. He grabbed a small pile of the thick green witch-hazel branches and threw them into the flames. They snapped, and the astringent aroma rose around him. The smoke brought back memories of the night they'd done it before—and reminded him it was possible to stop what was happening, as much as the doubts threatened to overwhelm him.

The lake stretched into darkness. When the branches had blackened and then turned to red and white embers, Corey picked up the final plants. These had taken him the longest to find, the tooth root plants with their tiny orange blossoms. Delicate on the tops—the petals all but falling off at the slightest movement—and stubborn below the ground, where the thick, pointed roots bit into the earth. He held the flowers in front of him and paused. It was going to work, or not. He feared not.

Don't be so clever, you're not so smart. Just say the words. It was as though Pannalancet was standing behind him.

"Fine," Corey said. He spoke the words—unfamiliar and awkward Pennacook—over the plants, moving them in a circle in front of his mouth as he chanted. He repeated the phrase four times, then tossed the plants into the orange flames. There was a *whoosh*, and the burning leaves rose on the heat, spinning and dancing above the fire before blowing off toward the lake. Corey was silent. He stretched his legs out. His body felt good, as though he'd spent a morning running and fishing, a morning of youth. He got to his feet—the effects of the winter thistle driving back the pain in his hips—and stepped to the water's edge, where he'd placed the other items for the ceremony. The easy part was over.

Now shut the gate.

Clenching his jaw, Corey leaned over and picked up the basket of clay from up the stream. He carried the basket to the water and took a step into the lake. As always, the water was icy— the sun couldn't warm it even on the hottest day of high summer. His feet slid into the soft muck. Holding the basket across his left forearm, he reached into it with his right hand and scooped out a palmful. The voices started up around him, just a few. Not loud.

"I can't find my arms."

"Be quiet," Corey said. He shook his head. They were always there, the voices of the dead.

"Norri slandia ra puk," another voice, guttural.

Corey ignored the voices and spoke the next set of words, dragged the clay across his forehead, down each cheek. Then, he tossed the clay out into the water. The voices grew in number and surrounded him. Whispers, screams, crying. He almost stepped back—he'd never heard this many voices before, nor this close. English, Pennacook, Abenaki. Other tongues.

He pulled out a second handful of the clay and leaned over, holding it in the water. He repeated the words. The water around his hand and ankles trembled. The voices grew louder. Horrifying whispers competed with shouts out in the darkness of the lake. Straightening up, he held the clay aloft, toward the stars and shouted the words a third time, yelling to hear himself over the dozens of voices that gathered around him.

A power shot up through his legs, spreading out across his torso like a swallow of strong whiskey. His arm shook. Holding the clay off to each of the four directions for a moment, he took a deep breath. He said the words a final time, drowned out by the torrent of voices around him. At the last word, he hurled the clay up and toward the center of the lake. It landed with a deep *ploomp* and sent out ripples that glimmered with starlight. A deep vibration rumbled beneath his feet, and the water shook.

Corey looked around, his head aching with the incongruity— his eyes saw a still, empty lake, but his ears were filled with the sounds of despair coming from an unseen crowd. He snapped himself back to what he needed to do. Turning, he reached back on the shore and grabbed the sack that lay on the grass. With a careful set of motions, he opened it, reached inside, and pulled out the skull of the tiny corpse he'd cornered in the woods at the break of day.

He forced himself not think about it.

He'd put the head into a pot of hot water, kept that fire well-fed, and let the boiling water do its work. The skull had no jawbone any longer. Even after hours in the pot, the tiny jaw had opened and clacked closed with surprising force—so he'd broken it off with a mallet. Now the skull was bare, the bone white in the moonlight. The touch of it repulsed him, still alive with whatever had entered it from the lake. He moved a step deeper into the water until its chill grip wrapped his knees.

"I've been killed, I've been . . ."

"Apat doh chu adonsett."

The dead spoke, too close. He tensed. What right did he have to do such a thing? And he was just moving ahead, as if he knew what he was doing. Pannalancet had been wrong to count on him

—what if he wasn't strong enough? He had to let whatever was working through him do what it needed to do.

"Pannalancet," he said, "help me get this right."

Corey balanced the skull in the crook of his left arm—the one that held the basket—and pulled out a thick handful of clay. He bit his lip but nothing came to him.

"Oh God, it's sticking through me. Ow ... ow ..."

"NO! NO! PLEASE ..."

How could he concentrate with this confusion of voices, some of them screaming right into his ears? The words, what were the words for the start of the skull ceremony?

"Kizos aalak nionakiya..." he began, then faltered. That wasn't right. That was the start of the blessing of the directions. A long drawn out wail came from in front of his face. The words weren't coming. He closed his eyes, knowing better than to chase after them—they would only slip further out of his grasp, like minnows darting away in a stream.

"Je suis morte ..."

The weight of the skull and the basket of clay strained his lower back. He chewed on the corner of his lip, eyes closed. He thought about Pannalancet's notes, the thin letters scratched on the old paper. His eyes opened.

"Alnobanogan nionakiya," he said, remembering the opening lines.

As he spoke, he held the skull out over the water. With his other hand, he pressed clay into the empty left orbit, then took another handful and stuffed the right orbit. His fingers pushed down the heavy clay, spreading it out so it sealed the openings. The skull grew even heavier, and his arm trembled with the weight of it. He repeated the words, using another handful of clay to seal up the nasal openings. Working fast, he pressed clay into every opening of the skull, saying the words over and over as he did. He felt the power passing through him, even as the voices of the dead babbled all around him. When he finished, the skull was heavy, its surface smudged with clay fingerprints. The packed eye-sockets stared up at him. Corey turned and tossed the almost-empty basket onto the shore. As he did, the skull slipped and splashed into the water, dropping to the bottom like a stone.

"No, damn it." He turned and bent over, fishing in the dark water with his hands. He stopped for a moment. Something shook the floor of the lake, a far off boom that came from . . . somewhere deep. "Where are you?"

His hands passing back and forth near his feet, dragging through the freezing silt of the bottom. Screams surrounded him, from men and women. His hands found the skull at last, and he pulled it from the water. It seemed to weigh thirty pounds. Water slipped from it, and some of the clay from one of the eye sockets had fallen out.

"Oh no," he said.

He turned and waded back to the basket at the edge. With a grunt, he squatted, pushing open the mouth of the basket. There wasn't much clay left, but he scraped around and came up with a lump the size of a chicken egg. He straightened.

The lake shook.

Corey stopped. The voices of the dead had stopped for a moment, gone silent. The noises came from deep below the lake.

A low rumble grew in strength. The surface of the water shook, the image of the moon breaking apart and then becoming solid again. The sound came up through his feet and deep in his chest. He chanted the words again as he packed the last of the clay into the left eye socket. They didn't sound right, the words. Before, the power of them had run through him and surrounded him—like the air before a lightning strike. Now they were just words, and he was an old man with a trembling voice.

The lake shook again, the water reverberating with the impact. Corey brought the skull close to his face, inspecting his work. He'd refilled the one eye socket, and everything else looked sealed. It would have to do: he had no more clay. Hoping that the last chant had worked, he waded deeper into the water. He grimaced as it touched his groin, but he kept going. Cold on his belly. A few steps more and the dark frigid water hugged his chest. The bottom fell off sharply. He held the skull up out of the water, using both hands. The dead whispered again, leaving behind their short silence. No screams, only whisper all around him.

The ceremony of skulls and clay to shut the gate, the ceremony of bloodfire to seal it.

He was ready to finish the first part. With the skull held up to the stars and out to the middle of the lake, he began the next chant. At the end of that first phrase, the air changed. The words came faster, as though his lips and mouth and voice were being driven, and not by him.

BOOM! BOOM! BOOM!

He fought to keep his footing. The water swayed and pushed him on the tide. Corey let the words keep coming, focused on holding up the skull. *Damn these skinny old-man arms*, he thought. He shifted his grip on the skull, bending his arms to ease the strain. *Close the gate, close the gate, close the gate.* He narrowed his eyes and continued. The words wrapped him in heat.

A rustling from the shore broke his concentration.

He turned his head. In the ferns to the left of the fire, a hint of white. Corey kept the words flowing through him while staring at the shore. He'd worried about the prowling dead interfering with the ceremonies. There was another movement of the branches and a glimpse of a figure. He turned back to the center of the lake, the prayer coming to an end. Whatever was on the shore would have to wait. He held the skull out to the four directions, seeing its faint reflection in the water in front of him as he did.

BOOM!

The lake shook so hard that he lost his footing on the bottom. He slipped into the deeper water, scrambling to catch himself. He pulled the skull against his body, afraid that he would drop it again and not be able to find it this time. Twisting, he got his footing just as his head dipped below the surface. A few panicky steps and he was back at a depth where his shoulders and head were above water again. He wiped water from his eyes and face. The noises and shaking grew louder.

Hurry.

With the final chant, he tossed the skull as far out in front of him as he could. It hit the water only six feet away with a deep splash and disappeared beneath the surface. Corey wiped his wet hair from his face, shivering. The dead were silent. Around him, the lake went still, surface flattening out as though it were smooth ice.

A vibration began, barely more than a feather shiver. He saw it on the water, the reflections of the stars and moon dancing. He took a few steps back. Water dripped off of him in rivulets. All around him, the water shook, the vibrations growing more powerful.

The ceremony of skulls and clay to shut the gate, the ceremony of bloodfire to seal it.

He moved toward the shore, trying to hurry through the water, but moving slow. The gourd near the basket contained the mixture he'd prepared for the bloodfire ceremony. If everything worked—and he kept telling himself that it had—then he'd shut the gate between the worlds. It wasn't sealed yet though. A loud noise came up from behind him. The center of the lake roiled, white with thousands of bubbles. The whispering of the dead started up again, fast and horrible.

"Bloodfire," Corey said, unable to tear his eyes from the center of the lake.

As he watched, a wall of water shot up into the air in a powerful spray, the droplets glinting in the moonlight. It rose high enough that he needed to crane his neck back to see the leading edge.

BOOMBOOMBOOM!

Three huge bangs shook the lake, one on top of another. Corey lost his footing, landing in the water on his backside. Something came out of the lake. Corey's mouth hung open as an enormous shadow lifted from the water, black and darker than heavy smoke, absorbing even the light of the moon. It rose, an inverted triangular shape that towered thirty feet over the lake. Around the shore, the trees blew, their branches waving and swaying in the wind.

Corey shook his head. "I'll seal that damned gate."

More darkness slipped out from the center, scurrying over the surface to the shores. Gusts of frigid air followed them, leaving trails of ice crystals floating in the water. The shadows shot to the edges of the lake and disappeared into the trees.

At the shore, a figure stepped out from the shrubs near the fire. "Corey Lane!"

Thomas Chase. The boy's face turned from him to the shadow behind him, his eyes wide, his mouth hanging open. Corey waved the boy off.

"Run!" he yelled. "Get the hell out of here, son!"

The boy looked back at him.

"Something bad happened to my family," Thomas said, "and my father told me—"

Corey struggled through the waist-deep water. "Run, right now! Go on, boy!"

The Chase boy stood as through rooted. His heart racing, Corey tried to get to the shore. The dead chattered around him. He tripped over something and nearly fell. Before him in the water, pale white below the surface, hands. Before he could step back, they shot out of the lake, slamming icy fingers around him. A face remained under the water, eyes shining a watery silver. In one horrible second, Corey recognized the face. The hands pulled him down and he couldn't resist, too weak now to argue with the iron pull of the sallow arms. His last look as he was dragged under was to the shore where the Chase boy stood at the water's edge, screaming, his face terrified. Yanked into the water, feelings flashed, lightning in a summer storm. Anger at being too slow. Shame for letting his closest friend in life down when it mattered most. Sadness he wouldn't see his daughters again. But as he took in his first throat full of icy black water, he had the strangest feeling of all: relief.

Relief at not being up above, up where the gate to the other world was open. At being away from what was now coming through the gate. Relief that his own death had come early and fast. Relief at no longer hearing the voices of the dead. Flashes of color exploded behind his eyelids as he choked and breathed in the water until there was only blackness.

20

A LITTLE LATE FOR OUR PARTY

Across the room, Pomeroy watched the men. With food and drink in him, he felt he could think clearly. He was about to ask Jude to refill his mug when the floor beneath their boots shook with a deep boom, strong enough to shift the logs in the hearth. Bright orange sparks swirled up the chimney, plates on the tables rattled. Conversation stopped. After, several of the militia talked at once. Jude stood up and looked out the door.

"See anything, Brewster?" Maguire called.

"No—"

BOOMBOOMBOOM!

Three loud booms, deep below the ground. They were stronger than the earlier one and flickered the flames on the candles around the room and sent a crockery mug crashing to the floor.

"That's got to be cannon fire," Maguire said, getting to his feet. He went to Pomeroy.

"You better tell us where your men are and what they got with them."

Jude stepped back in and closed the door. "Didn't you hear what I was just telling—"

"Damn it, Brewster," Maguire said. "That all sounds like a bunch of horseshit. That noise was cannons—and this fellah here knows how many, where they are."

To Pomeroy, the booms sounded nothing like artillery, and he had more than enough experience with artillery to recognize the sound, even at a distance. He may have paid more attention to the local spirits and women when garrisoned in the Highlands, but he'd still been an artilleryman.

"That wasn't artillery," he offered.

"Oh, please," Maguire said. "I ain't that dumb."

"You're sure?" Pomeroy said.

"Don't you insult me none, either. You'd better answer my questions. Now, where are they? And how many troops you got?"

Fine, Pomeroy thought. The man wouldn't hear anything else until he got the answer his mind had already sunk its teeth into. It might stir things up enough to give him an opportunity. "Two artillery companies to the north, one more to the west, across the river. Two battalions total." He didn't even blink when he said it.

"Good Lord in heaven," Maguire said.

"It's not true," Jude said.

Maguire spun on him. "I heard it with my own ears—he just gave us detailed troop information. I'm starting to wonder if you've been telling us a bunch of clap trap to cover for your own treachery, Brewster."

"Didn't you listen?" one other said to Jude, pointing at Pomeroy.

"He's lying to you, trying to shake you up," Jude said.

"You ain't making it any easier for us to trust you," Maguire said. "You might be spinning these yarns to us to stall for time while your Loyalist friends or a company of regulars comes marching in through the door."

The sound of a fast riding horse neared the front of the

tavern. A second later, the door opened and Eldridge Carrier burst into the room, his clothes dusty from riding, lank hair hanging from underneath his hat.

"My family," he said, his eyes wide in his grimy face. "They ain't right. They was waiting for me—but something's wrong with them. It ain't right, something ain't right."

Pomeroy suspected that his family wasn't much like he'd last seen them.

"Did you spot any troops, Eldridge?" Maguire said.

"Troops?" the man said, the word coming out of his mouth as though he'd never heard it.

"British artillery. They're all over."

The man looked around the room, confused. "What do you mean?" His eyes landed on Pomeroy and widened. His mouth pulled into a tight frown.

"Eldridge," Jude said, "what did you find?"

The man ignored him and strode over to Pomeroy. "What'd you do to my family?"

"Their eyes, what did they look like?" Pomeroy said.

The man looked at him, his own eyes widening.

"What did they say to you?" Pomeroy said.

The man started to speak several times, then just glared at Pomeroy. Without warning, he slapped Pomeroy hard across the face. Jude came up behind him.

"That's what's been happening, Eldridge," he said. "He's not lying."

The man whirled to face him. "Don't you tell me that!" he yelled, spittle flying. He looked around the room, his eyes wild. They landed on Elizabeth. He then turned back to Jude.

"We all left to fight," the man said, "all except you. And I see you still got yours, and then some."

"Eldridge, there's no—"

"Don't you talk! Don't you talk!" the man screeched. "We need not listen to a devilish Negro tell us right and wrong. Whoremongering tavern keep!" He swung back to Pomeroy. "And come to find it's the British, the ones we left to fight—and they's taken everything."

If he had some logic going, Pomeroy couldn't find it. The man wasn't making sense, and the situation seemed to be darkening by the moment. The man stared at them and lifted one hand off to his side, palm up.

"Cooper," the man said, "grab some rope. We're hanging him, and we're going to do it right now." His eyes never left Pomeroy. A log snapped in the fire.

Maguire pushed open the door and peered outside. "The horses is gone."

Morrill and one of the Cooper brothers pushed the door open and went out. They whistled and calling for their horses.

Carrier walked back to Pomeroy and leaned in close. "You know what I think?"

"That there's nothing a good game of whist can't settle?" Pomeroy said.

"You mayn't be nothing more than the bait," he said, "so as we might gather in one place with you and make for an easy target."

"Yes, we're clever ones, aren't we?" Pomeroy said. "Predicting that a handful of you would desert your company and come slinking back to this pissant little village—only to walk straight into our little trap."

Carrier punched him in the face hard enough to snap his head back. Pomeroy squeezed his eyes shut against the pain for a second, then spit as blood filled his mouth. His lip throbbed, numb and mashed.

"What'd you do to my family?" Carrier said.

Pomeroy spit again, a great bloody gob spattering on the floor.

"Why don't you go back out into the dark and ask them?" Pomeroy said. "You'll see soon enough."

Carrier threw another fist at him, but Jude reached out fast and snagged his wrist.

"You've got it all wrong," he said.

"I've got nothing wrong!" Carrier screamed. "And I'll see you swinging, too, before I hear any different."

He spun and looked at the stunned men standing around the tables by the fire.

"Get me that rope!" he yelled.

"But the horses are gone. All our stuff, too," Maguire said.

Morrill came back in. "I can't find them nowhere. Andy's still looking. Someone must've stole them."

"Brewster," Carrier said, "where's your rope? Rope!"

"No one's getting hung here tonight, Eldridge," Jude said.

"You traitorous, dark-skinned beast—" Carrier began but was cut off when Jude grabbed him by the front of his doublet.

"Another word and I'm throwing you out into the night to fend for yourself, so help me."

Carrier wriggled and scrambled.

Pomeroy saw it before anyone else did. "Knife!" he yelled out to the tavern keep.

Carrier pulled a wicked-looking blade from a leather sheath. Jude twisted fast and slammed him to the floor, knocking over a chair. The knife stayed in his hand. Brewster stomped on Carrier's wrist, and it broke with a splintering crack. The knife clattered out across the floor as Carrier screamed.

"Stop it, Jude," one of the militia said, pointing a musket at Jude's head. "Do it right now. Don't you make me."

Jude panted, trying to watch both Carrier and the musket at the same time.

"I'm not making you nothing, Ben Maguire," Jude said, "and you and the rest better listen to what I've been telling you."

"I don't trust him," one of the other militia men said.

On the floor in front of Morrill, Carrier moaned, cradling his broken wrist.

"Well, you'd better start," Pomeroy said. All eyes snapped to him. "The Devil is on the loose here in West Bradhill—or something just as foul. Hadn't you noticed that things were dark—no fires burning, no smoke on the air? If the British Army had come tramping through, don't you think you'd be able to tell? Wagons, torn up roads, burned houses, stables, businesses. Sentries, pickets, and the lot. Trust me, you'd have noticed."

Elizabeth spoke up. "And Jude here has seen it. He's a decent man who wouldn't deny even a prisoner a drink and a meal, and he's treated you men with respect and courtesy despite your lack of turnabout."

She paused, and there was a click as she pointed a pistol directly at Maguire. "So put that musket down, or I'll put a shot straight into your skull. So help me, I will."

Maguire swiveled his head back and around between the woman and pistol, Jude, and Pomeroy.

"Don't you do it, Mrs. Watts," Maguire said.

"Put it down."

"I've got my finger already squeezing tight on this trigger. Shooting me is gonna be shooting him," he said.

"It will still be shooting you, Ben Maguire. Don't forget that part," she said.

The other men in the tavern were still. Carrier sobbed and muttered to himself in a ball on the floor. A distant scream broke the silence outside. Gazes swung to the front windows.

"This ain't right," Maguire said.

Elizabeth kept the pistol steady. "Forget the rebellion, and forget the British. None of that matters here anymore. There's something much worse happening. We're telling the truth."

With a sigh, Maguire lowered the musket.

"Come," Pomeroy said, looking up at Elizabeth. "I think they're ready to listen."

The woman looked uncertain, but lowered the pistol. Maguire stared at Pomeroy, unsure of what was happening. The tavern door swung open, and the candles flickered.

Pomeroy looked over. "A little late for our party, I see."

Carolyn Bucknell stepped into the common room and looked around the fire-lit gathering. She smoothed the front of her muddy skirt.

"The dead are walking, all around," she said. Her voice held a tremor and Pomeroy noted that her hands shook. "Lines of them, marching on the green. All around the church. Everywhere!"

21

THEY WERE ALL GONE

Thomas lay still and covered in the tall grass, his head buried in his arms. The wind from the lake rose to a screaming pitch and swept right over him, tugging at his shirt. He couldn't get rid of the image of Corey Lane, pulled under the water. He'd watched the ceremony from the shore, afraid to interrupt.

He lifted his head. Looking through the weeds, he saw the surface of the water still dancing, shadows moving across it. To his left, he saw where Nathan had slipped below the surface. Now a terrible shadow hung at the far side of the water. It rose into the sky, higher than the tallest trees. The edges blurred, the stars behind dim, as if seen through water. At its center hung a heart darker than the night sky. No light passed. It filled with movement and brought on a dizzy feeling, as if he peered over the edge of the tallest cliff in the world.

It started with what they'd done with Nathan—he knew it. Just seeing the lake in the darkness again brought that horrible night back and sent a sickening wave of guilt through him. He only wanted to wriggle back into the forest—and then run as fast as he could in the other direction.

But he couldn't—he was the last.

They were all gone, taken one by one. And he'd been as useless as he'd feared. Not able to save them, not able to reach Corey Lane in time, not able to find Jonathon. Their words— Jonathon's, his uncle's, the major's—echoed in his head, urging him to give up, urging him to remember that he was just a scrawny deaf boy. He frowned and crawled to where the old man's fire died, the last red embers dragged off on the wind. Across the lake, the shadow moved out into the trees. Trunks snapped and leaves took flight.

In spite of Corey Lane's warning, he searched around the fire. He found an empty woven basket and tossed it aside. A small fold of leather had bits of plants. He held it to his nose and got the fragrance of fresh stems and leaves. He shoved it into his pocket and spotted a twisted up bundle of cloth. Thomas unwound it. It held a handful of smooth stones and a jar, the kind his father used for storing fruit preserves. Reaching in, he lifted the jar up and held it in the moonlight. It was half full with a dark liquid. Retying the cloth bundle, he continued searching around on his hands and knees.

The winds died and the water on the lake quieted again, the reflection of the moon appearing on the surface, an apparition. A huge shadow passed off into the forest. Thomas walked to the edge of the water. He looked to the spot where Lane had gone under but saw no sign of him. Mist moved across the water, gathering among the flowers and cattails that dotted the edge. He turned back to the fire. The embers glowed and brightened as they danced with the breeze.

Lane hadn't finished. The items in the cloth were important. They had to be. He searched the ground around the fire one more time, the moonlight painting it fine silver. He froze— someone moved behind him. He spun around and saw a figure rising out of the water, large with pale flesh, water dripping in heavy rivulets, hair hanging limp and soaked.

His uncle, Joseph, with eyes that shone quicksilver.

Thomas almost dropped the sack. He couldn't move for several heartbeats, eyes locked on the white face. He took a step back, then another, the back of his shoe knocking the dying embers out of their delicate pile. With a yell that carried over the entire lake—but lost to his own ears—Thomas turned and bolted for the woods, crashing into them, pushing aside low branches. He stumbled over a few protruding roots, but he didn't slow, not realizing he whispered as he ran.

"I'm sorry, I'm sorry, I'm sorry . . ."

The dark woods held his secret as he passed.

22

LIKE AN OFFICER IN THE KING'S OWN

The militiamen gave her dark looks, but it was better than fleeing through the darkness. She was about to ask one of them to escort her to her home when Eldridge Carrier—whom her father had never cared for—pointed at her.

"Who's lying now?" he screeched. "Look who it is. Her loyalist father can't be far behind—and you think they're out to stop by for an ale?"

A murmur passed among the men. The major—tied to a chair—made an exasperated sound. "Ask her what she saw and do it before you get yourselves all worked up again."

"She might be in on your crazy story," one man said.

"And her father's bringing the rest of them here right now!" an old man yelled.

"Ask her," the major said, "and please tell me you have a gag for this one."

The old man lunged at him, but the tavern keep caught him by the collar of his shirt and dragged him back, struggling. He whispered something to the man, and the fight stopped. The old man sat like a scolded child on the floor, cradling his wrist. All eyes turned back to Carolyn. She told her story: the road, the woods, what she saw on the green. She left out only Jonathon— she couldn't bring herself to put words to it. When she finished, Maguire looked around the room.

"It ain't possible," he said.

"See for yourself," Carolyn said. Maguire shook his head.

"What about them regiments the major there was talking of?"

"There are no regiments and no companies," Pomeroy said. "The only member of the king's army left here in West Bradhill is me. Hardly enough for a trap of any kind."

"I still don't like this," Maguire said.

After a discussion, they agreed to search the center of the village. A breeze gusted from the northwest, and thin clouds hurried past the moon. The men gathered outside the door. Morrill and his boys, Maguire, and Jude. Carolyn stood in the doorway.

"Don't see too much," Maguire said.

"You won't need to go far," Carolyn said.

"I think it's a trick," Cooper said. "They're trying to get us out of here, trying to split us up."

"Damn it, there's no trick. It's as I told you," Jude said.

"Then why don't you come with us?" Maguire said. "We need to round up our horses, and you can help us. Besides, if there are walking corpses around, we'll need an extra man with us, someone with another gun. If it means so much for us to believe you, maybe now you'll join us."

Jude looked at their faces and nodded. "Lock the door behind us, Miss Bucknell," he said with a glance behind her to Elizabeth, standing near the hearth, "and untie the major. There's another musket by the kitchen door—the back door's locked, too. Don't open the door for anyone but us—I don't expect it will take long."

After they'd gone a few paces beyond the circle of lantern light, it was difficult to see them. Carolyn watched the tavern keep and the other men walk across the street toward the green, disappearing into the darkness. She turned and closed the door.

"No one listens," the major said. "Well, that might be the last we see of them."

"They forgot to gag you," Carolyn said.

"Yes, well. Ha ha. How amusing. If I didn't have this rope digging into my chest and the other one turning my foot numb, I'd be stinging with enjoyment at your delicious wit, I'm sure. Now untie me if you would."

"I'm your servant now, Major?"

"Fine," he said. "Would you please be so kind as to untie me?"

Carolyn stepped around behind his chair and pulled at the ropes.

"Thank you for what you did, Major," Elizabeth said. Carolyn recognized her as the reverend's wife, though she'd never spoken to her nor had more than a glimpse of her at services.

"It was nothing."

"No, it wasn't," Elizabeth said. "Keeping everybody looking at you while I got to the gun. Things might have gotten worse if not for that."

The ropes shook loose, and the major slid forward on the chair and stood. He took a few slow steps, going lightly on his left leg.

"Things could still very well get worse," he said, "so let's not get too self-congratulatory."

Carrier watched them, his eyes wrinkled and glaring.

"I should do something about his wrist," Elizabeth said.

"We should break the other one," the major said. He walked to the window and looked out. "Going out there was a bad idea. Where are they?"

"You won't spot them. They're too far off."

"Fools."

"Would you believe that story?" Carolyn said.

He turned. "Well, why not? If nothing else, it's a reason to stop getting all worked up about uprisings and confrontations and the king versus the Colonies, Adams, Hancock, and the lot. What else are a few walking corpses good for, if not that?"

"You can't take anything seriously, can you?"

"I'm taking this more seriously than anyone else around the—"

"Oh, please."

"No, really," he said. "I'm the one who keeps urging everyone else to pack it up and leave. Why? It's not that this charming little village is full of people who I find a cut below my standing, Miss Bucknell. No, it's that this charming little village is full of walking corpses spitting up black blood. I'm not the one who insists on continuing to run around, looking for this person, looking for that, hiding from local militia. I'm the one who wants to leave here while I'm still alive. It all seems perfectly—"

"Well, yes—if you're not thinking about anyone besides yourself," she said.

"Hardly the point—"

"The rest of us aren't so selfish and callous and—"

"Excuse me, but I might well have been twenty miles from here by now, except for being selfish and callous enough to help the boy—and you, I thought at the time—hunt for your precious Jonathon."

She turned and walked away without another word to him.

"There's a lovely answer," the major called after her, "just walk away."

Carolyn spun. "Why don't you go ahead and do the same? Walk away, or run away, or slink off. Whichever it is that you're planning on. All this talk of being the only reasonable soul left standing, and yet you're still here."

"Yes, well, there was that little matter of being taken at gun point by the ever-vigilant West Bradhill militia and tied up to a chair." He put his index finger to his chin. "Hmmm. Now why didn't I leave?"

Carolyn pointed to the door. "It latches from the inside. Nothing is holding you back now."

"Except for the darkness full of walking dead. Thanks, but at this point I'll wait until daylight."

Jonathon could be vexing, but the major was on a whole new level for irritating her. She turned and walked across the room. There was a crash and a thud from the floor overhead.

"Major—" the reverend's wife said.

"Is there anyone else in the tavern?" Pomeroy said from over by the door.

"There shouldn't be."

"Blast it," the major said. He limped to the corner table. "Musket, quickly."

Elizabeth stood. She reached over and handed him the one in the corner.

"You have another?" he said.

"Only the pistol."

The tavern was silent, everyone listening. At the table, the major poured in the powder, tamped it, and pushed down a ball. A series of bumps came from the second floor.

"I'll go with you," Carolyn said.

"Hardly. As much as I'd prefer company, that's a bad idea. You wait here. If you shoot the pistol and miss, perhaps one of the fire pokers might—"

"I'm not one of your men," she cut in.

"Fine," he said. He extended the musket out to her, resting the stock on the floor. "Take charge, then. Here's the musket. The sound came from upstairs. Have a go."

She took the musket from him. Insufferable. Without a word, she breezed past him to the stairs. Her father had taught her to shoot a pistol—how different could a musket be, other than getting it up to one's shoulder? At the bottom of the stairs, she stopped. Trying not to let the others see, she hefted the musket up. It was heavier than it looked.

"Miss, don't do that," Elizabeth said. "Let the major go up there."

Carolyn looked over at the dim common room. "I'll be fine. I know how to shoot."

Starting up the stairs, Carolyn lifted the gun. It was difficult to keep the end lifted high enough. The stairs turned the corner into darkness—because they'd been downstairs, there were no lanterns or candles lit on the second floor. She paused at the turn. The top of the stairs was a black wall, the faint light from the common room below only hinting at the banister and the top steps. Footsteps came up behind her, and her shadow leaped up the wall next to her. The major had a fire poker in his right hand, a lantern in his left.

"I'm fine," Carolyn said.

"I'm not."

"Go back downstairs."

"Don't be stupid," he said. He looked up to the top of the stairs. The light from the lantern reached the upper walls, the lower part still in blackness. "Give me the gun."

"No, Major. I can shoot perfectly well."

"Good God, you're as stubborn as the boy."

"If by that you mean I'm willing to face a problem head on—"

"More how logic rolls off of you like water off the back of a goose once you've made your mind up." He started up to the top of the steps. "Be ready to use it, then."

She clenched her teeth. She lifted the gun to her shoulder again and started up after him. At the top, the major paused. The shadows moved across the walls. A breeze gusted in the long hallway, playing with the flame.

"That window," he said, pointing straight to the end of the hallway with the poker. "It's broken in."

Curtains waved on the cool night air. For the briefest moment, Carolyn thought she saw a shadow move outside the window.

"Did you—" she began.

He motioned for her to be quiet. "Listen," he whispered.

She leaned forward, taking another step. At first, she heard nothing—until a soft shuffling reached her ear, and an undecipherable whispering. The major pointed with the fire poker toward the last of the rooms on the left, next to the broken window. The doorway was solid darkness and silent. The breeze carried a stench on it, strong enough for Carolyn to turn her face.

"That's the smell of them," the major said. He took a step backward. "We should run. Get everyone out of here, meet up with the others."

His eyes held fear—and an earnestness she hadn't thought him capable of. Maybe he was right.

"Carolyn," he said.

It was the first sensible thing he'd suggested yet, but it didn't matter. All she thought about was Jonathon. What if he'd followed her here? What if that was him in the darkened room even now—and what if there was something that might help him? If they subdued him, kept him safe. Got her father to stop the terrible condition from worsening, save the fiery young man she'd half fallen in love with.

"No," she said, "there are two of us. We're armed."

She stepped up and onto the landing, keeping the musket trained on the door at the end of the hall.

"Good Christ," the major said. He followed her nonetheless. They walked down the hallway, silent but for the hissing lantern and the wind coming in through the broken window. Each step brought a deepening feeling of unquiet, the same as she'd felt at the carriage house.

"He knows we're here," Carolyn said, her voice at normal volume, shattering the quiet.

The major jumped. "Have you lost your mind?"

She took a step to her right, keeping the gun pointed at the doorway. "Not at all—there's no point in waiting."

"Oh well, in that case," he said, that mocking tone back in his voice.

"Please, Major Pomeroy—don't lose focus."

He looked over at her, face lit by the lantern. "You sound like an officer in the King's Own."

"It would be nice if you sounded a little more like one, Major."

The door stood halfway open, leaving more than half the room in blackness.

"Shall I charge in?" he said.

"Please, this isn't the time for—"

"There's no jest in there. I'll kick the door open and rush in as long as you're right in back of me with that."

Carolyn looked at him. He was serious. She nodded.

"Be careful," she said.

"Yes, well, be careful yourself." He stepped forward, looking into the room. "And try not to shoot me in the back of the head."

He took a trio of short breaths and sprang forward, kicking the door open with his right foot. Carolyn came up behind him. The major barreled into the room, spinning around, fire poker raised.

"I don't—" he started.

Carolyn spotted it before he did. A shadow shot a few yards across the ceiling and dropped on him. The lantern cracked and rolled off to the side, still burning. The major screamed, his voice muffled underneath the figure. A filthy cloak obscured the face. A dirty head, hair matted and muddy. The major screamed again. The fire poker knocked several times on the floor, but he wasn't able to lift his hand high enough to do anything with it. It was all movement and cloak and shadow. The major screamed again, his voice smothered. "Shoot!"

She wouldn't pull the trigger until she was sure. She stepped sideways. The skin of the face was pale, a faint beard showing. The hair was longer than Jonathon's, the nose was larger. An insignia decorated the coat—it wasn't Jonathon. The major grunted and tried to buck the fiend off, but the figure slammed him back to the floor.

Carolyn aimed at the back of it, near where she thought its top was. <u>But where?</u> For a desperate second, she froze. The end of the barrel moved back and forth, aiming at bits of shadow, bits of clothing.

She clamped her eyes shut and pulled the trigger. The hammer snapped with a tick and a spark, and the room flashed bright yellow. The shot kicked her shoulder back as though someone had grabbed the weapon and shoved it rudely. Through the smoke, a spray of tattered fabric and blood splashed the wooden floor. The figure rose for a second, craning to see her. Beneath it, the major cursed and tried to flip the creature over, getting his knees up underneath its torso. She threw the musket down as the major tried to scramble out. She skirted their thrashing limbs. Why wasn't it dead? It hadn't even slowed. The fire poker was a black line in the shadows. She picked it up, wrapping her fingers tight around the cast iron handle. She spun. The major was on his side, covering his head with an arm. From this side, Carolyn looked into the thing's face: gray skin, marbled with black; white dots of fungus clumped together near the nostrils and by the ears; lips black and shriveled, looking like dead worms in hot summer sun; the eyes glimmering points of quicksilver.

Carolyn yelled and brought the fire poker down in a swinging arc right onto its head, using both her arms. The hooked end of the poker connected with a muffled crack to the skull. She hung on and swung it again, even harder. With a sudden horror, she realized that the poker sunk right into the head, which had gone soft. It reminded her of the previous autumn when she and Jonathon had used an old walking stick to knock apart rotting pumpkins.

The figure reared up, reaching both hands to the fire poker. It wrenched it out of her grip and tossed it to clang on the floor. The eyes didn't leave her, shining out from the mottled face. With an unnatural jerk—limbs, elbows, and shoulders askew—the figure scampered to its feet and came at her. She stepped backward until she smacked into the corner of a dressing table. The creature reached for her.

Carolyn yelled and pushed forward with both her hands, hitting the creature hard in the chest. It didn't even budge, remaining upright with a sinewy strength. It pulled her in, its hands clamped on her wrists. The flesh that held her was cold and repulsive, smooth as leather but shifting, as though it might come apart. The heavy stink of rotten meat blew right at her. Black liquid covered its mouth and chin. She screamed and fought to pull away, yanking her arms and swinging her waist. The hands pulled her in as though she possessed no more weight than a paper doll.

Its head swung forward with a sudden thud. It jerked to the left and spun around.

The major stood behind it, his hands wrapped around the barrel of the musket. He swung again and connected the stock of the musket square into the thing's face. Pomeroy's shoulders bunched up as he swung. He pulled back—raising the musket to his shoulder—and let it swing again. This time, he hit with a solid connection and sent the figure reeling.

Carolyn backed off, wedging herself next to the dressing table. The figure stayed on its feet, bits of flesh hanging from the side of its face. It sprang forward at the major who hadn't had time to pull the musket back yet. Carolyn shot her right leg out. The figure tangled its ankle on hers and spilled to the floor. The major raised the butt of the musket to the ceiling and swung it in a brutal arc. It smashed into the back of the figure's head. Pomeroy raised the gun again and smashed it down even harder. Carolyn pressed back against the wall, unable to look away. Each time the major swung the butt, it crushed further into the back of the thing's head—and Carolyn couldn't stop thinking about pumpkins. Thud, thud, thud. Each hit punctuated with a grunt from the major. Wet bits of gore flew up from the musket in a spatter, hitting the ceiling and the wall. The figure stopped thrashing. The major panted, his eyes wide. He stilled the musket, leaning on it for support.

"Are you all right?" he said, his eyes not leaving the sprawled figure in front of him.

It took a second to find her voice. "Yes, I think so. Is it—"

"I don't know," he said.

Its head was a pile of sundered bone, hair, and flesh spread out in an irregular puddle of black liquid.

"It's not moving," he said. "It's the head, I think. Get rid of that, it'll stop."

He wiped his mouth with the back of his sleeve and spit onto the floor. Streaks of dark liquid lined his face. He hawked up and spit again, wiping his tongue. "It tried to put its mouth on mine."

Carolyn stepped out from the corner of the dressing table, keeping a good distance away from the thing on the floor. The major dropped the musket. He stepped to the figure and reached underneath, flipping it. The body rolled, one arm spinning out like a swimmer frolicking in a pond.

"Oh God—" Carolyn said, putting a hand to her mouth.

Parts of the head rolled with the body. Others didn't. The major grimaced. "Hutchison."

"What?" she said, looking at him.

The major shook his head and pointed at the feet. They shook, ever so slightly, thudding on the floorboards.

"The hands," Carolyn said.

They twitched, fingers closing and opening. The major leaned over and grabbed the fire poker.

"You won't want to see this," he said.

She turned and cringed at the smacking and tearing sounds that erupted, iron driven into wood, into bone, into flesh. After what seemed much longer than the minute it took, the fire poker clattered to the floor.

"There we are," he said. "Not bloody moving now. As I thought —the head must come clean off."

He turned and picked up the lantern. Blood glistened on the bottom of his leg, seeping from the thick part of his calf.

"Major, you're hurt," she said.

"Yes," he said, limping to the door. "You shot me."

He stepped out of the room. Carolyn didn't bother glancing at the body but followed the major. Neither one of them noticed the pale face that watched them from the shadows next to the broken window.

MINUTES LATER, Pomeroy tried not to shout. His eyes squeezed shut and tears poked out of the corners. The woman took his hand.

"That's right," Elizabeth said.

He sat in a chair in front of the fire, his wounded leg out in front. Elizabeth huddled over it, looking at the wound after having cut away the lower part of the leg of his breeches. It was a bloody mess. Carolyn returned from the other room with an armful of cloth. She pulled some of it out and dropped it on the floor underneath his outstretched leg, watching as the red bloomed on the cloth where it soaked up beads of blood.

"I don't think the ball is in there," Elizabeth said. She squatted, peering underneath. "Miss Bucknell, you might see if you can find bottle of whiskey, please. And a bucket of water, too."

Carolyn nodded and hurried. Her face was neutral, but she wouldn't meet Pomeroy's eyes. Elizabeth's hand was gentle on his calf, trying to wipe away the blood. Pomeroy drew a quick breath in, his hand tightening on her own.

"Sorry, Major," she said.

Carolyn returned, taking stuttered steps so as not to spill the heavy wooden bucket of water, a clear bottle in her other hand. She put the bucket next to them.

"I'll wash some of this blood off," Elizabeth said. She pulled a long-armed ladle from the bucket and poured a slow cupful of water over the leg. The water rinsed the blood off in a pink stream. Carolyn put a hand to her lip. The hole looked as if someone big had poked their thumb through the side of his calf.

"Found the other hole," Elizabeth said. "Went straight through the thickest part."

"Lovely," Pomeroy said.

"At least it missed the bone."

"If only it had missed the leg."

"I'm sorry, but this will hurt," Elizabeth said, holding the bottle of whiskey. She pulled the cork out. Pomeroy nodded and closed his eyes. She poured the whiskey over the wound, getting the stream straight into the hole. Though he was fighting not to, Pomeroy let out a yell and jerked his leg. Elizabeth tipped the bottle back.

"It's all right," she whispered.

She poured more. This time, the cords stood out on the back of his neck, but he bit back his scream.

"Good God, that's worse than the shot itself," he said, his voice trembling.

Elizabeth handed him the bottle. "Might do you good to take a sip or two."

Pomeroy nodded a thanks to her and took a long swallow. He grimaced and wiped his mouth with his sleeve, then took another pull from the bottle. He blew out a long exhale and handed the bottle back to her. She shook her head.

"You might need more," she said. "Careful, though. It smells strong."

He cradled the bottle in the nook of his elbow. "Have no fear. I have a passing familiarity with the finer qualities of such spirits."

She wrapped his leg as he looked around the warm common room. The stones of the fireplace were hung with colored fishing buoys. A painted wooden gull hung on the wall. Brewster kept the place neat—the sort of tavern that Pomeroy most enjoyed.

"Do you know, Miss Bucknell," Pomeroy said, "that if it weren't for the throbbing agony of my lower leg—not to mention the horrors that appear to have infested your lovely village—I'd almost be enjoying myself?"

He flashed her a smile and sipped from the bottle. The fire snapped cheerfully, even as the rest of the large public room was dim with flickering shadows.

"How interesting," Carolyn said before turning her attention back to the window.

"No, really. Seated comfortably beside a crackling fire, provided a delightful distillation." He held out the bottle, admiring the deep amber liquid in the firelight. "Sharing company with an even more delightful young woman who is, among other things, semi-good with a musket."

She flashed him a frown. "You're getting drunk, Major," she said.

"Now, that's an offensive suggestion, Miss Bucknell," he said. He waved the bottle. "Purely medicinal. Quite necessary to atten-uate the pain of my wound—which is rather excruciating." He nodded toward the bandages wrapped thick around his calf, now dotted with a pair of coin-sized spots of blood.

"Major, I'm very sorry that I shot you," she said, "and you know that. I did the best I could."

God, she was attractive. He'd noticed before, but in the fire-light with that earnest defensiveness on her face, it was all he thought about.

"Yes, yes," he said, "and don't think I'm not grateful. It was hardly your intention to put a ball right through my leg. Clearly, you're not fond of me"—he threw in a shrug—"but I don't think you'd want to injure me."

"Of course not," she said. "And it's not—I mean—it's not an issue of being fond of anyone. Or not."

He gave her a benevolent smile. "Delicately put. You're very kind."

"I'm not trying to spare your feelings, Major. But your suggestion implies—"

"No need to get defensive."

"I'm not getting defensive," she said, her voice louder.

"Your cheeks are flushing."

Carolyn straightened up. "Standing four feet away from a fire will do that, Major," she said.

What a marvelous chest she had. Up until that moment, he'd not really considered the way her hair tumbled down over the curve of her—

"Major," she said, folding her arms in front of her.

"Sorry," he said, looking up. "Trying to suss those things out."

"What things?" she said. She glared at him.

"You know," he said, "the bodies. The animated corpses."

"Perhaps you'd better—"

Elizabeth stood at the front window, having finished wrapping his leg. The woman looked forlorn. Pomeroy arched his eyebrows, sneaking another peak at Carolyn's figure as she turned to the window. He lowered his voice. "Dear, dear. I believe someone's in love."

"Whatever makes you think—"

"Oh, come on, Carolyn. Even I've noticed the little looks of longing she gave him, and the smitten eyes he gave back to her. And I was tied up and about to be hanged."

"But—"

"But nothing. Didn't it strike you as a little odd right from the start they were, you know, together here and apparently quite good at it? Or used to it at least."

"But she's married to the reverend."

He took another sip from the bottle, enjoying the warmth that slid down his throat and up into his head. He played with the cork, spinning it between thumb and forefinger. "Oh, please. The reverend looks to be about one-hundred and twenty-six, all white hair and wrinkles."

"But the tavern keep is a Negro," she said, lowering her voice to a whisper.

"Oooh, how scandalous, how unthinkable—"

She was naïve, and the expression on her face was priceless. A tumble of laughter fell over his words.

"Oh, that's right," she said. "My coddled existence of luxury. Sheltered from all but the most proper of scandals."

He shifted his wounded leg—still propped up on the chair opposite him—and grimaced. "Your words, not mine."

"I was only surprised that—"

"Hardly a thing to be surprised at," he cut in. "She's married to an ancient preacher—and if I've ever seen an arranged marriage, I see one there—but lives right across the common from the tavern, the proprietor of which is a decent, handsome fellow. She's in her prime, quite a handsome woman herself." He waved a hand through the air toward the front of the tavern. "One day, they pass a word. A smile. She brings him some cooked goods on the sly—or maybe he brought it to her, since the man clearly knows how to cook—and she grows all thoughtful, thinking of a future far more attractive than her present."

Carolyn shook her head, sneaking a glance at Elizabeth, her fingers drumming on her elbows.

"Then," Pomeroy said, dragging the word out for effect, "one day they meet somewhere else. In secret. A meadow or by a little stream. They talk and talk and talk, and the hours fly by—but before they part, they kiss. Ah, the forbidden kiss. It leaves them both a'tingle for days, and they think of nothing else. And when they see each other again, the conversation lasts for all of seven seconds until they're at each other, ripping each other's clothes off—"

"Yes, Major—you paint quite a picture," she said, cutting him off. She still had her arms folded over her bosom—which was a perfect shame—but he was pleased to see that the lovely flush of her cheeks had grown deeper.

"And more power to them, I say," Pomeroy said.

"I'm sure people will be scandalized," she said, keeping her voice low. "And that's not my sheltered naiveté showing."

He shook his head. "To hell with people. Always ready to dash everyone else's passion and enjoyment for whatever fool's reason they can muster, all to make sure that everyone around them stays as miserable as they are." He raised the bottle toward Elizabeth in salute. "Hear, hear, to Squire Brewster and Mrs. Reverend for embracing what matters to them."

He took a swig of whiskey, less able now to keep the inebriation out of his speech. "And everyone else in this backwoods little village can go rot." He turned to Carolyn. "Although it rather looks as though they have, haven't they?"

Three hard raps shook the back door. Elizabeth closed her hands around a pistol she'd placed on the table.

<u>Bang bang</u>. Two more. "Elizabeth, it's us. Open the door," a voice came, faint from outside the kitchen.

"It's them," she said. She ran through the common room to the back door in the kitchen and knocked out the wooden bars. The door opened in with a gust of chill wind, sending the flames on the candles dancing. Ben Maguire hurried in, followed by Morrill, his boys, and finally by Jude.

"Shut it," he said. Maguire slammed the door shut and fumbled with the crossbars, getting them to slip in straight. All the men panted, their cheeks flushed. Jude bent over, his hands on his knees, trying to catch his breath.

"Jude—" Elizabeth said.

"Is the front locked?"

"Yes, but—"

Jude hurried through the door leading to the common room. "Good. Because they're coming."

"No more chit-chat by the fire," Pomeroy said.

The rest of the men came into the room. Their eyes went to the front windows. Jude looked at Pomeroy's bandaged leg.

"Are you all right? What happened to your leg?" he said.

"Just a little scratch," Pomeroy said, "from when Miss Bucknell, here, shot me."

Carolyn told them the story. Whatever they'd seen outside, none of them appeared surprised. Jude checked the lock on the door. He stopped at the window.

"What did you find?" Pomeroy said.

"Bodies," Jude said.

Maguire sat at a table, eyes boring a hole through the floor. "You was right, Major. And I ain't never seen nothin' so terrible. It was little Hannah Perry, and I had to shoot her, Lord, help me. And it didn't even stop her."

Jude turned around from the window. "Major, there are dozens of them coming down the streets, filling the center of the village. Bodies are crawling all over the outside of the church."

"The hell we gonna do?" Maguire asked.

"We need to secure these doors and seal the windows," Jude said, pointing to the front of the tavern. "There's boards and nails in the cellar."

"Don't forget the second story," Pomeroy said. "We've already had one little problem up there."

Jude nodded and ran a hand across his cheek. "We should block off the second floor, right at the top of the stairs."

"And once we're nice and sealed in, then what?" Pomeroy said.

"We wait."

"Until?"

"Until sunrise," Jude said.

Soon, everyone was busy. Jude closed the inside shutters, getting ready to nail up boards they'd pulled from a crate of candles. The young boys dragged a heavy table in from the kitchen to block the door. Carrier sobbed in the middle of the room, his muttering ignored by the others.

"Major Pomeroy," Jude began. "How mobile are you?"

"If you give me my pistols, I can shoot. If I need to, I can run."

Jude nodded and one of the men brought the major his guns. Jude wiped rivulets of sweat off his forehead with his sleeve. The two young boys struggled with the table and he helped them lean it against the door.

Thud.

Pomeroy looked around. No one else appeared to have heard it. He looked toward the kitchen door where he noticed a hint of motion.

"Brewster!" he called out. "Maguire!"

Elizabeth screamed from the kitchen, and there was the crashing of glass. Jude dropped his hammer and ran to the kitchen. With a grunt, Pomeroy got his good leg beneath him and stood up, hands grasping the stones of the hearth for support. His right leg buckled, the torn muscle burning and cramping.

A shadow slid from the stairwell and across the ceiling.

Pomeroy took aim and shot at the shadow. The recoil was strong enough—and his leg weak enough—that he struggled to keep on his feet. The shadow crashed onto a table.

"Brewster," Pomeroy yelled, "in here!"

The fallen body writhed on the floor before standing again. A bloody hole gaped on the side of its head, yet it still moved. The shuttered windows rattled under blows from outside, and the front door shook. One of the front windows blew inward in a smash of glass and broken boards. A dark blur landed on the floor with the ruins of the window. Candles on the front table snuffed out with the wind.

"There's another—" Pomeroy said.

The new shadow rose: a thin and ragged figure with silver points for eyes. Eldridge Carrier—still sitting up in the middle of the floor—let loose a high, thin scream. The figure leaped forward, landing on him, crouching. Carrier's legs thrashed a frantic beat on the floor before stopping. The figure looked up, and Pomeroy caught a flash of Carrier's face, wide-eyed and smeared with black liquid. Another crash of glass came as the front door smashed open, splinters and pieces of broken latches tumbling across the floor. Two shadowed figures staggered in after it, one tall, one much shorter—a child, perhaps. Brewster ran over and pointed his pistol straight at the pale, filthy head of the thing that stood over Carrier. The shot took its head clean off.

From the second floor, heavy footsteps banged. Pomeroy looked up. If they were getting in from there, they were in a very tight spot. Carolyn yelled, pointing at the broken window. Another figure climbed in, a big man with a tangled beard. His skin shone white, flesh drained of blood. Pomeroy looked around and counted five intruders.

"Everyone back," he yelled. "To the back wall!"

Another pair of eyes shone from the kitchen. Pomeroy hobbled a few steps away from the fireplace, toward the back wall. A deafening shot exploded behind him.

"Tip them over," Jude said. "That's right."

The two boys knocked several of the tables onto their sides, in a barricade of sorts. Pomeroy slid against the wall. He pulled his powder horn from the large pocket of his jacket, along with the leather sack with balls. Twisting the leather strand that held it closed, he reached in and fumbled out another ball. His hands— whether from the whiskey or from the pain—refused to move with any precision. He dropped the ball, fumbled with the horn. Powder tumbled out in a puff onto his shirt.

"Christ," he said.

Carolyn huddled next to him.

"Can you finish loading this?" he said. He held the pistol out to her.

"Are you—"

"Yes, but you need to load this."

She took the pistol. Another musket shot exploded. A crea- ture took a blow between the shoulder and the neck, sending it spinning to the ground. It leaped up in a heartbeat, coming at them again.

"They're not staying down!" Pomeroy yelled. "Go for the heads."

Decapitation seemed the only way to stop them—and that realization brought with it a terrible feeling about their chances. Pomeroy tried to track the rest of them. One slipped in from the stairwell, clinging to the beams of the ceiling.

"There's one!" he said, pointing to the rafters. Carolyn pressed beside him and held out the pistol. He took it. He pulled back the hammer and aimed at the shadow creeping across the ceiling. Pomeroy squeezed the trigger and reloaded his other pistol. The shadow dropped onto one of the far tables. In a moment, it stood in the shadows next to the hearth, pale face catching the firelight.

Carolyn cried out, "Jonathan!"

"Your father understands our cause a little better now," he whispered. A fluttering giggle rolled out his mouth. "And I waited and waited, and supper grew cold, but you ran away. But don't worry, I tucked them both in. After tonight, we can all be together."

Carolyn put her hands to her mouth when the windows along the front side of the tavern blew in with a scream of nails and the brittle shatter of glass. Everyone shielded themselves. Pomeroy looked up, and the figure in the shadows rushed at them.

"No you don't!" Pomeroy said. He aimed his pistol at its head, using the shining eyes as a target.

Carolyn yanked his arm. "What are you doing? Don't, don't shoot him!"

He wrested his arm free and fired. The hammer clicked, but the spark fizzled in the pan and didn't ignite the powder. "We're done for," he muttered.

Jonathon stopped and arched his back, letting out a horrible cry, loud and bestial. Both arms raised, he twisted his head. The other creatures stopped and turned to him. In the silence, Jonathon lowered his head and looked around, eyes gleaming.

For a moment, no one fired a shot.

Everyone reloaded weapons, arms and hands frantic. Jonathon spoke—a long stream of harsh words, fast. The sound of them terrified Pomeroy: old words, older than him, older than the village, older than the valley itself. When those horrible words ceased, he motioned with his arm—and the bodies streamed out the door, out the shattered front windows of the tavern. Even the ones who'd been shot—as if the lead had done nothing more than knock them off balance.

"No—" Carolyn said. She watched Jonathon hurry to the window, clambering through the broken glass and frame. More creatures sped from the room. Another crawled across the ceiling, limbs like a huge spider, and slipped out the window.

"Careful," Maguire said. He stood up next to his boys and held out a pistol, sweeping it back and forth across the room. No one moved. In an instant, it was only them, the demolished room heady with the rank scent of rotting flesh.

"What's happened?" Jude said.

The room was silent save for the wind gusting through the shattered windows. Carrier stood. He moaned, holding his hands to his face.

"Careful," Pomeroy said.

Carrier lowered his hands and tried to speak.

"Oh!" Carolyn said, holding a hand to her own face. The front of Carrier's face was bitten off—the lips, the flesh on his chin, the tip of his nose. He moaned again and tried to speak, but all that came out were damp sibilants and groans. He held his hands back up to his face, running them over the ruin of his face. His eyes looked deranged.

"They got him," Pomeroy said.

Carrier stumbled forward, running headlong into one of the upright beams with a terrible crashing thud. He straightened himself. He grabbed a musket that had fallen, held it by the barrel, and bashed himself over the head with it.

Crack. Crack. Crack.

The moan he made was the worst sound Pomeroy had ever heard. The man knew exactly what was happening to him, what he was doing. Still, he hit himself.

"Would somebody please—" Pomeroy said.

The musket boomed four feet behind Carrier. Maguire. The back of Carrier's head shattered, much of it flying forward and splattering on the floor. Carrier crumpled and Maguire dropped the musket.

Outside the windows, the wind howled.

23

MAKING IT TO THE DAWN

Jude and Carolyn got Pomeroy up. The bandages at the bottom of his leg were soaked with blood.

"Can you stand?" Jude said.

Pomeroy clenched his jaw. "I can lean," he said. He steadied himself against the wall. Nearer to the windows, Morrill looked out into the night.

"They're gone," he said, "heading across the green."

"We fought them off," Maguire said.

"I wouldn't be so sure about that," Pomeroy said.

"They run out, didn't they?"

"You don't see what bloody happened, do you?" Pomeroy said. He held up an empty shot sack. "Another few minutes, and we'd have had nothing left."

"Don't matter, as long as they run off."

"Sorry. I hate to spoil the moment, but you've all just missed the point." He limped forward and gazed at the window.

"What do you mean, Major?" Jude said.

"That one in the middle—you all saw what he did."

"The one who yelled?"

"Very good, yes. The one who yelled. The one who spoke. The

one who ordered them all out—and the one they all listened to." He looked around the dark room at the faces staring at him. "They're communicating and giving orders. Worse still, they're working together with more coordination than we are. Does that spell it out enough—or do I need to tell you what that means for our chances of making it to the dawn?"

An icy wave of air rolled in. Jude stepped between two of the overturned tables to the window and saw that Morrill was right. More dark shapes crossed to the green.

"They're heading for the church," Morrill said.

His words sounded too loud. Jude wanted to clamp his hand over his mouth, so he wouldn't make a sound. Morrill must have sensed it too because he took two small steps back from the window.

"Right," Pomeroy began in back of them, "we'd better find a—"

Jude held his hand back, palm toward him. "Major," he said.

Pomeroy stopped talking. The floor of the tavern rumbled, and there was a sudden howling roar and the sounds of wood breaking. "What is that?"

The wind inside the tavern gusted from the broken windows and door. Morrill ran to the doorway—stepping over the fallen door—and out into the street, pausing after just a few steps.

"Zeke, what is it?" Jude said.

Morrill said nothing, just stared north with his eyes wide and his jaw hanging open.

"Get back here," Jude said. He didn't even need to see what Morrill was looking at—he felt it. The skin on the back of his neck rippled. He turned to the others. "Maguire, have your boys reload the guns. Now."

He went to the door and out into the wind. It was freezing, cold as deep winter. Leaves flew. Morrill pointed. A shadow rolled toward them, crossing Salem Road. It towered into the night sky, higher than the steeple on the church, higher than the tallest chestnut or oak in the village. Streaks of shifting colors coursed through it. As it moved forward, trees shuddered and then snapped. From within the shadow, a sickly light shone, rising into the sky.

"What in the hell is that?" Morrill shouted.

Jude didn't take his eyes from the approaching shadow. "Back inside!" He grabbed a handful of Morrill's collar and gave him a tug. It was like looking into the pit of Hell—a picture worse than any that the reverend had ever painted for his small parish. Then he noticed the figure at the bottom of the shadow, gaunt and terrible. Long hair swirled around the head, tight skin wrapped over bones and the skull around the sunken eyes. The eyes turned to Jude, and a thin arm extended to him.

"Brewster!" Morrill shouted from the doorway.

Jude ripped his eyes away from the shadow. His skin tingled, and he was dizzy. In the green across from the tavern, a crowd stood—the creatures that had fled the tavern. They cowered before the towering shadow, before the thin figure at its base.

Jude pulled Morrill toward the tavern. They stepped over the fallen door and into the common room. "We need to get into the cellar."

The wind gusted, and the tavern shuddered, oak beams groaning. Scraps of glass blew in and skittered across the floor. Upstairs, more windows burst. The wind howled through them. Pomeroy slid to the edge of the chair he was on, getting his good leg underneath him.

"Boy, come here," he said to Maguire's older son. "Help me up."

The boy looked at his father.

"Go on and help him. Quick," Maguire said.

Pomeroy got his arm across the boy's shoulder and stood up. "There we go. Easy." They hobbled toward the kitchen. Queer light shone through the window openings, falling in on the broken room. The tavern shook again.

. . .

A FEAR he'd never known rolled over Pomeroy. Something was moving outside the windows in the light, something large. They burst into the kitchen, Pomeroy hopping on his good leg and clamping his jaw against the pain in his bad one. The stable in back of the tavern was lit up with the shifting colors, the trees behind bending in the wind, branches whipping and turning. The boy with the lantern ran ahead and got to the door.

"What's taking them so bloody long?" Pomeroy said. He was looking back to the doorway to the common room. The others still hadn't reached the kitchen, though their shadows danced against the near wall. Carolyn disappeared into the cellar. Pomeroy glanced back toward the common room again and then turned.

"Let's go," he told the boy.

He gritted his teeth as he hopped forward, leaning on the boy. There was a deep groan, loud enough to be heard over the howling wind. The ceiling shifted and bits of wood and plaster dropped, dust filling the air as the rest of the windowpanes snapped and flew out. Light flared, bright enough to throw their shadows stark against the cellar doorway and wall. The boy turned and started down the stairs, taking them three at a time. Pomeroy turned. Someone ran at him.

"Down!"

It was Maguire, though Pomeroy could only tell by the voice as the light was so blinding. Pomeroy turned and then felt hands on his back, pushing. He fell. As he crashed into Morrill's boy, light from the kitchen flared impossibly bright. The whole building shook. With a tremendous ripping and tearing of timbers, it all came down. A board hit him in the head, and he tumbled into the cellar. He fell in a painful tangle, the wooden steps smacking his face and ribs. The pain in his leg exploded, washing out everything else.

Above them, the tavern collapsed with the loudest sound he'd ever heard.

24

YOU HAVE TO FIX IT

Alma Lane pulled her horse up at the wooden bridge that crossed the Shawsheen River. Below the bridge, the water murmured slow and clear. Alma's legs ached and her backside was numb, and each step of the exhausted horse brought a spike of pain to her head. She'd ridden through the night along roads alive with soldiers—minutemen farmers, craftsmen, husbands, and fathers, all converging on Boston to drive the British into a pen. She'd ridden north as they'd headed south, passing in long lines. They'd all eyed her. Not only because a woman riding a horse was an unusual sight on a normal day. And not how men eyed her sisters Ina or Nessa, both delicate beauties. No, Alma got stares of a different sort—she wasn't a small woman. Still, she didn't shrink under their gazes, knowing she could carry men like them under each arm and barely notice it.

The road forked after the bridge, and Alma reined her horse to the south. From there, she would cut east at Salem Road and head to her father's cabin. Each step forward reminded her why she'd left a decade earlier: it was in the air, in the darkness of West Bradhill, on the silent roads, in the drear sense of fruitless duty. The sky brightened, the slant of early morning light cutting through the trees. She passed a few houses that sat between the road and the river. All their windows were dark, their barns closed and noiseless.

All off to join the fight, she guessed. And no one begrudged them leaving.

She'd been the last daughter to leave, and it had been a blow to her father. Not that he'd grown any less stubborn. For years, she'd tried to get him to leave the cabin and join her in Boston. Be closer to her sisters, nieces, and nephews. Just last fall, she'd told him, again, that he didn't need to be tied down to the lake for his whole life. That he'd done enough.

That had gone about as well as ever. Hand-waving. Sighing. A thick dose of Irish martyrdom. And, again, the guilt: <u>she</u> was the one who was supposed to stay; <u>she</u> was the one to carry on the tradition of watching over the cold, silent lake; <u>she</u> was the one who would grow used to loneliness.

"I made a vow," he'd said.

"But I didn't," she'd answered, resigned to having the talk yet again.

"Do you think Pannalancet worried that he was missing out on balls and reels and dancing?"

Not that she was fighting off invitations to go to a ball. "Pannalancet was born into it. You know that."

"You were born right next to the lake."

"You made sure of that."

He didn't understand, he never would. Maybe they'd never understand each other. Maybe no one would ever understand her. Alma didn't want silk dresses, ribbons in her hair, a doting husband or bouncing babe on each knee. No, she wasn't cut from that cloth. Doing things, making things, thinking things—living in the midst of life. That's what she wanted.

"And what happens when your hip keeps you from getting up when you slip in the snow?" she'd said.

"That's why you need to be here."

"Or that's why you need to come to Boston with the rest of your family."

"I can't leave the lake. I made a vow."

And so the argument had gone, for years now.

Alma rode along the small lanes that led to her father's cabin. She was tired—but with the fighting breaking out, she and her sisters decided that the time had come to bring him to Boston. Time for arguing had passed.

From where her father's cabin sat, a swath of scraggly pine and oak filled the slope down to the narrow end of the lake. It opened like a giant thumb, then widened out into a fist, becoming broad and round. Trees stood right up to its edge all the way around, save for a few places where granite outcroppings leaned out over the water.

Once, she'd rowed a small raft out into the middle of it when her father and sisters had ridden off to Ipswich for a day to visit an old neighbor. Even the water that had rolled down the paddle onto her fingers had been freezing. In the middle of the lake, she'd leaned over the edge of the raft and dropped rocks into the depth—some the size of chestnuts, some small gourds. Each had shimmied down in the water, clear at first, then fading from the light. Finally, she'd pushed over the biggest rock she'd been able to wrangle onto the wooden raft, one larger than her own head. It had splashed into the water, disappearing.

Down and down, then gone.

Watching it, she'd almost flipped the raft and had to scoot back from the edge in a panic. Even now, fifteen years later, she could still taste the fear that had sent her paddling as fast as she could back to the shore: fear of the black cold depths below the raft where the stones she'd dropped might still be sinking; of the enormity of that much water, going down that far; of what the lake was and could do.

Dawn cut through the trees and dappled the front of her

father's cabin. It was here where she'd grown up, her home, her childhood. Corey Lane had tried to show his youngest daughter the way of the lake and done his best to make his vow into hers. Much as she loved him, it hadn't worked.

The door to the cabin was open. She didn't see O'Malley, her father's old stallion.

"Pa?" she called out.

Like the rest of the village, it felt empty here. No answer from the cabin. A pair of sparrows zipped by, landing in a thick bush near the cabin. She climbed from her horse and stepped up to the door, pushing it the rest of the way open, worried that she'd find him helpless on the floor. Or, worse, lifeless in his bed.

"Pa?" she said again.

Sunlight fell in across the wooden floor. Alma stepped in, her shadow in front of her. It was empty, and muddy footprints littered the floorboards. Furniture was knocked over, drawers smashed, windows broken in. She walked across the cabin and leaned down in front of the small fireplace. There was no warmth from the gray embers, and the stone was cold to the touch: no fire there last night. With a pop of her knees, she straightened up and looked around.

It was the lake, all of it. The lake.

Her eyes told her what her heart feared—the cabin had been attacked, her father was missing. She cursed as she searched the cabin. The bedding was rumpled and held the scent of old man. What now? He hadn't gone off to fight the British. She was about to head to the lake—a small voice inside her grew louder—when she spotted a hint of movement from underneath the bed. Squatting, she found an elbow, the back of a head. Without pausing, she grabbed and pulled. The figure jerked, smacking up against the bed, and cried out as she dragged him squirming out into the light, avoiding the fists and kicks that flew.

"Hey, hey," Alma said. She recognized young Thomas Chase.

Alma reached over and turned his face to her, gentle but firm. "Thomas—it's all right. It's me."

The boy stared at her with wide eyes. "Alma?"

"What are you doing here?" She helped him sit up now that his thrashing had stopped.

"I—I didn't know. Where to go. So I came here. And I was so tired, I slept—until I saw you. Outside. I had to . . . go."

He looked terrified. She remained squatting in front of him so he could see her lips when she spoke. "That's all fine, you're always welcome here. Where's my father?"

"The lake," Thomas said. Before he stood up, he reached back underneath the bed and dragged out a sack. "He was trying to stop it. He didn't get to finish it."

"Finish what?"

"Stopping the bad things from happening. And then one of them got him. Pulled him underneath the water." Thomas frowned. "He didn't come back up."

Alma felt the blood drain from her face as the boy spoke aloud the dread she'd long ago locked away in her heart.

"And I took these," Thomas said. He held up the sack and then put it onto the table. Reaching in, he pulled out the wrapped bundle of stones. Alma stared at them. "And this." He lifted a preserve jar from the sack and placed it next to the stones on the table. Alma picked up the jar. It was half-full of blood, and the blood had things floating both on the surface and objects at the bottom. She tilted it. Teeth and claws.

"I also found these," Thomas said. He brought out a fold of papers. "He sat at a fire, reading from them. Then he did something with a skull and put stuff into it. He held it over the water but dropped it. He found it, but I don't think it worked right."

"What do you mean?"

"Well, he dropped it, but some of the stuff came out. Then the lake vibrated with loud bangs. And the water shook. And something came out."

"What came out, Thomas?"

"Something bad. And big. Like a thundercloud. Worse than the bodies."

Alma put the jar down and looked at him, feeling like she'd just been smacked on the head with a board. Why hadn't her dad listened to her?

"You have to stop it," Thomas said.

She snapped out of the thoughts that spun and spun, her pulse hammering, her stomach fixing to unload. "Stop it? I can't."

"You have to."

Alma shook her head. "You don't understand. I don't know what to do. Only my dad knows—knew."

"But he was your father."

"Do you know everything that your father knows?"

"My father is dead," Thomas said. "They got him, and now he's one of the creatures. They got my uncle, too. Maybe my brother, Jonathon. And the village is dying. It keeps spreading. My uncle started it, I think. It was our fault that this happened."

Alma's eyes widened.

"I helped him," Thomas said. "So it's my fault, too."

25

INSIDE OUT

"Push," Pomeroy said, grunting. Sweat trickled down his neck, mixing with plaster and dust. He had his shoulder on one side of a beam. Morrill was on the other side, pushing with both arms. In the lantern light, the veins stood out on his trembling arm. Maguire's older boy crouched on the next step up, also pushing. The thick beam moved a little, no more. They let off pressure.

"It ain't going nowhere, Major," Morrill said.

"Indeed," Pomeroy said. He rubbed at his shoulder where the corner of the wood had dug in. Below them, lanterns flickered. Carolyn was down there with Maguire's younger son. The others hadn't made it. After the tumble and crashing, there had been only silence. In the darkness, none of them had moved or spoken. Something had passed above the broken floors above them. Pomeroy had curled into a small ball, pressing his arms over his head, too scared to breathe. He'd never had a worse feeling. Eyes searching for him, foul limbs and tendrils wanting to work their way into his eyes and skull. It wanted to devour him, to shred him from the inside out.

Whatever was up there destroyed the tavern. The sound of

the wind had moved off, replaced with silence, with an occasional muffled crash or thud. None of them spoke. Pomeroy had straightened out and found that his face was wet—tears had spilled down his cheeks. The others whispered or sniffled. Morrill had sparked a lantern to life. In the sudden firelight, they'd exchanged looks. By unspoken consent, nobody mentioned what had passed over them upstairs. Down below, a store of food, blankets, lanterns, and oil was promising—though less so if they were sealed inside the cellar with no promise of escape.

"Anything?" Carolyn said. She was standing at the bottom of the stairs.

"Well, we almost all broke our shoulders, but nothing was giving beyond that," Pomeroy said. He went down the remaining steps, holding the railing. Morrill and the boy dug at the piles of plaster and framing that blocked the stairwell.

"We have to get out," she said.

"This might well be the safest place for us at the moment."

"Major, I need to find my father–he might still be alive."

"Well, there's a little problem of a fallen tavern directly overhead."

Her eyes repeated her plea to him. He hopped over to a barrel and sat on it.

"Your father is a smart man. He'll know what to do," he said. He motioned for the younger boy to step over and be a crutch. "Let's see what we can find." He leaned on the boy and used his good leg to straighten up. The cellar stretched forward for twenty paces before turning right in an L shape. The lantern rattled in the boy's hand as they staggered forward in a slow three-legged march.

"No other doors or stairs you haven't mentioned?" he said.

"'Course not, sir."

"Then what's that?" he said. He pointed at a small door past the turn in the room.

"Root cellar?" the boy said.

"Don't guess. Find out."

He steadied himself on the wall with one hand. The boy pulled the door open. He leaned in with the lantern.

"Potatoes, sir," he said.

The boy came over and helped him inspect the rest of the cellar. There was no smell of must in the air, and the corners were free of cobwebs. Brewster kept it neat. In the far corner, several large wooden kegs stood next to smaller casks and sacks.

"Not exactly the way I'd hoped to find it," Pomeroy said.

"Sir?"

Pomeroy sighed. It was the famed Brewster's Tavern & Inn ale, a stack of wooden hogsheads: ale so good that each mug was a meal, according to a certain Lieutenant Sorrel—one of the few officers in the regiment whom Pomeroy could stand. Sorrel and another officer had passed through West Bradhill a few weeks ago en route back from Haverhill, stopping at the tavern here for a drink after paying a visit to a friend of his father's. When he'd returned to the regiment, he'd spent half an hour praising the "finest ale ever to pass his lips" to Pomeroy—who'd been in his cups, holding a letter from his own dear father. That conversation had put an idea into Pomeroy's head.

"Major?" Carolyn came up behind him, holding another lantern. "Have you found anything?"

"We won't go thirsty," he said.

She looked over the casks. "Anything that can help us get out of here?"

"I'm afraid this ale, while heavenly, only seems to get one into trouble, not out of it." He pointed at the casks. "This is why I'm here."

"What do you mean?"

"The ale."

"What about it?"

He shifted his weight, leaning on Maguire's boy. "It does take a certain genius—a flare for mucking things up. I suppose I have that at least."

"Major, what are you talking about?" she said.

He pointed again. "I led my men from the city garrison to find this. Told them it was a secret powder hunt when it was in fact nothing more than my personal ale hunt. I can't let the moment pass unremarked."

He turned away from the casks. "I have carved out a special, unimpressive niche for myself, you see. So inept an officer that even my dear old father, Lord Pomeroy, cut his losses. Mind you, I'm a fourth son and not the heir to the estate—leaving only the military as a path to Pomeroy glory. As that was not forthcoming in spite of the many commissions he's bought for me—well, he sent a letter. The first letter I'd ever gotten from him. He informed me that even should all three of my older brothers die, I would never, ever inherit the Pomeroy lands, titles, and wealth."

He picked up a pewter mug from a shelf next to the ale. Hefted it and placed it back, carefully.

"So, why not? Why not leave the King's Own Regiment, take liberty of the finest ale in the colony, and say goodbye to the King's Own for good? A nice little black eye for Lord Pomeroy in the process. Seemed a stroke of brilliance," he said. Pomeroy brushed the top of one barrel. "Of course, I couldn't even desert without turning it into a giant cock-up, now could I? Perhaps Father and the other officers are right."

"We need to get up those stairs," she said.

"You do remember what was up there, don't you?" he said.

"Do you mean the others? Or is it my family you're referring to? Or perhaps you're thinking we should stay down here so you can wax melancholy over a few barrels of ale?"

"Hardly."

"Oh, I see," she said.

"See what?"

"You're craven."

"Pardon me?"

"Might it be that you don't want to face what you yourself helped to cause?"

"What are you—"

"You just said yourself why you came here with your men in the first place, so perhaps you don't want to deal with the mess you—"

"I don't want to deal with the mess, do I? Is that why I used the butt of a musket to bash in the head of one of them—one of my men—that was attacking you. Because I didn't want to deal with the mess?"

She turned away. Pomeroy urged Maguire's boy onward, leaning on him and hopping on his good leg.

"And as far as causing things," he said, raising his voice, "you might want to rethink that. I merely had the bad luck to be here when this insanity started. I hardly caused the local militias to erupt into rebellion, and I certainly had nothing to do with people dying with blackened tongues and marching around this nothing village as shining-eyed monsters. It's been nothing but one bit of bad luck after another for me, and I've only managed to avoid even worse luck through sheer wit."

"Fine," she said. "Use some of that sheer wit to get us up the stairs so we can find the others, Major."

Morrill leaned down from the stairs, his face smudged with dust and sweat. "Major, sir," he said, "think I found a spot."

The boy squirmed out from underneath his arm, hurrying up the stairs. Pomeroy put his hands out for balance.

"Damn it, boy, I can't—"

Carolyn stepped over and steadied his arm. He put an arm across her shoulders.

"Thank—"

"Don't," she said. "Just make sure we get out of here."

He nodded.

Two minutes later, Pomeroy was back on the stairs. They had

a crowbar and two axes. The lanterns hissed on the stairs below them, shining through the dust thick in the air.

"Right," Morrill said. He worked the bar in next to the beam, each wiggle letting fall a tumble of plaster dust.

"It needs to go higher," Pomeroy said.

His leg throbbed with each beat of his heart, but he rested his weight on his other leg. They'd given up on trying to move the beam. Morrill had found a narrow triangle of space filled with debris that they were trying to leverage out.

"Andrew," Morrill said, "tap it with the axe handle."

He leaned back, making room for the older boy to swing the axe handle. One, two, three taps, each one causing rivers of fallen plaster to tumble onto the stairs in a cloud of dust. Pomeroy looked the other way, squinting his eyes.

"Good," Morrill said, "that's good enough."

"Is there room for a good yank?" Pomeroy said.

"We'll make room," Morrill said. He scooted off to the side. Pomeroy climbed another step, high enough to get his hands around the rod.

"Ready?" he said.

They nodded.

"Right, then. Pull!"

They pulled as hard as they could. The debris moved and the bar bent in the middle.

"Harder," Pomeroy said.

It shifted and fell. Bits of wall dropped with a tumbling rattle on the stairs. A large piece loosed a whole cascade of debris. The pieces poured down the stairs.

"Careful," Morrill said.

They moved aside. The stairwell filled with plaster dust. Larger pieces came through, thudding on the wooden stairs. The light from the lanterns was shrouded. Pomeroy coughed and wiped at his eyes. Light fell in. Daylight.

"Good Christ," he said.

The air cleared. Pomeroy moved up below the beam. The hole upward was a triangle, with debris hanging out over the sides. Over the edges, he saw the sharp blue sky of early morning.

"What is it, Major?" Morrill said.

"Do you remember the kitchen?" Pomeroy said.

"Yes."

"Do you remember seeing right through the ceiling to the sky?"

"No, sir."

"Neither do I," he said. He wedged himself up through the hole, reaching up to wrench a few boards out of the way. He almost fit. It was awkward. He pulled back into the darkened stairs. "Brace me."

Morrill shouldered his legs and lower back as Pomeroy poked his head through the opening once more. As he went up, he had to squint his eyes against the sudden light. He got his head and shoulders through.

"Shove me up, boys," he called out.

They pressed him upward. When one of them bumped his lower leg, he clamped his jaw against the scream that wanted to peal out of him. He stretched both arms out and grabbed another wide beam, pulling until he could get his good leg up and onto the surface. Wriggling like a fish, he got himself all the way out without knocking his bad leg. He lay on his back for a moment, gulping in the cool morning air. The sun was rising through the trees. A handful of chickadees swirled overhead and darted off. He got up and knocked the plaster dust from his breeches.

The tavern was destroyed. All about lay broken wreckage, a chaotic pile of beams, bricks, stone, and cracked walls.

"Major?"

The face of the older boy rose through the hole he'd climbed through. The boy extended a hand.

"Of course," Pomeroy said. He reached down and wrapped his hand around the boy's wrist, pulling. The boy wriggled through much more easily than Pomeroy had, getting to his feet. Once up, the boy looked around with wide eyes shining through the plaster dust that covered his face, looking over the damage and up at the trees and field beyond the stable.

"We're lucky not to have been up here," Pomeroy said. "Help the others up."

The boy turned and helped his brother. Pomeroy looked around and spotted a musket buried underneath stone rubble. He yanked it free as he put his weight on his leg. The barrel was bent right at the end. It wasn't loaded.

"This will do," he said.

He tucked the musket butt underneath his right arm and used it as a crutch. Choosing his path with care, he worked his way across a wide piece of a fallen wooden wall, feeling it crack further beneath his weight. Across the way stood the town green and the fallen chestnut in the center. Beyond that, the church was bright in the morning sun. It couldn't yet have been seven o'clock.

Where were the others?

Surveying the debris, his hope they'd found a way out of the building quickly faded. No one could have survived the fall of the building. As to what had happened afterward—the presence that had passed over them—well, perhaps they were better off having perished when the walls and second story fell in on them. He stepped over the wreckage of the inn, leaning on the bent musket. It was difficult to even tell where he was in relation to how the inn had stood. The kitchen, or the common room—he couldn't get any bearings other than the hole that Morrill was now coming out of being the stairs at the end of the kitchen. Parts of the building were still high up while parts of the second story had come straight down.

Then he saw the boots. They poked out from beneath a section of ceiling. He hobbled over the debris and slid at the bottom of a pile of plaster. It was the tavern keep on his stomach.

Pomeroy came to a rest next to his shoulder. The bottoms of Pomeroy's boots crunched on the broken plaster.

"Brewster," he said. He reached out and tapped the tavern keep's cheek, which was white with a dusting of plaster powder. "Don't you be dead. Come on now, don't do this."

The tavern keep stiffened and inhaled sharply.

"There we are, man," Pomeroy said. "You're alive."

The tavern keep coughed and groaned. His eyes opened and blinked several times.

"What—" he said. His voice was thick with confusion.

"Rise and shine, Brewster," Pomeroy said.

Jude spat, blinking his eyes.

"Major Pomeroy?" he said.

"No. George the bloody Third."

Jude wriggled and turned his head to look up at him. Fear flashed in his eyes.

"Where's Elizabeth?" he said.

"We're looking," Pomeroy said. "Are you hurt?"

"Shoulder," he said.

"Can you get out from under all that?" Pomeroy said.

"Something on my back."

"That would be your tavern," Pomeroy said. "Here."

Back over the pile, Carolyn climbed from the cellar. She and the others were dusted in white, looking like actors made up to play the part of ghosts.

"Morrill, boys," Pomeroy called to them, "this way. Brewster is alive and needs our help."

It took them half an hour to pull off bits of roof and wall and ceiling, then get at the beams crisscrossed over Jude, pinning him to the ground. If it hadn't been for the cabinet that had fallen across the table, the beams would have broken him in half. They pulled the last beam off of him, everyone lifting one end, straining while he wriggled out. Jude got to his knees, then his feet. He held his left shoulder.

"How bad is it, Jude?" Morrill said.

"Busted up pretty good."

His left arm hung at an odd angle. Just looking at it made Pomeroy's own shoulder hurt. There was a tearing sound. Carolyn ripped off a strip of cloth from the hem of her dress. When it was free, she stepped over to the tavern keep.

"Hold your arm close," she said.

With a grimace, he pulled his arm to his chest, bent at the elbow. Carolyn wrapped the cloth around him, a crude sling to keep his arm from moving.

"Is that all right?" she said. He nodded.

"I have to find Elizabeth," he said.

Pomeroy turned and surveyed the rest of the wreckage. "How close were the others when it came down, Brewster?"

Jude shook his head. "Not sure. I know they were behind me. After the crash, I heard screams before—"

He didn't finish the thought. In a way, he didn't have to. The look on his face was enough, and even remembering how it felt in the basement was enough to send an icy shot up Pomeroy's spine. It had to have been worse up here. Much worse. Pomeroy turned back to him.

"What was it?" he said.

Jude locked his dark eyes on him.

"The Devil, Major," he said, "only worse."

They searched the debris, working their way through the fallen timbers and stone, trying to cover the wreckage between where they'd come up from the basement and where the common room had been.

"They just bloody disappeared then?" Pomeroy said. He limped around the bricks from the chimney.

"Come on, you've got to be somewhere," Jude said.

One of Maguire's boys called out. The older one peeked over one of the higher piles of stone.

"Major," he said.

Morrill and Jude hurried over to the pile. Pomeroy made his way over, too, muttering as he went. Morrill was over the wreckage first, but he waved the boys off.

"Andrew, take Daniel out of here," he said. "Now!"

Pomeroy skirted leaning timbers and—bracing himself against a portion of wall—got up high enough to see what Morrill was looking at.

And he wished he'd not.

"Maguire," Morrill said. His voice was weak with grief. Pomeroy wasn't sure how he'd recognized the body as Maguire's. Process of elimination, perhaps—a shred of clothing that wasn't a dress. Maguire had been turned inside out. The torso was easiest to identify as it was the largest. Rolls of grayish intestines were knotted and folded over beside dark-colored organs. Up the arms and down the legs, the skin had been flayed, revealing bunches of muscles and fascia, lined with burst veins. The head itself was so mangled that Pomeroy had to turn away from it. None of them said a word, but Pomeroy was sure they were all thinking the same thing—thinking back to the terror that had flooded them when whatever had destroyed the tavern.

"How could it have done that?" Morrill said. His voice had a tremor to it.

"I'd imagine that if we saw it, we'd know all too well—and I, for one, hope to never acquire that knowledge," Pomeroy said.

"We have to keep looking," Jude said. "Elizabeth has to be here."

"This isn't encouraging," Pomeroy said.

"Doesn't matter. I have to find her," Jude said.

"Forgive my bluntness, but I'm not sure I'm prepared to spend the rest of the day sifting through huge beams and stone only to find another shredded corpse—and risk still being here by nightfall," Pomeroy said. He walked past Carolyn. If he were smart, he'd turn and hobble off away from everyone.

"Don't," Carolyn said.

"Ask Brewster what he saw over there," he said, "and you might leave, too."

He pointed to the destroyed tavern. Over the piles, Jude and Morrill moved about. Carolyn looked back at him. Patches of plaster dust colored her hair white. There was something in her eyes—uncertainty, a searching. Pomeroy didn't wait. He turned and walked up the road, leaning on the musket.

"I'm leaving," he said. Why was she looking at him that way?

Voices raised behind him. He wouldn't look, damn them.

"Ho, Major!" It was Morrill, waving furiously for him, cupping his hands around his mouth to call to him. "We found her, Major. We found her, and she's all right. Help us."

"Fool, fool, fool," Pomeroy said to himself. For days he'd been trying to leave but had let himself get caught up with Thomas. Now this. Yesterday, he wouldn't have cared one whit what Carolyn Bucknell thought of him, nor the others. He could have lived with himself quite well. Shaking his head, he stopped, feeling her gaze on him even from behind. He turned around, back toward Morrill's frantic waving. Carolyn watched him return and pass her. He ignored her and said nothing.

26

JUST A CRACK

They split up, an idea that the major made a point of underscoring as ill-advised. Carolyn ignored him—they had to find survivors. Morrill and the grief-numb boys crossed the green with Jude and Elizabeth to look for horses and check in on the church. Pomeroy followed Carolyn up the hill to her parents' house. They didn't speak as they climbed the narrow lane.

The walls of her house showed through the trees as they hurried along the flagstone path to the front. She stopped at the door.

"Tell them to hurry," Pomeroy said. "I'll wait here."

She didn't bother with a reply, surprised he'd even come this far, seemingly unaware that other people besides him had gone through the events of the night before.

"Father? Mother?" Her voice carried through the house. Several pairs of shoes and a collection of walking sticks lined the entryway. "Hello?"

She stepped into the elegant foyer with a staircase leading up to the second floor. A large, formal room stretched off to the left, while a hallway ran to the back of the house next to the stairs.

Carolyn followed the hallway back to the dining room. Three places were set at the table. One chair lay on its back. She took a step forward and something crunched underneath her foot. She crouched and picked a pair of spectacles, one lens now cracked and the frame flattened.

Her father's.

"Mother?" she called out.

Carolyn put the spectacles on the table. In the kitchen, windows looked out on the backyard. Bread crumbs dotted a wooden table in the center of the room. She stepped forward, letting the door swing closed behind her with a squeal. She walked to the middle of the kitchen. Ashes lined the hearth. A few bowls and pots sat on the table, vegetables next to them. The back door was closed and bolted. She left the kitchen and moved through the formal room, finding nothing else amiss. At the bottom of the stairs, she paused.

"Father?"

She started up the stairs. Her heart beat fast. At the top, she paused. Muddy tracks marked the floor. She wanted to call for the major, but her mouth had gone dry. Her mother should be here, even while it was normal for her father to miss a meal or be out at all hours. The horrible words of Jonathon came back to her, an icy knife in her belly.

But don't worry, I tucked them both in.

She girded herself and walked down the hallway.

"Mother?"

Her father's study stood empty. She headed the other way, toward the front of the house. The door to the room on the right was open, her parent's bedroom. It appeared neat and tidy, except that the bed itself was askew. With a step forward, she scanned the room. Nothing by the dresser or the small reading table near the window. A narrow closet door was shut. At the bed, she lifted a corner of the coverlet.

A pair of heels faced her.

Carolyn yelled and stepped back. With her face pulled tight, she pushed the bed forward. It moved easily over the wood floor. A pair of feet and legs poked out.

Before she had time to think, she grabbed the ankles and pulled, stepping back and sliding the body out to the center of the floor: her father. One of his eyes was open, just a crack. Purple-and-blue bruises lined his throat, and a black substance crusted his nose and mouth.

Carolyn ran out of the room, calling for her mother. She ran to her mother's sewing room at the end of the hallway—the door smacked into something heavy. A bureau blocked the way, brushes and ivory combs scattered across the floor. There were dents and raw wood on the inside of the door as if someone had slammed the bureau again and again into the door. The top canopy of the four-poster bed hung down, a corner post broken. A long tatter of fabric poked out from beneath the door to a closet in the corner.

"Mother?" she called.

Carolyn pushed her way in. The room beneath the windows was bathed in sunlight, clothes strewn about. Her mother sat in the corner, on the floor.

"Mother!" Carolyn cried, rushing over. Her mother looked up at her, her eyes like quicksilver and shimmering in the sunlight.

"Sit with me, child," her mother said. "I'll feed you as I used to."

A twist of black liquid spilled from her cold lips. Blood pooled on the floor beneath her, and her mouth and nose were blackened. She held her arms up to her daughter.

Carolyn screamed and kept screaming.

DOWN THE HILL, the church looked empty. Jude and Elizabeth stood out front, listening. Not a sound floated out.

"I was a fool," he said.

She didn't reply.

"When I thought I might have lost you, too—"

"Easier to say now that your tavern is lying in ruins," she said.

"That's not it."

"Isn't it?"

"You told me that part of your heart was a room, boarded up," he said. "It's even more for me. It's a whole floor, a wing. Walled off. There are dark places in my heart, Elizabeth."

"Then I won't be more darkness for you," she said, stepping into the church. "Let's see if there's anyone here, so we can leave."

She led the way, already certain what she'd find. She felt it. The door stood wide open, a perfect silence inside the entryway. Their footsteps felt intrusive as they headed toward the main room.

The windows had shattered. The benches were thrown about, most of them knocked over, others pushed together up against the wall. One of them was broken, long bits of white wood showing among the dark varnish of the surface. The silence of the room took on a weight. Elizabeth stood in the doorway, amazed at how different it felt. She'd taken no comfort or joy from the little church, dragged there by duty and finding herself daily shutting out what her life had become. There were occasions when images of the church burning to timbers had helped her fall asleep at night, but this was different. Filthy tracks ran across the floor.

"Where did they all go?" Jude said.

"I don't know," she said. "The Simpson girls, their mother, old Liam Waters, the Dornans."

Jude stooped by the window. He picked up a tiny shoe in his hand. Without a word, he set it on the windowsill.

"Could they have gotten away?" he said.

Elizabeth looked around, remembering what had attacked the tavern, the way the creatures lurched, climbing the walls, through the windows. The way they had coordinated and communicated. The shadow that had devoured the darkness. She said nothing. Jude pushed a pile of hymnals with his boot. She walked along the front wall, pieces of broken glass grinding and snapping beneath her steps.

"And I heard no horses," she said.

She looked out of the window. The town was still.

"The tracks go up the stairs. Lots of tracks," Jude said. They both caught the scent on the air—rot and putrefaction—wafting from the belfry where the tracks led. Elizabeth crossed the room but stopped when she noticed dried blood on the floor. The pattern was strange, with drops moving evenly out from the center.

"Let's go," he said. "We should tell the others."

"Jude, wait," she said.

He turned from the doorway and looked up.

"There's something—" she began.

"Elizabeth," he said, cutting her off. She looked over and followed his gaze. She stepped back and craned her neck.

It was Adonijah—staked to the slanted ceiling, long triangles of wood from the smashed bench driven through his shoulder, his belly, his neck. His eyes and mouth hung open. His arms stretched down as though reaching for her. Elizabeth put a hand to her mouth. Several long moments passed before she could take her eyes off of him. The scream inside her stuck, and she didn't let it go. She straightened the torn front of her dress.

"Do we have any weapons?" Pomeroy said. They stood out in front of the rubble that had been the tavern. A wounded lot they were, too—and more than just the cuts and bruises. To one extent or another, they each appeared to be in shock. Carolyn had gone—and remained—white as a sheet, hands trembling. He couldn't blame any of them.

"I've two pistols," Morrill said, "and Daniel has one of the muskets."

"Now's when that bloody weapons cache would come in handy," Pomeroy said. Morrill looked at the others and then back at him.

"Williams the cooper."

"Pardon?"

"Williams the cooper, sir."

"Williams the cooper what?" Pomeroy said.

"Ah hell, Major. Never did think I'd be telling this to a lobster-back, but that ain't the only thing I never did think until last night." He turned and pointed to a pair of shops across from the green. "There's our powder store, the whole thing. Should still be plenty of muskets and shot. We moved it there a few days back when we got word you'd been tipped off to our old spot. Boy died moving it, too—broke his neck."

THE COOPER'S SHOP STOOD NEXT to the blacksmith's, a half-barrel hung out in front of the overhang. Pomeroy pushed open the front door into one long room, a workshop. To the left, windows ran along the walls, the many small panes letting in watery light. Two long benches stood by the wall, a third out in the middle of the floor. On the other wall, tools hung: planes, chisels, mallets. Piles of wood chips gathered beneath the benches and on the work surfaces, and the air hung with the scent of wood and pitch.

"Now, prepare to make note of this moment," Pomeroy said. "My finest action as an officer of the Fifth of Foote. The culmination of years of loyal and dutiful training."

"You don't sound too fond of it, if you don't mind me saying," Morrill said.

"I could think of a hundred more interesting ways to spend one's life."

"Well, why didn't you?"

"I'm a Pomeroy, and that's all one needs to know. And while I assumed it to mean gambling, whoring, and occasionally ordering my men to march around in tiny little circles, let's say that wasn't quite what my family had in mind. It's occurred to me that our friend Brewster has the right idea; in spite of everything else that happened last night, I shall always remember that ale I had. An ale worth throwing away a career for, without doubt. Once we're miles and miles from here, I'll have to ask him how he does that." Pomeroy ran a hand through his dirty hair. "Now, the guns—where are they?"

Morrill took a deep breath and then slid one of the benches from out along the wall. Behind the bench, floorboards were missing. The space below held muskets, two dozen of them. Next to those stood crates of lead balls, packets of powder. Pulling another board aside, he revealed barrels full of black powder, priming fuses, and a stack of cannon balls.

"Morrill," he said.

"Sir?"

"Don't 'sir' me, Morrill. You realize that I could have you all hung for this?"

"But—"

"And in doing so, I could rescue my faltering career. The very bloody powder stash I set out for."

Morrill reached for a hammer on the bench next to the door.

"Oh, don't be stupid, Morrill," he said. "I'm jesting. We've enough fire-power here to shoot our way through a whole sodding army of those corpses, which is all that matters."

He motioned, and Morrill handed him out a musket.

"And as far as my career," he said, "I'm sure I'd end up in the stocks even were I to return to the garrison with the head of Sam Adams tucked under my arm. Now, the wagon and the horse."

They took a few more muskets into their arms.

"Oh, and I want to burn the church," Pomeroy said.

He considered it an insurance policy of sorts. Morrill and

Maguire's boys brought the weapons to the wagon, now loaded with a dozen muskets and enough powder and ball to last through several nights like the last one. Pomeroy took a tin can of oil he'd found and worked his way across the green toward the white church. The pain in his leg had fallen off to something of a dull throb, though putting much weight on it would raise it back to a roar again. He tightened his jaw and kept moving. The others watched him from the wagon. Pomeroy stepped up to the doorway, the floor filthy with tracked mud and footprints. The smell of decomposition reached him even before he stepped inside.

"Ha-llooo!" he called out. "Anybody in here that's alive? You need to leave now because I'm about to burn this church down. Are you there?"

He put a hand to his ear and tilted his head. There was no mistaking the tomb-like silence. Pomeroy pulled the cork from the tin and poured the whale oil, splashing it across the wooden floor of the entrance and up onto the walls and the doors to the congregation. Shaking out the last drops, he tossed it to the floor.

"Right," he said, "this ought to save us some trouble."

His new pastime, apparently: arson.

He hopped back out, careful not to slip on the oil. A movement caught his eye. In a narrow window along the side of the belfry, a child stood outlined in it, arms moving in jerky arcs. The child swung back and forth, head lolling side to side. Eyes gleamed silver.

"Come help, come help, I'm frightened," a strange voice called to him.

Sodding bastards, Pomeroy thought. *See how you like this.* He pulled the tinderbox from the inside pocket of his jacket and struck sparks. The fourth strike did it, sending a blue flame racing across the oil with a loud rush. Even at the bottom of the steps, he felt the heat from the fire. The giggles of a child soon disappeared beneath the roar of hungry flames.

27

IT HAD TO BE

It was worse than Alma imagined. They crouched behind a small rise that fell off into the water. A stream gurgled beside them, sluicing between a pair of large rocks. Beyond, the edge of the lake splashed up against the muddy banks in agitated little waves. A churning black ceiling of shadow emerged from a point near the middle of the lake. No light, just a blackness that roiled, veined through with a flash of color that hurt her head.

Alma tore her gaze away. Thomas stared up into the darkness, his eyes wide, a look of pain and sorrow pulling at his face. Alma reached over and shook him hard by the shoulder. "Don't look at it." She spoke slowly, so he might read her words. Thomas nodded.

Alma wriggled farther up the rise. She kept her eyes from the darkness and looked at the water instead. Rough, small white-tipped waves blew across the surface. The air that gusted from the water was cold enough to make her eyes water, forcing her to squint. Near the center of the lake, the water dropped off into a rounded depression. At the far lip, water rose, fat at the bottom and twisted to a rounded tendril that extended up into the air, like an old tree trunk made of water. Little waves, and even a fallen leaf, moving within the strange shape.

People stood round the closest edge of the water. Dozens of them, some knee-deep in the lake, others in past their waists. One or two were out even farther, so that only the tops of their heads were clear of the water. All of them faced the strange protrusion of water that lifted out of the lake. Alma recognized many of them: the oldest daughter of the farmer whose fields ran along Salem Road; Ichabod Clarke, the cooper who'd once courted her; Nell and Purity Ward, whose father tended the burial yard. Others were in worse condition. A few of them had skin that had gone dark colors—streaks of dark green and gray— their hair hanging in filthy locks, their clothes ripped. H ere and there, a large wound gaped, bloodless.

Alma motioned for Thomas. He slid up next to her.

"Where did he start the ceremony?" she said.

Thomas nodded and pointed to a spot twenty-five yards to the left of where they were. Alma spotted the blackened remains of a campfire next to the water.

What had her father attempted?

Something was coming through the lake, following the bodies. And how far that had spread, she didn't want to guess— Pannalancett and her father had always stopped them before. But the darkness and the moving shadow, the strange form in the middle of the lake... What did those mean? The ground shuddered and shadows moved across the water. Alma grabbed the boy's arm and pulled him back.

"We have to go," she said.

She worked her way along the small stream and cut back up into the pine. The boy followed. The farther away they got from the lake, the warmer the air grew. They found the horse—he was snorting and rolling his eyes, jumpy. Alma ran her palm alongside the animal, trying to calm him.

"What are you going to do?" Thomas said. He was breathing hard.

"I have no good idea, and that's the truth."

"But what about the lake?"

"I understand the problem," Alma said. "I just don't know the answer."

"But there's only a few more hours until nightfall—"

"I know what nighttime brings."

Thomas set his lip and lowered his eyebrows, crossing his arms in front of his chest. "Finish what your father started." He pointed back toward the lake. "Close the door and make the bodies go away."

"And how am I supposed to do that?"

"Use the things from your father," Thomas said. "The wrapping with those smelly leaves. Put some of those in your mouth. Your father did that. Use the stones. Probably put them into the water. Maybe pour in that blood, too." He paused. "I don't know what words you should say."

"You're guessing."

"At least I'm trying."

Alma threw up her arms. "I could make a bunch of wild guesses, too. That doesn't mean—"

"I just told you—" Thomas said.

"No, you didn't. Those old Pennacook ceremonies don't work that way. If I don't do it properly, nothing will work. Nothing. I need to do the right steps. Even then—look what happened to my father."

"He almost made it work," Thomas said.

"But he didn't. Even if I understood exactly what to do, those dead are everywhere. There's no way to get by them."

"At another part of the lake. The far side."

Alma shook her head. "Has to be done in the same spot. Or I think so—I don't remember. And stop looking at me like that. I'm trying to think of something."

She wasn't sure. Her father had shown her a few things, which she'd only ever half-believed. Her sisters knew less than she did.

Was the village getting what it deserved? The thought stuck in Alma's mind. She looked at the boy, wondering what he knew and if he'd ever been told that even his father and his uncle had been part of the tragedy that had driven off the last of the Pennacook, save for Pannalancet. Her father blamed the damned pastor for stoking the violence. No one ever learned who'd killed the farmer, but that hadn't stopped the mob from chasing the Pennacook—mostly women and a few old men—into a cabin. Shooting. Shouting. Burning. Pannalancet never spoke of the tragedy after that, but he'd stayed to keep his watch by the lake, as his family had always done. And when there'd been no one else left, he'd turned to his friend Corey Lane.

Alma rubbed her eyes. How could <u>she</u> be the only hope left? She lifted her head. Legends, rumors—her father's stories once seemed a thing of the past. But all she had to do was go back to the lake and look.

The boy grabbed her arm and pulled. "We have to do something."

"I need to get down into that water," she said. "That's the only way."

"If I can get help, will you try?"

"What help?"

"Against the bodies. Will you?"

"Still might not work."

"You have to try. Because of your father. And mine." He shoved the satchel at her. "Wait here."

Thomas swung himself up onto the horse before she could stop him. He pointed toward the village, where a column of smoke rose. "I see our help."

"That's my horse—get down." She reached for him, but he spurred the horse away.

"Nothing a little fire couldn't take care of—that's what the major said. He's still near!" Thomas said.

"What are you talking about?"

"Just get ready—I'll be back with help!" With that, he yelled and sent himself and the horse off down the lane. Alma watched him go, wondering if she'd just gotten what she'd deserved for leaving West Bradhill years earlier.

Or maybe for coming back.

28

___

NEVER COMING BACK

The road curved up between a rolling orchard and a tended field. Pomeroy turned and looked behind the group of survivors. The smoke from the church rose in a big, black column. Good riddance. Once they reached Ipswich, he had every intention of offering Morrill the wad of pound notes he'd kept tucked in his breeches for the horse. And from there, who knew? Out west, perhaps, toward the reaches of the Adirondacks. Or head south, see Philadelphia, or even Richmond—some place where rebellion hadn't taken hold. All he'd need was a change of clothes and he'd be as anonymous as he wanted. Perfect for starting a new life.

Morrill stopped at the high point of the rise in the road, silhouetted against the afternoon sky.

Pomeroy pulled up on the reins, bringing the wagon to a stop. "What is it?"

"Look," Morrill said, pointing.

The road sloped into a small valley of sorts, with a stream twisting a path at the bottom. Beyond was a wall of trees, the start of the thick forest north of the village. A great blackness roiled in the sky over the trees from deep in the woods.

"Good Christ, what is that?" Pomeroy said.

Behind him in the wagon, Maguire's boys scrambled to see the mass of swirling darkness that towered upward into the blue.

"Don't look at it," Jude said. "None of you. Not even you, Major. It's dangerous, just looking at it."

It certainly was different. Despite the admonition, Pomeroy didn't turn away. It was no thunderhead, that was clear. The edges of it shimmered, full of motion, thin strands of black spreading out. At its center, blurry points of light shone through, turning—a patch of night sky seen through water. Between and around the lights, faint colors shifted and pulsed. Something akin to despair ran across Pomeroy's neck and scalp. Hands grabbed his shoulders, shaking him, turning him away from the vision in the sky.

"Major!"

Pomeroy tore his eyes away. It was Carolyn.

"Of—" he said. The world shifted out from under him in a terrific wave of vertigo. He closed his eyes and leaned forward. It was as if he was tumbling through space.

"Major?"

He opened his eyes and gave his head a shake. The horizon still spun. He took in a deep breath and rubbed his eyes. Opened them again. The spinning slowed.

"Are you all right?" she said.

He nodded. "Remind me to listen to Brewster. Always."

"The hell is it?" Morrill said.

"Further reminder we need to get as far away from here as fast as we can and straight away," Pomeroy said.

He spurred his mount. Morrill paced him, keeping the boys distracted from the darkness. The road crested at a small rise and cut its way through the thick woods of the eastern half of West Bradhill.

"I don't think it's darkness," Jude said. He shifted his weight, grimacing as he did. "It's emptiness. Like we're seeing through a window onto someplace else."

Pomeroy nodded. "As ludicrous as that sounds, I believe you're right."

Carolyn laid a hand on Pomeroy's arm that held the reins. She pointed up ahead of them. A horse appeared at a gallop, with a small rider. Pomeroy slowed the wagon.

"Morrill?"

Morrill rode on ahead. "Can't tell, Major."

The rider got closer.

"It's Thomas!" Carolyn said.

The boy rode up to them, the horse breathing hard. He looked half ridiculous up on such a big horse—but no worse for the wear since the day before.

"They were out of ponies?" Pomeroy said.

"Where on earth have you been?" Carolyn said.

Thomas struggled to keep the horse still. Morrill nudged his own horse closer and reached over and grabbed the halter, steadying the animal.

"Thomas Chase," Morrill said. "Is your father here?"

Thomas looked at him and then shook his head. "No. They got him. They got all of them. But I know where they are, and we can get them." He pointed to the darkness in the sky beyond the woods and told them what he'd seen. After a few moments, Pomeroy held up a hand.

"Not likely. You're coming with us. Now."

"He's about to fall off that stallion and break his neck," Carolyn said. She climbed from the wagon and walked over to him. She reached up and tried to get him down from the horse. Thomas shook his head.

"Thomas," Carolyn said, looking up at him, "are you hurt?"

"We need to hurry. It's getting late," he said.

"My feelings exactly," Pomeroy said. "Carolyn, get him into the back of the wagon."

"Come, Thomas—" she said.

Thomas turned to Pomeroy. "You can help me. I helped you."

"And I helped you right back," Pomeroy said. "And I'll even do it again and help you get out of here with us."

"No, I mean with the lake. It's all at the lake—the one we were at. The creatures are there, and also the shadows. You need to help. Help me and Alma. Alma Corey."

"Far too late for that, boy. It's too big. We're leaving. You're coming with us. What's-her-name will have to help herself."

"She can't, there are—"

"And we can?" Pomeroy said. "Look at us. I've a wounded leg, the tavern keep a broken shoulder, Mrs. Reverend a bruised everything. Beyond Morrill here, we have two children—not counting yourself—and two women. Not exactly a crack fighting force."

"But—" Thomas said.

"As much as I'd love to march in there at the head of a strong battalion of troops and send every last one of those things back to Hell, it's not going to happen. We have little in the way of options, boy."

"But we need to do something," Thomas said. "I won't leave without Jonathon."

Carolyn turned her face up to him. "Thomas, you've been very brave ever since this started. You might not care for me, for my family, but you need to listen. Jonathon is gone."

"But I found his—"

"I saw him, Thomas. At my house, and later. He's one of them. I'm very sorry."

"No, he's not!" He looked to Pomeroy for support. Pomeroy looked away. "Don't say that!"

She took the reins from his hands. "Jonathon would be proud —you did what he would have done, everything. But we can't do anything about what's happened here, and the longer we stay, the more danger we're in. We have to leave."

The boy deflated. He certainly had gumption, and Pomeroy was glad to see Carolyn treating him with care.

"But the others," Thomas said, his voice quivering, "they're gone, but not Jonathon. I don't want to be all alone. I don't want them never coming back."

Carolyn leaned forward and wrapped her arms around him. Tears of her own rolled from the corner of her eyes. Pomeroy frowned—two fine people, and they'd just lost all they had.

"I know, Thomas," she said. "I know."

He watched the boy sob into Carolyn's embrace and said nothing. Something hardened in his chest. A minute passed, nothing but the wind rising and falling in gentle waves. The boy cried.

"Carolyn," Pomeroy said softly.

She looked up at him and nodded. She gave Thomas a final squeeze and then stood up and took his hand, leading him around to the back of the wagon. The sun was low enough to sink behind the trees that bordered the side of the road as it curved before them. Darkness wasn't far off—they needed to get away from here before the sun set.

"Right," Pomeroy said. He flicked the reins, and the wagon rocked forward. The wagon bounced on the rutted road. "Morrill —do you recognize that name, the one the boy mentioned?"

Morrill nodded. "Sure. Corey Lane's youngest daughter. She moved away years ago. Boston, I think. Her father lives out in the woods."

"And the lake he mentioned?"

"Up in that same area. No good for fishing. Seen it a few times. Coldest damn water you'll find."

They moved forward, passing through lengthening shadows. As they rode, Jude glanced over at the boy; he didn't look too good. There were circles under his eyes, and his skin was pale. The boy looked like his mother, the same eyes. It stirred up memories.

"You hungry? We've some crackers," he said.

The Chase boy shook his head. The rest of them were still too numb to do much more than sit. Elizabeth wasn't speaking with him, wouldn't even glance at him.

"You're a Chase, all right," Jude said. "Always in the thick of things, making something happen. Rest of your family, always been the same way."

"They're gone," Thomas said.

"I'm awful sorry to hear it. Your father was a good man, and your mother was even better. But listen, you aren't gone. Don't forget that, hard as it is. You've done them proud, taking care of yourself. A lot of folks older than you weren't so brave. Most folks ain't deaf, neither."

The major turned. "Trust me, if the rest of the rebels have half the courage and stones of this one, then His Majesty is in for a shock."

"You knew my mother?" Thomas said to Jude, who nodded.

"She helped me out, more than once. Meant a lot." He looked at Elizabeth, who continued to ignore him.

The darkness loomed above the trees to the north, a shadow of something terrible lurking on the edge of the village. Looking at it, Jude couldn't shake the feeling it was meant to be there; that it wasn't any different from what West Bradhill had always had for him and for others: darkness always near, full of secrets.

29

SECRETS OF THE DARKNESS

None of it should have happened the way it did, not for Jude, not for Thomas's mother, April. Not for his aunt Constance, Joseph's wife. The darkness held their names for Jude, images of Constance—her eyes, her voice, her laughter. How many nights over the past six years had he seen them as he stared out into the night, alone at the tavern, listening to the wind that moved through a world without her?

It'd been Jude's fault, as he saw it.

Jude had worked at Joseph's mill before buying the tavern, and it had started there. Both of them felt it from the start, that was clear enough. Constance would smile at him, bring him food when Joseph was off on a delivery. Conversations ended in laughter and an accidental brush of an arm. He'd made the first move. She'd responded. And so it had gone, taking on warmth like the start of spring, even though it had been the shortening days of autumn in the world beyond the one they were creating for themselves. Stolen afternoons, early morning rendezvous, planned detours on the way to town. Each time bringing them closer, stoking what grew between them. In time, even Joseph understood—he just didn't know who it was. To him, it made little difference; he wouldn't suffer being cuckolded and a black rage simmered. One afternoon, he even told Jude about it, his voice shaking with anger and humiliation over it. Jude said nothing.

And then Joseph heard who it was, heard it from the reverend himself—only the name wasn't Jude's.

It was Daniel Turner, the one who'd owned the tavern before Jude had bought it, when it had been called the Gray Mare. The way the reverend told it, there was no surprise: evil congregated at a tavern, drawn by a brew of alcohol and gossip and braggarts. Joseph's eyes had grown hard then, his face pinched, as his anger took shape into something sharper, more deadly. By then, it grew even worse—for Constance was with child. Not Joseph's, she was certain. Too much had happened then, too much for Jude to search out the right things to do, the right course. Nights and days were spent in a state of panic and fear that the wrong move would bring Joseph's wrath down on him. Constance herself had been terrified, too, and had turned to her sister-in-law for help. They'd made a horrible decision. They'd decided that they should still the child in her womb, still it before it could take good root, before it could come forth and damn all of them with the darkness of its innocent skin. To do this, Constance and April had traveled one cold winter day while Joseph had been off, went north to the Abenaki village on the shores of the Merrimack River, where it turned to meet the sea. There they had bought the tincture of Wolf Bark that would bring her blood back to her and still the child inside, not yet even showing.

But they had bought something else there, something paid for by the sins of Jude and Constance.

When they returned to West Bradhill, talk was that Daniel Turner had run off, driven out for want of money to pay back his mounting debts. Fled west to the frontier in search of a new start. Not everyone in the village believed that story, however. A few had heard—from the reverend, from others—that a tavern keep is bound to reap what he sows, and Daniel perhaps had sown his fate. A few others may have noted that Joseph Chase had closed his mill for a day and not been seen, though his dray and team were in clear sight out front. The forest was deep around the village. Go far enough into it, and a man might hide just about anything with nary a chance of it being found in a decade of summers. And few could blame him for shunning the company of others, of avoiding the tavern, once the pox took hold of his wife. People in the village stayed away from Joseph, away from the dreaded illness. Constance slipped from the world at the side of her husband and her sister-in-law, April, who risked what little she had left exchanging brief notes between Constance and Jude, knowing they couldn't again see each other. April, the poor woman, caught the same sentence, covered in sores and dying in a delirious fever not long after—leaving both the Chase brothers widowers. How they'd come by the illness had been a mystery to most, but not all. The final tally of those who had lost loved ones in the tragedy was unknown by most, but not all. And the secrets that the darkness held—the stains on the human heart hidden by the shadows of the forest and the always cold lake within—well, that also was a mystery to most.

But not all.

30

ALL IN

The wagon wound its way up through the low hills that rose on the eastern side of the village. Beyond was the long stretch of woodland that separated West Bradhill from Boxford. An owl hooted off in the trees, and there was a sudden rush of voices up ahead.

"Christ," the major said.

Jude cursed himself for a fool—he should have known. That owl hoot sounded a little too much like a person, too little like an owl.

"No farther. Don't move."

Men with muskets emerged from the trees that bounded the road. Jude counted a dozen muzzles pointed at them, some on Morrill on his horse. A company of militia surrounded them, with more stepping out on the road behind them. Farther down the road, there were even more men—a small artillery company with horses drawing a cannon. One of the militia stepped up to the wagon, pointing a pistol. Several more of the muskets swung over to the wagon as men spotted the British uniform on Major Pomeroy.

"Who's in charge?" the man with the pistol said, "and where are you headed?"

"Colonel Brewster here's in charge," Morrill said. He pointed to Jude and then at himself. "And I'm Captain Zeke Morrill. West Bradhill militia."

The commander looked over the wagon and then back up at him. "And what are—"

Thomas stood up in the back of the wagon. "The king's men attacked the village!"

All heads turned to face him.

"A whole brigade," Thomas said. He was speaking loud and slow, as clear as he could. "And they came in and shot people, and they burned the church, and now they've set up a camp next to the lake over here. They got prisoners—women and children."

Some of the militia passed a few words among themselves, looking as though word of a British presence had been rumored. The one with the pistol turned to the wagon. "That right, Colonel?" he said.

Jude didn't have time to think—he nodded his head. "We were outnumbered. Most of my company already headed to Boston—we were rounding up the rest when they came in. They sacked most of the town. Destroyed businesses, burned the church, killed the citizenry."

"I told you," one soldier near the commander said.

The soldier in command silenced him with a wave of the hand. "What about him?" he said, pointing at the major.

The major lifted his hands. A pistol appeared in Jude's hand, pointed at him.

"Prisoner. One of their officers."

Thomas pointed at the major. "He knows where they are—he can lead us to them. We can surprise them."

An angry murmur swept through the company of militia that was now crowding around the wagon. A minute later, Morrill and Jude stood at the side of the road with Captain Silas Adams of the

Portsmouth militia. The troops were forming up in the road, the artillery moving up from behind. A pair of soldiers kept their muskets trained on Major Pomeroy while another pair moved the wagon with the women and children.

"We saw the smoke off over the hills and got a little more cautious," Adams said. "I worried it might be the British—there'd been talk of it on the roads. Our company leaders were down in Menotomy when the fighting broke out, sent us a rider telling us to form up and head south."

"We were as surprised as you, Captain Adams," Morrill said. "They'd driven their troops out under cover of darkness last night, riding and marching hard."

"And him?" he said, nodding his head toward Major Pomeroy.

"Caught him at the tavern. Got separated from his men," Jude said.

"Get him over here," Adams said.

The men guarding him prodded him with their muskets, and the major limped over. All the eyes of the militia followed him. When he reached the officers, he looked up and down the line of men.

"More hayseed soldiers, I see," he said. "We'll make quick work of you, too."

Jude saw they were all in, playing their roles just so.

"How many men have you?" Adams said.

Pomeroy smiled. "More than enough to deal with the likes of you lot."

The captain stepped close to him. "And is what the boy said true? Your brigade is bivouacking near here?"

Major Pomeroy gave him his haughtiest look. "Precious little good you'll do against them. Your best bet would be to turn around and hightail it off."

The captain nodded and then motioned to one of his men. "Tie his hands. He'll lead us there."

31

ECHOES OF THE PRAYERS

The sunlight in the cabin deepened. Alma stood in front of the table, looking at the objects: the stones, the blood mixture. She held the wrapping of raven's tongue, its pungent scent strong. None of it meant anything to her—one reason she'd left. Thinking of the horror that the lake had become, she knew she should have come up and fetched her father years ago, when they'd first argued about it. Just taken him, protests or no. Instead, she'd left him watching the days and seasons and years go by with nothing but his memories and the rituals handed down by a long-dead friend. Standing guard over a cold, deep lake.

But she'd done what she'd done, and here she was. Alma looked at the items on the table again, knowing she couldn't run away now. *Wouldn't* run away.

"What else?" she said, re-reading the fragile letters again. She lifted four of the slender leaves from the leather wrapping. They were growing dry. She folded the leaves, twice.

"Fine," she said.

She slipped the leaves under her tongue and grimaced at the bitterness. After a few minutes, she sat in the chair, face to the sun coming in the window. Alma sat still, her mouth growing numb from the strong plant. She stared at the sunlight on her hands, the long spidery shadows on the table. When she began speaking, her voice sounded strange in her ears. The shadows moved across the table, shifting as she repeated the words. Over and over—and the words deepened with meaning. She lifted her eyes. The sun was molten orange, a lake of burnished copper. Shadows gathered outside the window: the dead.

Alma repeated the words and sensed their power grow, holding back her doubt, her surprise, and the wave of grief for her father that rose around her heart.

Even from where she was, she reacted to the power at the lake. She saw it filling the afternoon air. It coiled around trees and settled in low spots, sent streams of darkness to poison the sky. Alma stood, trembling with energy, and gazed out the window. The dead gathered around the cabin. A dozen or more watched her, washed out—as void of color as they were void of life. Their talk was loud and agitated.

". . . sent me to this hell, and all I wanted was my Lorulei, but my eyes are gone . . ."

The voices.

". . . the water is always so cold and the fishes move across me and pick away at my face and neck, and the cold mud is choking me . . ."

One who looked to be a soldier lurked nearest the window. With the powers of the raven's tongue, Alma saw the man's skin, his hair, his eyes. His face was full of anger and despair. The sunlight passed through him and cast no shadow.

Alma didn't panic, but she needed to know what to do. The back of her neck tingled. Alma opened the door. The deep sunlight warmed her skin. She had one hope, one way to find the answers. She looked around, searching. The dead filled the yard. They turned to her. An apparition just before the window turned to face her.

"Pa," Alma said. Her heart crushed in her chest; it was him,

Corey Lane, a faded vision, eyes the color of washed out seashells.

His hair and clothes hung damp while his blue lips leaked lake water, his voice gurgling as he spoke with lungs soaked and full of water. "Not much time, lass." There was no comfort in his voice. "I can't speak to you much—so let's hurry."

"Who are all these spirits?" Alma said.

"The dead of the lake. Once you touch the power there, they're drawn. Drawn like fish below the surface rising to the moon. They'll stay with you."

Her father's shape grew indistinct, breaking apart in shards, then connecting. She wondered what the plants had done to her mind. As she stood in the doorway, her perceptions shifted. Colors leaped out and danced. Her whole body tingled, shuddering in waves.

"It's opening up—and there's more than the dead about. Worse is coming, drawn from the other side."

"What are they?" Alma said.

Corey's spirit reached forward and passed a hand through her, through her face and eyes. And she saw it, a vision from beyond the lake. A gasp broke from her throat, and she stepped back with a shudder. Every bit of her flesh crawled. Even the dead were a welcome sight.

"They'll lead these armies, the armies of the dead. They'll move out to hunt down the living, wherever they are. Villages, towns, territories far from here. You've got to stop it, now." He turned to the lake and pointed to the darkness rising into the sunset sky. "Shut the gate before it opens all the way, Alma. Shut it. Now."

"How?" Alma said.

"I'll help you, lass."

Soon, she had a fire going in the shed behind the cabin, built right on top of the pile of ashes she'd found there. The dead stayed outside, except for her father, who sat across from the fire

—but whose eyes didn't show a reflection of the flames. Alma shuddered with chills from the raven's tongue. She opened the jar that the boy had brought back from the lake's edge, from her father's failed ceremony. Her ceremony now.

"This will focus the power. It will fill your veins," her father's spirit said. "You're strong, Alma. You've always been so strong. You can do this."

Alma nodded, not quite believing it.

"You've run from it and fought with it, but you're bound up in this. But I'm here with you."

"Why?" she asked.

"Because I've loved you since I first set eyes on you."

Alma looked at the faint shade of her father. A tear spilled down her cheek.

"It's time to start," he said.

She wiped her face and closed her eyes. She chanted the strange Pennacook words, written out by sound. They may have been only the echoes of the prayers, but they held a power. As Alma sang the words, she heard her father's voice clearly. After a quarter of an hour, she opened her eyes and looked at her hands: they shimmered like the embers, coated with a layer of shifting red—the bloodfire. It ran up her arms, through her shoulders, and up onto her scalp; nothing to scoff at, no figment of a lonely man's imagination, no legend. The flames moved over and through Alma, hot and strong. She looked up for the shade of her father.

He was gone.

"You're ready," came the whisper in her ear.

The bloodfire flared. Alma opened the door, the light from her hands shining on the wood and the iron latch. The night air was chilly. The dead gathered when they spotted her. As she stepped out, their chatter grew, but they parted before her. Alma shut them out, their calls and yells and cries. She passed them and crested the small rise. By the wide spruce, she found the path and headed to the lake. The dead trailed her.

As she passed beneath the boughs of pine, the light on her hands grew brighter. Root, pebble, branch—all shone clear, with shadows as crisp as printer's ink. Alma reached the end of the path and groaned as she looked out over the lake; she was too late.

The gate was open—wide open—and the winds from beyond roared up into the sky, blotting out the stars with their darkness. Something else was coming through—she knew it in her bones, heard it in the panicked yells of the dead around her, saw it in the shifting of the light in her hands and arms. She hurried to the water. The bloodfire shone on the agitated waves, red as rubies. She looked back over her shoulder. The crowd of the dead had grown, lining the shore behind her.

Alma ignored the din and recalled the words. She raised her hands out in front of her, seeing the heatless flames dance. When she tried to speak, her voice failed, her throat and mouth dried out in fear. She began again, her voice trembling.

The flames on her hand grew. She repeated the verse, finding her voice. By the sixth repetition, the bloodfire filled her. The dead behind her murmured and cried out. Movement from the lake drew her eye. Bits of darkness broke away, moving. Coming toward her. Silver eyes, dozens of pairs. More. They rose from the deeper water. The bodies slunk toward her, slow in the muck of the lake bottom.

Alma held her hands out and yelled. "Get back!"

They kept coming. A wind ripped across the lake, frigid enough to steal the breath from her chest. The ground shook and a deep green light came from the center of the shadow in front of her. Flames danced around her hands, her body. A memory came to her then, just a fragment but as tart and strong as a cranberry on her tongue: being led to the edge of the lake, her small hand wrapped safe in a large dry hand; the sun turning the water into shimmering jewels; looking around as the cool air of October wrapped her face; tottering against the wind and pale blue sky; gazing up at her father.

Time to seal the gate.

Alma took a step forward, toward the bodies with their bright eyes, toward the cold of farthest space.

32

A LITTLE BIT OF HELL SPRUNG LOOSE

The sunset faded while the darkness deepened over the lake. The militia readied themselves, the captain at the head of the line, a cannon at the rear. Pomeroy's hands were bound, a pair of militiamen guarding him. He looked up the line of soldiers. A motley lot. A handful of them looked to be competent soldiers. The bulk were craftsmen, farmers, and attorneys—little use in real combat, he guessed. As the tale that the boy had spun made its way up and down the line, he faced ill looks and curses. One thick-necked soldier—looking like he belonged behind a plow, not a cannon—hawked up and spit, hitting Pomeroy's shoulder.

"That's for your king," the soldier said.

Pomeroy didn't glance at it, didn't wipe it off. Another soldier smirked.

"You won't be laughing long," Pomeroy said. "Not when you learn what's waiting for you up ahead."

"They won't even see us coming," the thick-necked soldier said.

Pomeroy sniffed. "This is the King's Own Regiment you're facing, boy. We'll cut you down just as fast as we cut down the sorry lot of bumbling farmers in West Bradhill. Look at you. Can't even stand in proper formation."

The men glanced at one another. Pomeroy was amused when some of them straightened up their muskets.

"If you think you will simply march into the woods and demand we hand over our prisoners without a fight, you're even duller than you sound," he said, knowing such a comment would rile them up.

The militia captain walked over, Brewster and Morrill with him. He couldn't read their faces.

"Major Pomeroy," Adams said, "you will lead us to the British encampment, under guard. If you attempt to flee or signal to them, you'll be shot on the spot."

"Listen, Captain whoever-you-are, you don't have a prayer," Pomeroy said. "The smartest thing you could do would be to turn about and march straight away."

"No chance, Major. Not after what your men have done. We're going to serve them a taste of their own."

"We'll see about that, won't we?" Pomeroy said.

The column of men and their cannon began their march, up and down the low rises and turns of the road. Night wrapped the woods. Soldiers prodded Pomeroy along before the column, a pair of bayonets at his back. He scanned the dark road for familiar landmarks, wishing the boy were here—every chestnut and break in the pines looked the same to him. They'd sent the Chase boy along with Carolyn and the other women and children, the wagon headed west.

Dark trees and meadows stretched away on either side of the road. The wind rose, stirring the trees and tossing his cloak about. Pomeroy peered forward. He turned to the north side of the road and paced along the edge, scanning thickets that bordered it. The guards followed him, exchanging a glance. The rest of the company followed.

"Path," he said. "Where is the bloody path?"

One guard bumped him with the tip of his weapon.

"Easy," Pomeroy said.

"Stay where I can watch you," the guard said, a tall fellow with a hook of a nose.

"Don't go getting all—" Pomeroy began. A pale face leered out at him from the darkness between tall trees. The two guards had their back to it. The face disappeared, darting back into the blackness. "Ah—here we are."

Adams gave the orders, moving down the line of troops. Pomeroy stood with Morrill and Jude before a trail black as a tunnel through a mountain.

"Well, gentlemen," Pomeroy said, keeping his voice quiet, "this is it. As soon as we get into the woods, we bolt to the right. Lose them in the dark and catch up with the others." Spoken like the scamp he was. Living down to his father's low expectations of him once again. He leaned closer to the pair of villagers. "Or—we can see what a cannon and a score and a half of muskets can do to help out young master Chase's Indian friend out by the lake."

"But—" Jude said.

"No buts, no ifs, no whys. This is our one chance."

"We got fighting men now," Morrill said.

"I'd be surprised if three of them were fighting men, Morrill—the others are just scared farmers," Pomeroy said. "But they all have weapons, and there are a lot of them. I have more than a passing familiarity with artillery—the one thing the king's army ever found me useful for."

Captain Adams made his way back to them.

"What say ye?" Pomeroy said.

Morrill nodded his head. "We do it."

"Brewster?" Pomeroy said.

"Running won't make it go away. I know that now," Jude said.

Pomeroy looked back and forth between them. He nodded. "We stay, and Lord help us. Young master Chase can thank us later."

"You're a better man than you give yourself credit for, Major," Jude said.

"Or the biggest fool to wear the uniform of this king or any other," Pomeroy said.

They headed into the woods, careful to stay on the narrow trail. Pomeroy and Morrill had two of the militia men with them, their weapons trained on Pomeroy. Jude and Captain Adams followed with a line of men trailing. Only moonlight illuminated the path, faint through the trees. The air changed. Pomeroy recognized it as the way it felt when they were around—the walking corpses.

Something moved in the darkness ahead of them, a figure. It stood motionless, a pale spot. "The children are waiting for you, yes. They want to hug you and tell you secrets. Come along and don't disappoint." The voice was a cruel whisper. The shadow moved. "We're watching you."

And it vanished. Men aimed their muskets at nothing.

"The hell was that?" one of the militia said.

"They're taunting you," Pomeroy said. "Try not to wet your breeches."

The militia pushed their way forward until they reached a granite outcropping. Before them, two score bodies stood in the lake. The longer Pomeroy looked, the more he spotted. And that wasn't what worried him. He stared at the middle of the lake. His resolved threatened to crumble. Above the lake, blackness. No moon, no stars. In their places hung a swirling mass of shadow. Streaks of color moved through it in irregular patterns: thin lightning, or wider, churning waves. The colors—sometimes faint, sometimes bright—made him ill. The sickly light from the sky lit up the scene.

A hole gaped in the middle of the lake; huge, bigger than West Bradhill's village green. On the other side, a spindly shape rose. Pomeroy stared at it for several long moments before he realized that it was made of water itself, rising from the edge of the hole. He craned his neck and put it at two hundred feet or more. It branched out into smaller parts and reminded him of the tree-like structure of arteries and veins he'd seen removed by butchers. A stream of shadows shot up into the darkness above, ragged and tearing. The effect brought to mind the tops of the giant waves he'd seen during a horrific night storm on his Atlantic crossing; winds so strong that the foaming white caps tore straight off howling spindrift. Dread swept away his earlier confidence.

"We are so stupid," he said.

"What happened to the sky?" Jude said.

"A little bit of Hell sprung loose, it would appear."

"But what—"

"I don't know."

"But how could—"

"Really, I don't know," Pomeroy said.

Jude looked at him. "Then what are we going to do?"

"First, we hope to Christ that we haven't horribly miscalculated," Pomeroy said. "Then we find a good spot to put the guns and keep the men distracted—and away from seeing any of this business." He pointed to another outcropping of rock fifty yards to their right. "If we put the four guns there, then line up the men every few feet in the cover along the shore coming this way, we can hit most of the bodies on the flank. Just the way we'd prefer."

"You think the cannon can take care of those things?" Jude said.

"I bloody well killed one with a spent musket. Cannons are sure to do something useful." The ground shook beneath them. Pomeroy turned and realized the horses wouldn't be able to pull the guns through the dip and rise before the outcropping. "We'll need to unlimber the cannons and have the men haul them."

Captain Adams and the nearby militiamen turned to him. "What did you say?"

"The horses will never get up that with them, but the men can."

"You're our prisoner, sir."

"Take a good look about, Captain. At the lake. At what's in the lake. I may be your prisoner, but we're facing something far more dire than this side or that with muskets, opinions, or differing loyalties. Furthermore, I'm a prisoner who's led artillery companies far more experienced than this, through terrain far worse."

Adams stared out into the scene before them, his mouth open. Several of the pale bodies turned toward them, eyes glimmering.

Adams broke the men up into teams to have them pull the guns by hand up over the other ridge. The first of the guns was free from its limber and being half-rolled, half-carried toward the ridge. There were eight men heaving and lifting the gun up the short but steep incline, their feet slipping on the forest floor.

"More effort, boys," Pomeroy said. "Just imagine you're slipping it right into your friend King George's arsehole. Grunt a little. Push it right up to the trees."

One man straightened up and turned on him. "I thought we was here to kill lobsterbacks—not take orders from them."

"And you'd regret every second you wasted doing it, trust me," Pomeroy said.

"Only take a second."

"I'm not anyone you bloody need to worry about," Pomeroy said. "Bloody worry about what's out there! Death, darkness, and misery—that's what's out there. And believe me, as one who's seen both sides of this conflict, that's actually worth fighting. None of our disagreements matters one whit in the face of that. Believe me."

He turned and walked over to Captain Adams. The middle of his back itched—right in the spot they'd shoot him. Each step forward made it itch more—but no shot came. "We have a slight high-ground advantage here. Lower the barrels and have the men wheel them forward until they clear the branches. Then we'll loose one giant volley—artillery and infantry. Have them loaded and prepare to fire. Go for the heads. Keep the aim high. If we don't take the heads off, we don't stop them. I'll watch and dial in the cannon for the next volley."

Adams stared at him. "Tell me you know what you're doing, Major."

"Forethought may not be my strength—just ask Brewster here—but I've never been more certain of anything." He straightened out the front of his uniform. "Now let's see how well those silver-eyed bastards enjoy a few dozen rounds of minié ball and four barrels spitting four-inch shot."

"Yes, sir," Adams said.

The sky crackled with flashes of muted light through the thick tree cover of their location.

33

HELP ME STAND

They rode alone under the stars, their escort of two militia men walking alongside the horses. The smell of the night woods was strong. Carolyn's back ached, her legs and buttocks ached—just sitting in the driver's seat of the wagon a strain.

"We should have all left," she said.

"You can thank young Master Chase for that," Elizabeth said, not unkindly. She turned. "Thomas?"

The Maguire boys turned, looking out into the darkness. Thomas had vanished.

The argument was short but heated. Their escorts were adamant: they had their orders. Carolyn wouldn't have it. She'd find Thomas, and that was that. She flicked the reins, getting the horse to speed up.

"Please," Elizabeth said, "no farther than the border of the village. If we don't find him before then—"

"I know," Carolyn cut in. "He can't have gotten far."

Thick woods came right to the road along the northern side, and rolling meadows and fields disappeared off into the darkness to the south. She scanned the road ahead of them, pale in the moonlight. Empty. The wagon banged over a rut in the road left over from the spring run-off. They soon reached the border of West Bradhill proper, three miles from the center of town, and no sign of Thomas.

"He's gone," Elizabeth said.

"He must have cut north earlier, through the woods," Carolyn said. If Jonathon were here, she'd slap him and scold him, and she'd scream at him. Scream at him for being so strong willed and for being so stubborn. For being everything that a younger brother would emulate. She climbed down from the wagon, holding on to the side.

"What are you doing?" Elizabeth said.

"I'm going to find him," she said.

"But you agreed that if we—" Elizabeth said.

"Yes, and I'm sticking with that. Please. Go. I'll catch up with you once I've found him."

"You can't expect to march into the dark forest and find the boy by yourself."

Carolyn walked across to the side of the road, looking out to where the path led. "We'll see."

"We can't stay," Elizabeth said.

"I wouldn't ask you to," Carolyn said.

"The children."

Carolyn nodded. Elizabeth turned the wagon around and headed east, away from the town.

"Be careful," she said.

Carolyn raised a hand in agreement and farewell, then turned and faced the entrance to the woods. The darkness made following the path difficult. A rumble and flash of light passed through the trees. Loose, old branches shook free, falling around her. The sky turned a strange blue in a quick flash—the blue of a corpse's lips. Each step became a trial, but she hurried, breaking into a jog so that she might stay ahead of her panic. Eventually, a medium-size oak stood silhouetted ahead of her. She'd reached the forest where it met the lake. The water lay just past a dozen yards of soft ground and ferns.

She gasped.

Body after body stood in the water, slouching, all facing the center of the lake where a huge column of darkness rose, full of movement and flashes of light. The water danced, waves rising and falling. Whatever will she'd had before dissolved. She tore her eyes away from the huge shadow and searched the shore. Maybe Thomas was nearby. In a sudden fit of horror, she turned back to the bodies and searched for any that looked like a boy. They were old and young, tall and short. Some looked normal, others filthy with leaves and mud. A few looked sunken and rotted. They stood so still.

Carolyn paused. Nearer to her, a large woman stood in the lake, her hands raised, shining as though with a deep fire. She sang as the bodies in the water came toward her. Her voice grew loud enough for Carolyn to hear the words, though she couldn't understand them. Carolyn's pulse raced as she saw the silver eyes draw near.

And then the shore of the lake exploded in a line fifty yards long.

Flames spit out from the trees, followed by a gut-shaking boom. A buzz ripped the air into loud screaming whistles. The water around the bodies jumped, spray shooting off to the left. One body nearest the singing woman tore in half. Another lost its head, the hair and bone lump of it tumbling up into the air and then landing in the water with a splash. Carolyn looked over to the shore where the firing had come from. The major was behind it, she was certain. Turning back, she saw the woman struggle. The rows of bodies had been thinned as wheat before a scythe— but there were still dozens moving toward her.

And we need to help because Alma can fix it. Was that what had Thomas said? So, this was Alma.

She watched Alma try to stand, holding her leg and grimacing. The glow around her hands and arms faded, a trick of the eye, a glimmer floating around her fingers. Carolyn ran out across the muddy shore and splashed into the water. The air was freezing and wild, blowing in all directions, the water icy. As Carolyn reached her, Alma looked up in shock.

"I'm not one of them," Carolyn said. "I'll help. I'll help you."

The blood leaving the woman's leg shocked her. Carolyn reached down and tried to get a grip underneath the woman's powerful arms.

"No, don't," Alma said.

"We have to get out of here."

Alma pulled away. "I have to stay."

"It's too dangerous—"

"Help me stand."

"But—"

"Help me stand."

A pair of silver-eyed women pushed through the water toward them, bringing with them the rank odor of decay. Carolyn lost her footing and fell on top of Alma, both of them sliding into the icy water. More bodies rose from the lake, dripping black streams of water.

34
———

LOST TO HOPE

Not far off, Thomas spun his head around to the right at the flash of bright yellow. He felt a concussion in his chest and in his ears. It wasn't thunder, and it wasn't the rumbles that had shook the ground. He broke into a run. The trees ended, and the lake opened before him. Blackness stretched into the sky, an angry wound pouring forth violence and death. Air colder than a winter midnight washed over him.

And the bodies.

They filled the lake near him: men and women, children, old people. Staring and hunched, backs arched, silver eyes gleaming, slouching toward the shore. Some wore only nightclothes. Dirt and filth covered them. Some had pale skin, others mottled patches of decay. He knew most of them—his neighbors, friends of his father, children who went to the schoolhouse. But they were all gone now, lost to days and light and laughter. Lost to hope. Like his own family, their lives had been snuffed out, embers blown away into cold darkness.

The water was black and choppy, stretching out into the night. Thomas took a deep breath and sprinted to the shore.

35

HOLD FIRE

"Hold fire!" Major Pomeroy yelled, waving his arms. "DO NOT FIRE!"

Jude ran up to him.

"Did you see that, Major? We punched a hole right through—"

"Don't let them fire again! It's Carolyn."

Confusion broke out among the men. Jude raised his voice, trying to get them under control. "Load and hold, men! Load and hold!"

"There," Pomeroy said, pointing to the main group of the bodies. "Right into the center there. Keep their shots away from the left. Hit neither of those two people down at the edge—don't even aim near them. Do you understand?"

He pushed his way through the branches. Jude followed.

"You'll give them the order," Pomeroy said. "Get them pointed toward the center of the lake, toward that towering . . . thing. Give me half a minute and then have the men fire. Cannons toward the middle, muskets toward the bodies."

"Where are you going to—"

"No time to waste," Pomeroy said.

Past him, scores of bodies rose out of the water, farther out than the ones they'd just shot at. Their eyes shone, a hundred silver candles reflecting off the turbulent water. Jude caught Pomeroy by the arm and turned him to the water. Pomeroy looked at the bodies that had just appeared and then back at Jude.

"Right," he said, "shoot them, too."

Pomeroy patted him on the shoulder, then broke into a running hobble down through the trees that bordered the lake. Bursts of color, bright and quick as lightning, shot out across the lake from the center. The ground rumbled.

36

THE SECRETS OF THE LIVING

A shot rang out behind Jude, the ball clipping through the leaves. He shouted at the men to hold their fire as he ran back up to the guns. Several of the men had their weapons raised, getting a bead on Pomeroy as he ran off.

"He's getting away," one of them said. Another shot rang out.

"Damn it," Jude said, "lower them muskets right now!"

"But—"

"But nothing. He's one of us, don't you see that?" He ran over and reached out, pulling down the barrel of the last musket trained on the disappearing figure of the major.

"But if he goes to tell them what we—"

"Tell them? The British? Boys, open your eyes. Ain't no British but our major over there, and he's doing all he can to save some good people." He pointed at the lake. "Now, go on and a take a good look at what our problem is here, because we don't have time to stand around jawing about it. Go on."

The men moved up into the trees. A few already knew they weren't facing companies of the king's troops. Morrill watched the shore across the way, where Pomeroy headed.

"The rest of you," Jude said, "get on over here and see if you can't take out some of them down there, down where he's headed. Go for their heads—a good shot can slow them down, and that's what we need. Morrill, get these cannons barking. Straight ahead, where those others are coming on us."

"You'll eat your sins tonight." The voice was high and piercing, coming from the darkness. "The water will soften your cold flesh down below."

Whispers surrounded them.

"Jude?" Morrill said.

"Don't know."

Jude strained his eyes and saw movements beyond the outcropping, shadows in the trees. Some of the men fired off their muskets, a few toward the lake, others into the surrounding forest.

"Now, don't all start firing without a plan," Jude said.

Captain Adams—just off to his left—dropped his musket to the ground. He craned his neck and looked above them. Jude followed his gaze. Pale faces with silver eyes looked back at them. They were in the trees, more than a dozen of them, surrounding them. The bodies hung upside down—grotesque bats.

"Your secrets will follow you as the light fades," one voice whispered.

They dropped from the trees, gray and filthy skin, cold to the touch. Men cried out in terror. A handful of shots went off, and then there was an awful silence as the men struggled to wrest themselves from the bodies that landed on or next to them. Jude saw Captain Adams's neck snapped by a young woman, who didn't even give him time to cry out before clamping her mouth over his and spraying black liquid. A harsh shriek split the air— one body stood behind one of the cannons, an old man with wild hair and beard, the flesh of his lips torn and hanging loose. He yelled in the terrible language they'd heard at the tavern, before it fell. Others ran over to him.

The dead turned the cannon.

Jude used the bayonet on the end of his musket to keep back one corpse, catching it hard in the throat and using both arms to slice the neck near to clean through. After a violent struggle, the body fell and lay twitching, struggling to regain its footing. More came at them from the trees.

"Fall back, fall back!" Jude yelled.

His foot caught on a root and he slid down the incline to the lake, losing his musket. The other men panicked, driven back on top of him. Here and there, a musket shot sounded. Jude struggled to get to his feet. Silver eyes tracked him. Screams filled the woods. A hand got him under his arm and yanked him to his feet —it was Morrill.

"What now?" he said.

Jude turned. The lake was at their backs. A dozen pairs of silver eyes were coming through the darkness of the water toward them. A handful of the militia were down at the water's edge with Morrill and Jude, some with guns, some—like Jude now—without. Up the outcropping, the yelling grew more infrequent.

"They're on one cannon," Morrill said.

"Got to get them back, all of them," Jude said. The ground shook again, harder this time, hard enough to rattle the water of the lake itself, sending it up in jumping waves. One of the militia men came running down toward them with no weapon. Jude raised his hand to signal the men, and just then the cannon manned by the dead went off with a deep boom that echoed off to the other side of the lake. The man running down the hill landed at Jude's feet in two pieces and a shower of blood. Several of the militia men fled. One of them ran in the direction that Major Pomeroy had gone, only to be chased, caught, and pulled into the water by two corpses.

"This way!" Jude yelled. He traced the shore in the other direction. Hellish voices came down from the cannons. Jude kept calling, making sure that the militia men who'd gotten down from the onslaught were with him. They waded around the end of the outcropping, pushing through the water with all the speed they could manage. An eerie light seeped from the darkness at the heart of the lake.

There were sixteen men with him, by Jude's quick count, most with their muskets. The ground rumbled, a slow and heavy movement that made him think of a heavy wagon train passing.

"Get everything reloaded," he said. "We're taking those cannons back."

The wind kicked up into a billowing force, tearing the words from his lips.

"How we going to fight them if they have the cannons?" one of the men shouted.

"We get up there before they can turn them this way."

"What the hell are they?" another said as he tamped a shot into his musket.

"The end of us all unless we can get the cannons back."

Light brightened over the lake as though a rotten, green sun shone through a thunderhead. Soon as the men finished reloading, Jude traced out a plan, pointing along the overgrown shore. They would wind their way along the rocks and trees, up the steep side of the outcropping, then line up and shoot two volleys into them. Morrill would lead the men, and Jude would bring up the rear. Jude gave the order, and the men followed Morrill and snaked through the weeds and rocks, reaching for good handholds as they reached the steep incline. The men didn't speak— most of them didn't even glance over at the lake, a scene grown even more hellish and worrisome. As the last of the men set off, Jude looked off behind himself one last time. Still, none of the bodies had followed them around the outcrop. He turned and hurried after the line of men. Another cannon shot boomed out across the water. Jude hoped the major was in the clear.

"She tried to end it—but instead she ended herself and the babe and William's wife." The voice was a hiss. Jude stopped in his tracks and turned. There along the muddy edge of the rocks was a shape, big and hunched, eyes shining bright and locked on his own. Jude's breath caught in his throat. "I knew what she was doing, and I let her do it because the child wasn't mine. And you let me do what I did. You let me get away with it."

Jude couldn't move. Even when the musket shots erupted from up in the trees above, he couldn't move. The light from the lake brightened, and he saw the weed-and-mud-covered figure of Joseph Chase, clothing torn, flesh gone the color of dried corn husks, grown over in spots with dark mold, blackened lips over yellow teeth.

"She died covered with pox and bleeding out of her opening, a bleeding that never let up. Even old Corey Lane couldn't save her nor her sister-in-law—no matter how hard that limp brother of mine apologized to him, or begged, or promised to make it all up to him. But make no mistake, Negro—never once did she call your name—and all she kept saying was what a mistake she made with you. Mistake!"

Chase took a slouching step toward Jude.

"I tried to bring her back, did you know? Dug her up and brought her stiff corpse right here. She came back, all right. But she weren't looking for me—she were looking for you, but you'd up and left for a time, wandering and sniveling, I'll wager. Well, we took care of her." A cruel grin split the swollen face. "And she's in here, in bits and pieces. A bit here, a piece there. I feel her all around. Had to cut her up to stop her. Couldn't let her make a fool of me a second time."

Joseph leaped and landed right in front of Jude, fetid air coming from his muddy mouth.

"Oh, and I made a mistake—but you knew, knew it all along. The tavern keep never had anything to do with her. Told me so. Swore on the Lord it was so. Cried that it was so, even as I drug him out here and choked the life from him, choked him till his face turned blacker'n yours."

Another volley of gunfire blasted up in the trees. Yells and orders echoed off the water.

"But it was you that made fools of the both of us and kept your secret all these years. We've both got a thing or two for you now, yes we do, and we didn't think we'd get the chance, didn't think so, but I sensed you as soon as you stepped in the woods, sensed your secret like it was the North Star itself, bright in my new mind." He came a step closer. "And he can't talk, but I'll wager he feels the same. Just look at him–he don't look to happy, does he?"

From the trees stepped a figure that Jude first mistook for branches. There was precious little flesh left on it and a tatter of clothing, here and there—the rest was soil and the white of bone and a glimmer from the eye sockets. Jude staggered back from the corpse of the long-dead tavern keep. Joseph Chase reached and grabbed Jude by the arm, pulling him off balance with a surprising strength.

"She said you cried like a babe for her, and that it disgusted her, didn't she? Yes, she did. She wanted a man, not a reedy boy Negro."

A shot rang out, just behind him. The head of Joseph Chase exploded in a shatter of moldering flesh and bone, and the hand on Jude's arm let go as the body tumbled. Jude yanked his arm free.

"Come on Brewster—we almost got them!" Morrill yelled from up the ridge, lowering the musket he'd just fired.

Jude turned from the bodies and scrambled up the incline, not looking back, not looking at the moving bones by the water, ignoring the words of the dead, the dark reflections of the secrets of the living.

37

BLOODFIRE

The bloodfire drained away.

One moment the words flowed and vibrated and pulled forth the power that Alma needed—and then a minié ball drove into her thigh, sending her sideways. The water and air exploded. And now this other woman was on top of her, yelling, trying to pull her out of the lake. Alma's leg burned, and the lake and night around her kept wanting to slip away in a wash of white. She had to finish the ceremony. As she struggled to stand, another pair of hands grabbed her right arm, pulling.

The Chase boy.

This was the help he brought? A young woman who wanted to do nothing more than pull her from the lake?

"Let's go," the woman said.

"No," Alma said. She tried to shake them both off, but didn't have the strength to wrench herself free—and she knew she wouldn't have the strength to stand up if they let go. She looked down to find blood running from her leg into the water. The bloodfire sputtered in her hands, the glow fading.

It wasn't working.

The lake rumbled, the water shaking and splashing around

them. Alma tried to move forward. The hands held her back. Alma turned to the boy.

"Deeper," she said. "I need to be deeper to make this work."

Thomas stared at her lips and then nodded, leading her out. The woman held them back. Thomas leaned around her and shouted, the two of them arguing. The dead came toward them, drawn to Alma and the power—but they were nothing compared to what emerged from the center of the lake. A power larger than anything she'd imagined.

But she was the only one with a chance, the responsibility hers. The boy dragged her out until the water rose over her knees. She began the song again, trying to find her voice, trying to find the power even as the world went white around the edges of her vision. She took two quick breaths and continued the song.

"Thomas, they're coming!" Carolyn yelled. She tried to pull Alma away again.

"We need to keep—" the boy shouted, his next words lost beneath the deep boom of a cannon from the shore. The deadly projectile cut out into the darkness.

Alma kept repeating the proper words, praying she recalled them properly. A connection tugged at her mind—she wasn't far off. She leaned on the woman and the boy. That's when the voices filled her ears: the voices of the dead.

Screaming.

38

A HELLISH BANNER

Pomeroy ducked at the sound of the cannon. It hadn't been half a minute.

The single shot cut the air over his head. He sprinted around the narrow inlet that marked the southern edge of the lake, through the branches and bracken, running as fast as his wounded leg allowed. Calls filled the night—voices from the bodies in the lake, voices returning their calls from the dark woods, the stony words of the dead.

"Bloody coordinating themselves better than we are," he muttered.

As he pushed from the thicker undergrowth to the shoreline, he came to a stop. The glow from the middle of the lake threw its eerie light across the water and ground and trees. The corpses closed in on Carolyn—and now the boy, he saw. Another group moved to the shore where the cannons were. But that wasn't what stopped him. The woods were full of movement, up from the direction they'd come.

God, no.

The dead came through the woods. A line of them, four

abreast, stretching back into the darkness. Their skin gleamed of raw flesh in spots, blackened and burned in others. Glimmering eyes shone with hatred. Most had no hair left, nor any clothes. Pomeroy understood: the fires—the fires at the mill, the church. Even that didn't stop them.

Among the marching corpses were a few that didn't appear to have come from the fires, including one in a soiled British uniform, holding aloft a broken musket with a bloodied shirt tied to it, a hellish banner. Others had muskets, the bayonets catching the light from the lake on their wicked edges. At the head of the line, a pair of skeletal figures lurched, their eyes burning, the night around them darkened with something not of this world. Trees, plants, the ground itself—all appeared to shrivel and die as they passed. Even the dead behind them gave them distance. Pomeroy had no idea how to stop them, not even with cannons. The ghastly army of the dead would sweep a merciless path through the surrounding countryside, growing ever larger and more deadly.

"This is bloody ridiculous," he said. "We're all going to die."

He turned and ran, ignoring the searing pain in his leg as he splashed out into the water, keeping his pistol up, rushing forward, legs slowed by the water and muck. A musket shot and then another whizzed by him—the dead were shooting at him.

Where were the cannon shots?

"Carolyn!" he yelled out. Even over the sound of the freezing wind, she heard him and turned to look. As she did, the water crusted over with a thin layer of ice. The wind stung his face and eyes and sucked the air from his lungs. He reached the trio.

"We have to run," he said. "Now."

She shook her head and held on to Alma. The woman chanted something, or sang, her voice nearly lost on the wind. Silver eyes in a shadowed form burst from the water in front of them. Pomeroy didn't pause but lifted the pistol and pulled the trigger. The ball caught the thing right in the face—it spun around to the right and fell into the water like a child who spins in a circle too long and falls down dizzy. Another sprung forward, leaping clear of the water and hitting Carolyn from the side, sending them crashing. Pomeroy tossed his other pistol to Thomas, who caught it before it hit the water.

"Shoot anything that gets close!" he yelled, then dove forward. His hands gripped a wet cloak, filthy with mud. He yanked, but the fabric tore. He kept working his hands forward, pumping his legs through the silt and waves. The smell of the tomb filled his nose, but he didn't stop. His head slipped beneath the water for a second, but he got his arms around the waist of the thrashing figure and pivoted on his heels, lifting it up clean out of the water. He cried out in fury as he tossed it sideways, following it below the surface. Wiry, cold hands worked across his ribs, trying to spin him and hold him under. In a panic, Pomeroy thrashed, pulling himself away and getting back up for air. He took in a huge breath that was part air and part water. Coughs racked him as he tried to get a breath. His throat pinched tight.

"Major!" Carolyn shouted.

She pulled him backward by the collar of his cloak. He coughed and struggled to get his feet beneath him. She pulled hard enough to right him. The water was up to their thighs. The wind howled, and the light from out in the lake flared a blinding white-yellow as the wind snapped trees like they were twigs. He struggled in the shallow water before a group of clawing bodies. Behind them, the army of corpses took up positions at the shore.

"We should have run!" he yelled. "We should absolutely have run!"

In front of him, the large woman staggered. Carolyn and the boy struggled to hold her. Pomeroy pushed forward and helped them pull her from the water, yanking hard on the woman's arm. He pointed back to the shore, but Thomas shook his head.

"There's no chance!" Pomeroy yelled. A crowd of bodies in the water closed in, and the dead on the shore fired muskets. Water kicked up from the nearby shots.

Carolyn put a hand on his back. "Just help Thomas!"

39

CHATTER OF THE DEAD

Something pushed through the gate.

Even as she struggled not to swoon, Alma sensed it. Even with the chatter of the dead surrounding her and drowning out all else, the entity from a distant place froze her blood. Alma was ready to sink into the dark water and be done with it. It would be a fitting end—sink and drown in the lake itself, the heart of the place she'd run away from. Without warning, the talk of the dead trailed off, reduced to whispers and mindless chatter. The shadow continued to rage on the lake.

Alma didn't know who squeezed her ribs or that it was the sole reason she stayed upright. The boy reached out and grabbed her hand. The words: Thomas read her lips, not deafened by the howling winds like everyone else. She slowed and let him watch her mouth. He followed her lead and they chanted together.

The light of the bloodfire ran from her hand to his. Up his arm. The light grew. A pressure grew behind them, a mountain of energy. A weight grew in front of them, enormous as the moon. They hung in the balance.

Alma opened her eyes and squinted at the swirling glow of power shining out on the water, shining along her arm, shining around the boy. She looked up, across the water lit by the energy of the gate, seeing for the first time the shadow that had crossed over. It was tall, and its shape was foul: appendages that stretched and coiled, skin like armor, long mouths, dozens of eyes that shone with colors. Half in their world, half in another. Long sub-limbs covered in pinchers that opened and closed dragged behind it, larger than the tallest oaks she'd ever seen. The blood-fire let her peer into the veil of shadow that wrapped it—and the fiend turned to her.

Alma focused the energy that surrounded them.

The dead howled, screamed, and shrieked as they converged. On the shore, dozens more, an army. Their hair blew around their heads on the frigid winds, their blackened teeth seen in hollow mouths. They raised their hands, one in front stepping into the water and coming toward them. The wild water all around them roiled with impacts from the branches, the bodies, stones the size of heads. Alma ducked as a fist-sized stone tore through the air next to her.

A wide wave of red light spread out from her hands and the boy's, shooting across the lake, through the air, into the darkness in the sky. It hit the edges of the shadow. Veins of bright red and orange filled the air. A collective howl from the dead shook the bottom of the lake and rose over the hills and trees. Energy exploded, meeting head-on. The sky filled with a blinding mix of jagged lines, blood and lightning, comet streaks above the lake. And it pushed back—pushed back stronger than she had imagined. Alma staggered—the boy, too. A crushing power threatened to smother them both. The shape above the lake moved forward, its revolting form poisoning the wind and the water. The air crackled.

40

THUNDER OF THE GUNS

The men hugged the edge of the trees, digging in and firing. In the growing light from the lake, the scene around the cannons was terrible to behold as the dead fought to protect the big guns. They'd turned the one cannon off in the direction that the major had gone, and a handful more were turning a second to the ridge. Jude ducked as a shot screamed over their heads. One of the dead had a musket and set about reloading it—his uniform shone a deep maroon in the glowering light, the uniform of a British soldier, torn and dirty. Several more staggered or twitched on the ground, ghastly head wounds not stilling them.

"If they get that cannon turned, we're through!" Jude yelled. More corpses approached from the lake itself, still a ways off.

"We charge them?" Morrill said.

"Got to," Jude said.

As they fought, the dead yelled back and forth to one another, their harsh language filling the air. Jude aimed at the reloading soldier and got him right in the mouth, cracking his head back and felling him. The soldier struggled to get up, trailing a flow of dark blood and teeth. Jude knelt and reloaded the gun.

"Volley, then bayonets!" he yelled. They were down to just under twelve men. Two of their original survivors fell before stealthy corpses who'd slid along the ground and took them. Another had taken a shot to the head, killed by a dead man. Jude waited until they were all ready, then he gave the signal. The guns sounded as one, covering the ridge with powder smoke. And with that, they charged forward, leaping over logs and trampling underbrush, yelling as they did. They swarmed the remaining dead at the cannons and fought them with blade and bayonet, always going for the eyes.

"Cut the heads off, even when they're down!" Jude yelled.

He hacked off the head of the British soldier, glad to see the light snuffed out from the silver eyes. Then it was gore and grunting and slicing and pulping until they stood breathing hard, leaning on their weapons over the headless torsos that covered the ground. The wind ripped leaves off of branches. From the center of the lake, the strange light grew blinding. Bodies—dozens of them—slouched toward the shore. That's when he spotted the major and the others, standing in the water near the edge.

"Turn the cannons back!" he yelled, motioning. "Right to the center, right into that light."

"There's more of them at the shore firing on the major," Morrill said.

"The major's going to have to handle it himself until we get a round off."

Morrill nodded. Jude turned and helped the men with the guns. After a scramble of turning, shouting, and loading, all four cannons pointed out over the lake. Bodies rushed up the incline, swarming around the outcropping, their eyes trained on them, their faces in the dark shadows cast by the glare. The soldier lighting the fuse sticks had trouble—his hands shook.

"You'll want to hurry with that," Jude said, trying to keep his voice calm.

The soldier kept his face grim. In a moment, he had it lit and used that to light the other three. They sprinted behind the guns, ready. Jude held his hand in front of his eyes, keeping out the blinding glare. He looked over at the artillery teams. In the shifting light coming over the lake, he saw the men steady themselves, their faces blackened with powder, their eyes taking in the horror.

Time to take a shot right into hell.

Jude straightened up and bellowed at the top of his lungs. "FIRE!"

The guns thundered.

41

TO LOSE EVERYTHING

The cannons boomed again, the balls screaming through the night to where the abomination loomed, where the prism eyes glittered. Alma squeezed Thomas's hand. "Now—push hard now!" They shouted the words in unison and flung the power forward. The foul being coming through the opening reeled, the balls connecting with its heavy mass. Thomas forced the strange energy forward.

They both strained, and more power came through them. Shadows and bits of tumbling darkness shot out into the water. Thomas felt the strange power pour from him, up his arms and back and neck, into Alma's arm. It was like the air before a lightning storm, the powder in a musket, the fire in the hearth at home, the starlight falling in his own bedroom window. The horrid shape before them staggered back.

Thomas wrenched his gaze away—and his heart froze. Coming toward him through the water, not ten feet away, cloaked in the shadows cast by the blinding light: a torn cloak, hair askew, a familiar hand outstretched.

"Jonathon!" he cried.

His brother's eyes shone silver, his face twisted into a grimace as he pushed through the water. Thomas's bladder let go even as he wanted to run to him—to tell him they needed to leave, that Daddy and Uncle Joseph were dead, that they were all they had left so they needed to run away, run from West Bradhill so they could at least take care of each other, that Thomas didn't want to be all alone. He pulled away from Alma, but the major grabbed him.

Jonathon kept coming. "I see you, Carolyn. You're all I can see."

Carolyn screamed as he reached for her.

"We'll make a family together so I can crawl inside you. We can all huddle together in the water and the mud and never need to be warm again."

He lunged at Carolyn. Pomeroy threw himself between them, pushing back on the corpse. "I don't bloody think so."

His hand slipped off the clammy flesh, and Jonathon shot his own hands up, grabbing him by the throat. He picked Pomeroy up, lifting him up from the water. Pomeroy tried to peel off the cold fingers, but they wouldn't budge. Jonathon spat stinging black liquid into his eyes and face. Carolyn clawed at Jonathon's eyes, trying to get him to drop Pomeroy, who was on the verge of blacking out. His legs kicked at the water.

"Drop him, drop him, let him go!" she screamed.

"The sleep will come," Jonathon hissed.

The lake shuddered, and the light flared.

"He's killing him!" Carolyn yelled. Pomeroy's kicks slowed. Carolyn's feet slid out from under her, and she fell forward, her head against Jonathon's stomach. Jonathon turned his face down to her—and the top of his head blew off, shattered by the shot that hit it at close range.

Pomeroy dropped to the water with a gasp. Jonathon's body slumped backward into the water and sunk below the frantic surface in a swirl of filthy clothes and pale flesh. Pomeroy turned. Thomas stared at the water, his arm outstretched, a twirl of gray smoke rising from the pistol in his grip, his face running with tears.

Alma grabbed him and turned him to look up into his face. The pistol dropped into the water. "Now! We have to finish this!"

Thomas took a last look at the shape of his brother, then he closed his eyes and cried out. Alma gave his hand a squeeze, and Thomas knew what to do. He focused his energy, every bit, every bit of pain that was tearing his heart into pieces. All of it. They both did.

The night and the lake exploded in their faces. Sparks and streaks of light spilled out from the shadows and the monstrosity, traveling up and along the underside of the darkness that had hung like a low ceiling over the lake and the valley. Trees blew backward, cracking, tearing, and falling. The ground shook as though a giant hammer smashed it, making the lake water itself jump up in the air. The screams of the dead rose in a choir of agony behind them, echoing out over the water. Their gaunt corpses and the bodies fell, dropping into the water, collapsing on the shore, eyes extinguished.

Alma's hand went limp as the power left them. She staggered. A huge wind roared—not coming from the center of the lake but from all around it, heading in to the center. Thomas had to reach over to Pomeroy and grab onto his arm. The water spun, flowing as fast as a river.

"That's it—out of the lake!" Pomeroy took hold of Thomas's arm just after everything blew apart. The water rushed around them in a circle, yanking at his legs, trying to pull him off his feet. They turned to fight their way back to shore. Thomas slipped from the major's grip.

POMEROY SPUN AROUND, then lost his footing, swept out after him. Bodies floated around them in the black water. He swung his arms around, catching Thomas by the shoulder, locking his fingers—he would not let anyone slip away again.

Thomas flailed, the water up to his neck. He struggled, trying to swim against the torrent, choking on water. Pomeroy pulled him in close, his arms around his neck, nearly strangling him.

The militia men gathered on the shore. Carolyn stood waist-deep in water, straining to hold up Alma. The men worked their way out to them, linking arms and forming a human chain.

"Hold on, boy!" Pomeroy said. "Just a little swim. We'll be out in a minute."

A sudden rush knocked him loose again. The current grew deadly, sweeping him to the depths. A hand grabbed Pomeroy's ponytail and then his shoulder: Jude. Thomas kicked his feet, helping. Water was tugged at his legs, pulling at his breeches, his jacket, his shoes. They inched back toward the shore. Beneath his feet, the bottom of the lake shifted, rocking. The soldiers pulled at Pomeroy and Thomas, fighting the massive current. By the time they reached the shore, Thomas felt like a shivering sack. They stood in silt and mud and slimy rocks, exhausted. A huge roar came from behind them. Carolyn came up next to him, drenched.

Pomeroy grabbed her arm above the elbow. "We have to leave. Everyone. Now."

The roar from out in the lake rose in volume, drowning out even the wind. The soldiers lined the edge of the shore, staring out into the howling darkness. Bodies littered the ground while others whirled off in the rushing water. A deep, muffled crack shook the ground. The water of the lake drained away, spinning into the earth, all of it. A handful of men ran toward them, their faces dark with powder, their hair slick with sweat. Morrill was at the head of the group.

"He all right—the boy all right?" he yelled, out of breath.

Pomeroy nodded, raised his hand, and motioned toward the woods lined with fallen trees. "We need to leave, fast as we can!"

The men didn't need to hear it twice. Pomeroy kept one hand on Carolyn and the other on Thomas. Two soldiers helped Alma. The wind screamed, and another rumble shook the ground. There was no easy way through the fallen trees and burned corpses that littered the ground. The soldiers scrambled over them, cursing and yelling, branches breaking beneath their feet. Thomas followed and had to be lifted more than once. The sky lightened, bringing the woods into a faint blue-gray focus.

THE STRANGE POWER that had coursed through Thomas vanished. He staggered, often dragged by Pomeroy. It became a blur to him, a haze of exhaustion. At some point they reached the path, and that made the going easier. The ground quieted beneath their feet the farther they got from the lake, where the pine and spruce stood undisturbed. The soldiers were scattered now, most up ahead. Pomeroy wasn't able to run as fast since his leg was hurt— but he didn't let go of Thomas, either.

The path opened out into a clearing. The sky to the east faded from black to a deep indigo that lined the horizon through the trees. There was dew and mist across the grassy clearing. Carolyn tumbled to the grass, landing on her knees. She fell in a heap and shook with sobs. Pomeroy fell to his knees next to her and put his arms around her. She tried to beat him away, landing several fists onto his face, but he held on, pulling her in to him. He buried his face in her hair and pulled her into his chest. They rocked back and forth.

Thomas didn't know what to do. He watched them, and then he turned back to the woods the way they'd come. A strange gray ash covered the tops of the trees. There were no birds in the sky. A giant graveyard, no life. Something jabbed his leg. He reached into the soaked pocket of his breeches and pulled out one of the keys from the broken fife—it had twisted and was poking him. He let it fall to the ground.

"We have to go," he said.

Pomeroy looked up at him. His eyes were red, and he had snot running from his nose. He nodded and stood up. Gently—as though she were injured—he helped Carolyn to her feet. He said a few words to her that Thomas didn't catch, and then they started off from the lake again. Thomas led the way, soaked and shivering, just as Pomeroy was himself. Up ahead, Jude stood at the end of the path. Pomeroy hurried them forward, still holding Carolyn by the hand. They came out onto the road.

"Thought I'd have to go back and find you," Jude said.

"I'd hate to imposition you like that," Pomeroy said.

"Too late, Major. You already imposition'd me plenty. But you didn't do too bad, for a lobsterback."

"We have our uses."

The surviving men gathered next to the road, staring back they way they'd come.

"How are we getting out of here?" Pomeroy said.

"With us," came a voice.

Elizabeth came toward them on the wagon, spare horse in tow. She climbed down and rushed over to Jude.

"I had to come back," she said. "I couldn't lose any more—and I don't care who knows it or not or where we go or how we're together. As long as we are."

Jude pulled her tight into a hug.

Pomeroy looked around and pushed his hair out of his eyes. "Now—might we finally leave?"

They set off minutes later, the injured loaded into the back of the wagon. Pomeroy leaned against Thomas, who stared at his feet. A soldier helped Alma tie a bandage around the wound on her leg. No one spoke. The wagon climbed the hill and then started down the other side. The soldiers followed behind them on foot. Most appeared stunned. They'd done well, Pomeroy thought—but they hadn't seen everything those in the wagon had seen, nor lost what those in the wagon had. The sun broke over the horizon. Around them, the mist burned off. Plowed fields caught the morning light. After a time, Pomeroy looked back. West Bradhill lay beyond the forested hills, out of sight. They'd made it out.

Carolyn looked over at him, fixing him with a hard stare. "Is it possible to lose everything?"

Pomeroy almost said something flip but stopped himself. "Yes. I suppose so."

The morning air grew warm as the sun climbed.

EPILOGUE

SIX YEARS LATER
GREENCASTLE, PENNSYLVANIA

SHADES OF THE DEAD

Thomas ran the small hand scraper along the violin neck clamped in the wooden vise and then leaned over to check the smooth plane he'd made on the curving surface. A neat furrow, though there was a slight wiggle in it that Nathaniel Longstreet would notice. Longstrect was a local instrument maker that Thomas had been apprenticing with for the past several years; demanding, yet patient. Thomas enjoyed the work. The detail of it, the fifes and fiddles. The feel of the wood and the tools, the smell of sawdust, turning something rough into something that could shine and sing. When he'd first told Pomeroy what he'd wanted to do, he'd more than expected a stinging barb: *Ah, yes, just what the world needs—a deaf fiddle maker.* Instead, Pomeroy had bought him the finest tools he could find and made space for him in which to work.

Thomas checked the edge on his scraper again with his thumb, then leaned in and took another pass. A curl of wood spun out beneath the edge of the scraper. The sun came in through the dusty window of the barn, shining on the pile of wood scrapings he'd made. A square of light appeared on the wall as the side door to the barn opened behind him. Thomas stood up and turned around.

Lizzie stood in the doorway. "We got a letter, and Papa wants you to be there, Thomas."

With that, she spun around and ran back to the house. Thomas crossed from the workshop area in the barn to the tavern. The leaves in the trees were still green though they blushed with a hint of the reds and yellows to come. Sunlight, warm for September, dappled the ground. He opened the back door to the tavern, inhaling the aroma of fresh beer and bread. Two hot loaves sat cooling on the table.

In the public room, Pomeroy leaned in the doorway that opened onto the street in front, wearing his customary apron and loose shirt, his long hair pulled back with a tie. "There you are. I wondered if you'd gotten lost."

"What?" Thomas said. "I came straight away."

"Remind me not to send you running for help if there's a fire."

"Ah, more sarcasm," Thomas said, "I never tire of it."

Pomeroy sniffed and approached the long bar. "I thought you might have the honor of reading the letter we received by post," he said. He held up a letter and broke the wax seal on the back, then handed it to Thomas.

"What's it say?" Lizzie said, impatient as always. She was only five. Carolyn looked up at him from where she sat polishing the pewter utensils for the tavern. She was going to have another baby, though she didn't look it yet. Pomeroy had told him the night before after they'd closed up for the evening. He'd poured Thomas an ale as a toast, and the two of them had tossed back and forth ideas for names as the logs in the hearth had faded to embers. It had been well past midnight by the time Thomas had gone off to bed.

"It's from Mr. J. Brewster, Brewster's Inn, Ipswich, Massachusetts," Thomas said. He opened the letter, brushing off the last of the wax.

"Who's that?" Lizzie said. "Where's Ip-stich?"

Carolyn shushed her. "Read it, Thomas," she said.

Over the years, Thomas had become good at reading both of their lips. He cleared his throat and held the letter in the sunlight. The writing was strong and clear, from Brewster himself.

"Dear Pomeroys and Chases, I hope this finds you all well and prosperous this autumn. We are all fine, and business is good. We've developed the reputation as the finest tavern north of Boston and are always busy with travelers and locals. A few bits of interest you ought to know about: firstly, Elizabeth and I have now a charming and delightful set of twins, nearly a month old. They are beautiful and healthy. Isaac and William, and more than enough to keep both of us busy round both sides of the day."

Pomeroy chuckled. "Good Lord, twins." He smiled at Carolyn. "Try not to do that, dearest, if you would be so kind."

"Please. As if I have a choice," Carolyn said. She shook her head and smiled. "Poor Elizabeth. Go on Thomas."

Thomas shifted the letter and continued.

"The second big news here is that Ipswich has a new mayor. Mayor Zeke Morrill, in fact. He and Alma and their boys are busy with their dairy farm, and now Morrill has transferred his knack for being the most likable fellow in town into being the most likable mayor in town. William, the third bit of news is for you: one of my brews from this spring past was called 'the finest in the Colony' by the Boston Courier. I've called it English Revolutionary Ale—you might appreciate it, since it's named for you, the finest English revolutionary I had the pleasure to serve with. Fine brew for a fine man."

Thomas looked up. Pomeroy shook his head, a smile on his lips. Thomas looked over at Carolyn and saw her eyes fill with sudden tears. She kept smiling and wiped them away with the hem of her apron. Pomeroy walked over and leaned down, planting a soft kiss on her cheek.

He picked up Lizzie. "Come here, you little dearie." The girl wrapped her arms around his neck.

"What's wrong, Mummy?" Lizzie said.

Carolyn shook her head. "It's all right, sweetness," she said. "Mummy was just thinking about some people she used to know."

Thomas finished the letter. "I trust that all is well out on the frontier where you are, and that your harvests and brews are bountiful. William, come on, give me some competition. Yours, etc., Jude Brewster, Master Brewer."

Pomeroy snorted. "Master Brewer, as if that's an official title."

"It might be," Thomas said.

"Please, boy. Try not to be so gullible." Pomeroy turned and pointed at a fresh cask brought up from the cellar. "Wait until I tell him about my latest and greatest. Brewster's Dark Porter. That'll scare him." He tickled Lizzie, who giggled and laughed. She could be a brat, but she was a fine little sister, as they had insisted that Thomas regard her as. Pomeroy turned around, his face lively.

"Oh, he'll love this," he said, tapping his temple. "I'm brilliant, really. My next brew: Morrill's Artillery Ale. Bloody brilliant."

THOMAS WALKED BACK to the barn a short while later. He would work with Lizzie on the alphabet that afternoon—it was one of his responsibilities. In the meantime, he wanted to finish the neck of the fiddle before Longstreet came by for lunch, as had become his custom on Saturdays. If it looked good enough, he'd show the fiddle to him.

He walked through the shade and sunlight of that warm September morning into the cool of the barn. Out of the corner of his eye, shadows followed him, faint in the daytime. They never bothered him, or even frightened him any longer. He'd grown used to them in the years since they'd left Massachusetts; in fact, he'd told Pomeroy and Carolyn about them, heeding the advice of Jude Brewster, who'd told him after they'd left West Bradhill behind them that a man could pay a terrible price by holding a secret too close, especially a secret of the dead. That's what followed Thomas: shades of the dead. They were always there, ever since the lake, ever since the bloodfire, following him in silence.

Still, the family he'd lost were worse than these shades— those memories stayed with him, too, and weren't as easy to ignore. Thomas picked up his scraper and looked down the length of wood in the vise. He went back to work.

THE LAKE: PART TWO

Seasons came and went, and years came and went, and still nothing thrived anywhere around the deep gully that marked the place where the lake had been. Eventually, even the name of the small village that had stood nearby faded, lost to time.

And while no land stands unclaimed for long, the land around the lake stood vacant longer than most. Other towns grew and spread and pressed into the old woods and fields. Their borders met, and the land had a name once again. So it was that, after the rocks had bleached in the sun of scores of summers and cracked in the deep throes of New England winters, it happened all at once, one October night long after the gully had grown silent and empty.

The lake came back.

From the deepest crevice, water flooded back in and rose until it was deep and black and icy cold.

KEEP *up to date on my upcoming books, novellas, and exclusives by joining my private newsletter.*

AS A WELCOME, *I'll send you a free ebook of* **Sorcery of the Stony Heart** *(the prequel novella to* The Books of Conjury*), along with* **A Spark of Will: The Trans-Atlantic Diary of August Swaine**, *an exclusive novelette you can't get anywhere else.*

IT'S EASY, *just sign up here:* **Join Newsletter**

Twenty-two minutes until sunset, maybe twenty-three.

Almost time to hide. I get jumpy even without a clock left in the house, from the light from the windows, creeping up the bare walls. The shadows gobbling up the dusty corners. Some afternoons, I stand in the hallway, watching. As the afternoon drains, I listen to the muffled sounds of life outside. Cars passing by on the street. Kids shouting after each other on bikes. Crows. Wind sighing around the walls and roof. A house sounds different when it's empty. The windows pop in their frames when the sunlight hits them long enough. The boiler coughs on with a rattle, setting the radiators to knocking. Boards and stairs creak as the house breathes with the weather.

Twenty minutes.

This is the first October I've been alone. I miss the sound of people. Footsteps. Plumbing running, shutting off. Whispers and coughs and throat clearing. Talking on the phone. Radio. TV. Enough to cover up the sound of emptiness. It's worse in October. Lower light. Shorter days. And me, by myself.

The world's dumbest ghost.

Trying to find new places to watch a day come to a close. Up in a corner of the ceiling. The attic crawlspace with the ancient insulation and abandoned mousetraps, filled with must and resin from the roof joists.

I didn't think death would be like this. I didn't think about death at all. What junior high school kid does? I guess if you'd forced an answer out of me, I'd have said: Something like sleep. Not emptiness, not that part of sleep. The other part, where you feel safe, lulled to sleep by all the familiar sounds of the house around you—except in death, you'd be hearing the good sounds of the universe around you. God clearing His throat. The spin of the planets. The low hum of the stars and the distant rumble of the universe's gears turning.

Well. Nope. It's nothing like that.

It's this. Watching the days pass by. Keeping an eye out for sunset, when the nightmare games begin. Stuck in this one place, the house I grew up in, apparently forever. And if there is something else to it, then I'm missing it. I've tried everything I can think of.

Eighteen minutes.

So when I hear a car door slam in the driveway, boy does it catch my attention. A minute later, a key works the lock on the front door. Takes a couple of tries—my family used the kitchen door, and it has the newer lock—but the door swings open. A woman steps inside. She's pretty, but old. Probably near forty. Dressed nice, jacket, long skirt, boots. Blond hair. I stand at the bottom of the stairs, unseen. No one's been in the house since my sister locked it up last winter and drove off with my dad.

The woman looks over the entryway with a quick eye, then purses her lips and looks up the stairs. She looks right through me, which is a weird feeling. When I was alive, there were plenty of times I'd wanted to be invisible, like at school. East Junior High. When a teacher like Mr. Fitzgerald was looking for his next unprepared victim in class—usually me. Or when a dickhead like Mike D'Angelo—one of our three class psychopaths—went stomping down the hall in his shit-kicker boots, training his beady eyes on anyone stupid enough to look in his direction. Then, not being seen was sweet relief.

But that's different from someone standing four feet away, looking right through you. Makes me feel like some kind of peeping Tom. Not that I can see her naked or anything. It's that looking at someone who's totally unguarded is weird. Like peeking into someone's head in a way you'd never be able to if you were actually there. She walks right in front of me. I'm close enough to see the mascara on her eyelashes, to see the smoky makeup on her eyelids, the light green pattern of her iris. She frowns, her lipstick a muted red.

I can't tell if she senses I'm there, or not. Some people can.

Back when my family was still here, a few did. My sister, Beth, had a friend in high school named Chrissie. This was seven years after I'd died. Chrissie made me think of a nervous mop. Quiet. Shy. But an amazing artist. She used to draw pictures of her pet rabbit that were better than anything I'd ever seen. Chrissie knew I was here. Every time I stepped close to her, she wrapped her arms in front of her flat chest and frowned. I'd follow them around the house as they did whatever they were doing—something for school, usually—and it was one hundred percent reliable. She also got chills when I blew on the back of her neck. I'd watch her get goosebumps, and tighten her shoulders as a chill rolled up her back.

After a while, Chrissie stopped coming around.

THE WOMAN WALKS RIGHT through me. Feels like a wave of warmth and force, uncomfortable. As a ghost, I can't stop her. Can't touch her. Nothing. After a quick shiver of my own, I follow her into the kitchen. She stops and looks around. Goes to the sink, turns on the tap. The water gurgles out and when she shuts it off, the pipe bangs. Her black heels clack on the linoleum as she opens and shuts cabinets, tries light switches, looks out the window into the yard. She goes through the door to the breezeway connecting the house to the garage. When she tries the garage door opener, I step up behind her and blow on the back of her neck.

Nothing. I get a whiff of perfume and a hint of coffee. I inhale. Life. Not that I care too much for either smell—but still, she woke up somewhere this morning, showered, shampooed her hair, filled her coffeepot and drank a cup or two, left her house, moved through an autumn day, alive. So wrapped up in being alive she probably doesn't even realize she is. That's what I drink in. Life. I'd almost forgotten what it's like.

She turns and walks through me again.

"Wait up, lady," I say.

She doesn't hear me, of course. The mice and spiders in the garage don't hear me, either. No one hears a ghost. I can hear myself.

I catch up to her in the backyard. The fence is gray and splintery, the tall grass next to it faded, leaning now that summer's gone. Leaves from the big sugar maple cover the yard and the corners of the roof. Orange, yellow, red. The wind sends a dozen more leaves floating down, twirling like dizzy birds. She walks the yard, stepping carefully, trying not to get her heels stuck in the ground.

I only follow her so far. I know from experience I can make it a yard or so past the fence, but no more. Trust me, I've only tried about twenty thousand times. Here's what happens: I reach a certain point, and something holds me back. It's like being a bug stuck at the bottom of a porcelain sink. Can't get a grip, gravity does its thing, bug goes round and round. The house and yard are the sink.

I'm the bug.

The lady takes something out of her pocket and taps it. Like a deck of cards, only thinner. Like a quarter of a deck. A little picture shows up in her hand. She points it at different corners of the yard. Tap. Picture. Tap, another picture. Coolest thing I've seen in years. Then, she holds it up to her face and talks to it. "Hi, Brittany. Call Phil over at Pine Street. There's a fence that needs to go, and a general cleanup for 162 Chestnut. Also, call Dave Sutton and schedule something for him. It's cold inside, and the paperwork mentioned something about the furnace being questionable. Thanks."

She taps the device too quickly for me to figure out what she's doing, and then it makes a noise like a miniature rocket taking off, and she puts it back in her jacket. She eyes the roof and the gutters, then walks through me yet again. I'm still thinking about the thing that took the pictures—it's like something from *Star Trek*.

After that, she walks through the whole house, trying light switches, running faucets, looking in closets, her boots loud and sure. At my old room, she pauses with her hand on the doorframe. I feel something then, a quick opening into her thoughts. A weird jumble of images, ranging from an office that looks like a house, with a board with pictures on it, to a kid about my age, her daughter, to a Halloween costume in a mirror. A fairy, with a sparkly wand, a poofy skirt, and a glittered gold mask. Hers, when she was younger. She knows the story, the history of the house. She remembers it from when she was a kid.

How do I know?

The other thing about being a ghost is that when people think about you—not you the ghost, but the life that you had—it opens up a glimpse into their life. Usually just for a moment or two, but sometimes longer. And she was thinking about what'd happened to me. And it got to her.

By now, maybe you're thinking about what happened to me.

Here's all you need to know: I died on Halloween night, 1981, at age fourteen.

I don't like to talk about it.

Ghost at Dusk is available now—read it today!

Click cover below to see it at your favorite retailer.

ALSO BY KEVAN DALE

The Governor's Witch

Ghost at Dusk

The Magic of Unkindness

The Grave Raven

The Halls of Midnight

Sorcery of the Stony Heart

The Books of Conjury: The Complete Trilogy

The Devil's Key

Shades of the Grave: A Horror Collection

Find out more at www.kevandale.com

www.ingramcontent.com/pod-product-compliance
Lightning Source LLC
Chambersburg PA
CBHW050241110726
47898CB00007B/2230